Also by Melanie Crowder

Audacity

An Uninterrupted View of the Sky

PHILOMEL BOOKS

An imprint of Penguin Random House LLC, New York

First published in the United States of America by Philomel, an imprint of
Penguin Random House LLC, 2021.

Copyright © 2021 by Melanie Crowder.

Philomel Books is a registered trademark of Penguin Random House LLC.

Visit us online at penguinrandomhouse.com.

Library of Congress Cataloging-in-Publication Data is available.

Printed in the United States of America

ISBN 9780525516743

1 3 5 7 9 10 8 6 4 2

Edited by Liza Kaplan.
Design by Ellice M. Lee.
Text set in Palatino.

for Elliott

NEBRASKA, 1959

-1-

IF YOU HOLD a map of the United States in both hands and fold it top to bottom, then again lengthwise, and open it back up again, chances are you've landed smack-dab in the middle of the Butterfield family farm. I should know—I spent half my childhood at my grandmother's hip, poring over her unruly stack of maps. I'd lie for hours on my belly, chin in hand, clacking my heels in the air, the braided rug over the old hardwoods in the living room digging permanent imprints into the skin at my elbows and knees. Nana says you have to know where you come from to have any hope of figuring out where you need to go—otherwise a compass is no better than a child's spinner toy, and a map is just a fussy drawing for folks to bicker over. I've hardly stepped foot outside Nebraska, so I can't say as I know one way or the other.

As any agricultural map will show you, the heart of this country is corn country, and my hometown of Fairbury is no exception. In the middle of town, you'll find the Frosty Top drive-in diner, where I spend my weeknights on roller skates delivering trays of burgers and fries, shakes, and ice-cold bottles of Coca-Cola. The giant ice-cream cone rotating high above the outdoor dining section is like a beacon drawing folks in from all over Jefferson County. Or maybe it's the weather.

Tonight's one of those sparkling spring evenings when the place is packed. Everybody's got their windows rolled down despite the chill, folks so eager to believe winter is finally behind us, they don't mind their teeth chattering so long as the sun is out. I take an extra second to steady the tray on my palm, toe the brake on my right skate, pivot the other, and holler, "Door!" before I clip it with my hip and wheel outside. The air is crisp, fluttering the pleats of my skirt and tugging at the pins that hold my Frosty Top cap on my head at a jaunty angle.

A song takes form in my mind like it does every time I get so much as a second to myself, building in my chest and begging to be set free as I skate toward the pickup trucks parked in V formation. This time it's "Getting to Know You" from *The King and I*. The notes are simple enough and the breath work isn't too tricky, but hitting those staccatos while you're sashaying around the stage shaking hands and dropping curtseys—it isn't half as easy as Deborah Kerr makes it look on screen.

Late last night when I should have been writing an essay on Senator McCarthy's steep rise and abrupt fall, I was poring over the Richard Rodgers score to see if any of his songs hit the sweet spot for my voice. I can reach the high notes, sure, but the mezzo range is where my singing goes from pretty darn great to ain't nobody in the room paying attention to a single thing but me. The judge at the state fair last summer said my voice was the best to come out of Nebraska in a decade.

I *think* I'm good enough for Broadway, but I won't know for sure until I get there. In the meantime, I'm studying the only way I know how. Our library in Fairbury doesn't have much in the way of a music section other than a few musty hymnals. But the librarian goes out of her way to set aside the theater section of the *Times* for me, and to request a steady rotation of scripts and scores from the music school in Omaha. They're teaching me more about technique than my voice teacher, Mrs. Muth, ever could. So I know to breathe in through my nose in the cooling air and hum for a good long while before I open up and sing.

I skate nice and slow to buy myself a little extra time, and so I don't spill the drinks. The owner of the Frosty Top, Earl, is in one of his moods today, so he'd probably take the ruined meal out of my paycheck. I've heard folks say, *Aww—he's more bark than bite*, by which I know they've never been on the receiving end of that particular bite. I swing a wide turn and sidle between a shiny red Chevy Bel Air and a beat-up Ford that's more rust than anything else.

"Two hot chocolates, two Frosty Burgers with extra pickles, hold the mustard, and an order of skinny fries to share." I set the tray on the window hanger, pull a stack of napkins out of my apron pocket, and flash my best smile. "Anything else I can get you folks?"

The driver takes his time looking me up and down. It's acting practice—that's what I tell myself as I freeze that smile in place and shift my gaze to the woman in the passenger seat, who's either oblivious or, more likely, willfully ignorant as to the kind of man she's with.

"Nah, you're doing just fine," he drawls.

Cretin. I don't meet his eyes—won't give him the satisfaction. I push off and skate back to the diner empty-handed. It's more of that acting practice to keep my hands from clenching into fists when I know his eyes are on my ass the whole way back to the diner.

The job does have its perks, though. Skating back and forth between the kitchen and the cars parked beneath that shiny red roof is a workout. I need the practice if I'm going to make the chorus line of a Broadway show my first season in New York. It may look easy bell-kicking across the stage with a big smile plastered on your face while you sing, sing, sing, but those people have built up more endurance than marathon runners, I'll tell you what.

The heat from the kitchen blasts my cheeks, the fry oil in the air sinking into every pore when I make my way back inside. "Hey, Marv, you got those milkshakes for table sixteen?"

"Sure do." He tops each whipped cream tower with a maraschino cherry.

"Hustle up," Betty says, eyeing the tray balanced on my palm and smoothing the sides of her Kool-Aid–red hair. "We're on in ten."

Every hour on the hour, us carhops line up in front of the diner's chrome bar and do a choreographed song and dance. Yep, on skates.

"I'll be ready," I call over my shoulder as I make for the indoor dining room. "Door!"

I skate across the black-and-white checkered floor, past the chrome barstools, and into a bank of curved red vinyl booths. Everybody's so happy to see the sun, the air is fizzy as a freshly poured soda pop. The diner's packed with families tonight, so the show should be a hoot. I set down the milkshakes with a straw and a long skinny spoon for each. A girl in pigtails goes straight for the cherry, plucking it off the swirl of whipped cream and dropping it in her mouth. A boy next to her with freckles like polka dots sprinkled all over his face dunks his straw straight to the bottom of the glass, eyes wide and cheeks pumping like bellows. The Mr. and Mrs. thank me, and I give them a genuine smile in return, no acting required this time.

I tuck the tray under my arm and scoot back to the kitchen quick as I can without catching a wheel on a chair leg and falling flat on my face. The other carhops are lined up, waiting on me. Patty pinches my cheeks, while Edna pries loose the knot at the back of my apron.

"Ready?" Betty stations herself at the door, peering out of the round window and watching the clock. Like he does every hour, Earl leans over the jukebox, his apron strap digging into the pink skin at the nape of his neck, wiry hairs curling out the back of his white T-shirt. He punches the button for "Moonlight Serenade," and the machine clicks and whirs, the record dropping on the turntable. Betty counts us off, and we glide into the dining room, moving in unison, like a bunch of slow-motion Rockettes on skates. The music is dreamy, and I fall into the familiar pattern of swirl and swish as we wind across the checkerboard floor. The whole thing is a Gene Kelly rip-off, to be honest, but nobody around here would know that, or care.

Although it's the same routine every night, the customers never seem to tire of it. No matter how many times they've seen it, folks my parents' age glaze over the minute the music begins. Oh, they're still watching us, but they're far away, too—lost in wartime memories of whatever heartbreak or glory or both this song always seems to call to mind. Earl knows it, and he's squeezing that nostalgia for every penny he can get.

We spin and twirl through the diner before landing in front of the bar for the finale, all in a line. It's a little like being in a musical, I suppose. Doing the same thing night after night, calling up the crowd's emotions and playing them for all they're worth. But I won't be satisfied until I'm doing the real thing on a real stage eight performances a week.

When we hit the last, sleepy note, the customers clatter with applause, blinking and glancing around like they're waking from a dream. Betty, Patty, and Edna skate back into the kitchen—they don't care whether they're dancing or waiting tables, so long as the tips are good. When Earl hired me two years ago, I made my six o'clock solo part of the deal. There was no negotiating the three dollars per week, believe me, but no way was I going to put up with milkshake stains on my socks and fry grease in my hair if there wasn't something more in it for me. Something bigger.

I take in a deep belly breath and let that first note scatter any noise left in the diner. Sure enough, the place goes quiet like a real theatre when the house lights dim. The fryer stops sizzling, and people quit clinking those long spoons in their sundae glasses. They just listen—and me, I *sing*.

I was born to do this. To draw in an audience with nothing but my voice, to hold them captive and wring raw emotion out of them, willing or not. The diner is too divvied up into sections to really do me any favors as far as acoustics are concerned, but I take that as a challenge. If I can't fill a small-town diner, how the hell will I ever fill a Broadway theatre? So I sing with everything I've got.

When the last note is done, a pang of longing hits—it happens every time. I hate working here. The plastic carnations in those beaded white vases that are always getting knocked over. The clamor in the kitchen so loud you have to shout every single order. The burns on my forearms and that perennial bruise on my right hip from the swinging kitchen doors. The way half the men who walk through that door ogle my body, like it's part of the appetite they've come to satisfy. But I'm not me if I'm not onstage, even one as humble and greasy as this. And that time in the spotlight is almost worth more than the paycheck.

Almost.

Still, the best part of my shift is when it's over.

I push through the front door, my skates knotted and slung over my shoulder. There he is, leaning against his grass-green Chevy, a smile brighter than both those headlights combined—all for me.

"Hey," Jesse says. He slides a hand through his sandy brown hair and pushes off the truck.

"Hey yourself."

The way he looks at me? I let it burrow between my ribs until my breath is short and that traitor heart of mine is banging against my chest like it *wants* him to know the effect he has on me. Then, whether I mean to or not, I'm beaming right back at him.

When I cross the parking lot, Jesse lifts the skates from my shoulder, snugs an arm around my waist, and kisses me like a soldier home from war, dipping me back over the hood just a little—enough that my knees give and I stop breathing altogether, but not so much that the reverend's wife will cross the street to give us a lecture on good Christian chastity.

Sparks dance around our heads, the bulb inside that goddamn ice-cream cone flickering above the Frosty Top sign like it's about to pop. Or maybe my brain has used up all its oxygen and that twinkling is its last, desperate plea for help. I pull back despite myself, suck in a breath, and pray some common sense comes in with it. I remind myself, like I do every single time, not to fall one inch further for this boy. Because much as I love Jesse, I am going to leave him and the rest of Nebraska behind—the first chance I get.

-2-

WHEN I SCOOT onto the Chevy's bench seat beside him, Jesse starts the ignition and drapes an arm over my shoulders. "Straight home?"

"Yeah." I move the stick into reverse while he pumps the clutch.

Jesse looks over his shoulder, but instead of taking his foot off the brake, he runs his lips along my neck. "You sure about that?"

I laugh. "Unless you want to explain to Momma why I let them wait around the table while the roast she spent half the day basting grows cold—"

Jesse coughs and sits up straight, the tops of his cheekbones flaring bright pink. "No. No, I do not."

I don't know what it is about seeing that boy blush—I can't take it. I grab his face in my hands and pull him toward me. His foot slips off the clutch and the truck lurches to a stop with a god-awful screech. There it is again, those cheeks blushing clear to his ears. I dive for them next, but Jesse only blows out a breath and clamps his arm around me again. He has to reach with his left hand to get at the ignition, and it's all so ridiculous—the truck squeals out of the parking lot, and before I know it we're both laughing so hard he can barely steer.

The fields on either side of the road were planted last week; now that the sun has gone down, leaving a periwinkle sky behind, the wind slices across the rows, kicking up grit into the air and reminding us all that summer isn't quite here yet.

I hitch to the side so I can watch Jesse's face while he drives. I run my fingers through his hair, slowing at the tips where the ends flick upward. He drops his head back into my hand.

"Your papa keep you out in the barn all afternoon?"

"Yeah," he murmurs. "Sorting seed and planning for the next crop rotation."

I can feel his exhaustion sink into my palm like a sack of flour. "And you've still got homework to do?"

He drags a hand across the back of his eyes. "Yeah. I got the calculus equations done pretty quick while I was waiting for Nelly to get out of school. That was easy."

"Course it was." Jesse is super smart.

"And that physics essay is all but written in my head. I've just got to get it down on paper."

I sit back with a groan. *Essays.* "That won't be so simple."

"No," he admits. "And Mr. Grange gave me a new article out of MIT on rocket propulsion that I've been wanting to read all day. I'm hoping to get to it tonight if I can keep my eyes open long enough."

I'd tell him to get some rest, to put the article off until tomorrow, but I know it won't do a lick of good. It's one of the reasons the two of us go together like Fred and Ginger. Or—as Jesse would say—like the pair of moons orbiting Mars. Point is, I've got big dreams, and he does, too. Sometimes I think it makes me even more determined to see mine come true since we both know he'll never have the chance. Jesse has the family farm to run, so all he has to look forward to is what he can grow out of this earth, no matter that he can't hardly keep his head out of the stars.

We pull down the curving drive leading to the Butterfield farm, and he glides to a stop in front of the old farmhouse. I jiggle the stick into first and he cuts the engine, then we scoot out and climb the steps hand in hand. Jesse walks me to the front door, keeping a respectable distance in case somebody's watching from the parlor. He squeezes my hand, then backs down the porch steps, his voice low and a little gravelly. "I love you, Mazie Butterfield."

I bite down on my bottom lip to keep a wobbly smile from taking over my whole face. "Don't I know it."

-3-

I DART INTO the entryway, drop my skates beside the armoire, and hang my sweater inside. "Should I wash up before coming in?"

Momma answers from the dining room—never a good sign. "Your father's belly is rumbling loud enough to call the pigs. You'd best have a seat."

"Yes, ma'am." I scoot into the dining room, going the long way around so I can drop a kiss on Momma's cheek, then Daddy's, then Nana Butterfield's before sliding into the empty wooden chair beside her.

Daddy bows his head the second my behind hits the embroidered seat cushion for the quickest blessing I've ever heard before the clatter of serving spoons on china platters begins. It doesn't matter whether it's a weekday after she's spent half the day mucking stalls with Daddy or Christmas dinner, Momma uses her grandma's wedding china for supper every evening.

She looks down the bridge of her nose at my uniform and away again with a *heaven help me* sniff. "How was school today?"

"Principal Echter is an imbecile—"

"*Mazie*," Momma chides.

I shove an oversized bite of rosemary potatoes into my mouth. "It's true! He won't listen to any of my ideas for the graduation ceremony. He wants the choir to sing the same tired song we do every single year. When I made a teensy suggestion, he said I was showing off and trying to angle for a solo."

"Want me to have a word with him, Mazie, dear?" Nana asks.

"Mother, please." Daddy levels his fork at me. "Mazie needs to handle this on her own. Us Butterfields face our problems head-on, so she'll need to figure out a way to speak up for herself and keep the peace at the same time."

Across the table, Nana winks, whispering none too quiet, "You just tell me when, honey. I'll give that nincompoop what for."

Thank goodness for Nana. And thank all that's holy I've only got another week left at Fairbury High. I'd leave in a heartbeat for New York City if I had enough money saved up. Every time I think I'm almost ready I add it up—the train ticket, plus a room to rent while I audition, not to mention dance classes and voice lessons in the meantime—and I know I'm nowhere close. But I've got this nagging feeling that if I don't go soon, I'll miss my chance. And that thought's like a cattle prod in my behind, shooting a bolt of panic clear through me. I can't stay here forever.

I can't.

Momma is eyeing my uniform like she does those crows that are always hopping a little too close to her kitchen garden.

"I wish you wouldn't work at that dreadful place."

I sigh. We've been having this conversation at least once a month since I started working at the diner. "It's just a job, Momma."

"I don't like the way all those men look at you."

I pull the standard-issue Frosty Top skirt down so it covers an inch more of my thighs. "We don't like the way they look at us, neither."

That earns me a long sigh in return. "If you'd only take your uncle Cal's offer to work in his office as a secretary like your older sister did before she got married."

I set my knife and fork down a little too forcefully, the china trembling on the brushed table linen. "Uncle Cal pays peanuts. Besides, you know I work where I do so I get practice in front of an audience. There's nowhere else in town that can give me that kind of exposure."

Daddy coughs into his fist. "I believe *exposure* is exactly what your mother's worried about."

I pick my utensils back up and stab a hunk of meat, sawing a little too enthusiastically. "If anyone is doing wrong, it's them. Those Neanderthals should keep their eyes to themselves."

What I don't say and what I hope to Jesus Momma never finds out—it isn't only their eyes that roam over some of the waitresses when their backs are turned. It's their *don't nobody dare tell me no star quarterback, Eagle Scout, deacon in the church* hands, too.

A few of them tried it with me when I started working at the diner—the first time I was so shocked I dumped a milkshake down the guy's shirt. That became my go-to move, along with a *don't mess with the bull* glare anytime I could sense it coming, and a tongue-lashing when I couldn't. Earl may be a bear sometimes, but he has no qualms about throwing their kind out on their rear.

Nana, bless her, changes the subject back to the graduation ceremony a couple weeks from now. Then talk shifts to when the next Vanguard will launch and the countywide competition for student-made rockets. I jump in to keep the conversation permanently shifted away from me and also because I am a veritable fount of information as Jesse's been talking about nothing but that dang launch all month.

After supper, I help Momma clear the dishes, sweep the crumbs from the tablecloth, and tidy the chairs around the table. Daddy makes a fire in the hearth, checks the mantel clock to see how long until the new episode of *Gunsmoke* begins, and switches on the radio, turning it up real loud. Daddy made it home from the war in Germany, which is more than most can say. But all that artillery going off right beside his head left him with an awful ringing in his ears. It's a good thing he has my older brother, Otis, to help with the farm, because each year the workload on Daddy's shoulders seems to grow a little heavier. A few years from now, Otis and his wife will move out of the house they're renting in town to come live with us, and then it'll be Daddy helping Otis for as many years as he's able.

I watch from the doorway, pulling a drying towel through my hands as he pours two whiskeys—one for himself and one for Nana—ice popping in the stout glasses. He sinks into the armchair, listening as the crackling broadcast runs down the day's news. There's plenty of love to go around this house, even if my folks will never understand why I want the things I do. If Momma had her way, I'd marry Jesse the minute we're out of high school, live right down the road the rest of my days, and have a whole passel of babies. Just like my big sister, Lucinda. Momma relishes being Daddy's partner in everything from the farm to the family. They depend on each other, and even after all these years, they're clearly smitten.

It's not that Momma doesn't try to understand me. Two years ago, when Rodgers and Hammerstein's *Cinderella* was broadcast live on television, she went with me to the neighbors' so I wouldn't miss it, and then she put up with me raving about Julie Andrews and trying to imitate her singing voice for weeks and weeks after. Then, when I won a ticket from the local radio station to see the touring company of *Oklahoma!*, she drove clear to Kansas City so I could catch the show, then turned around and drove straight back through the night to get Daddy's breakfast on the table before he headed out to the fields in the morning. She wants to see me happy. Momma just can't imagine any other kind of happy than what she's got: married to a farmer and living life the way God intended, hearts humble and hands in the dirt.

All right, so I *could* do with a pinch more humility. But hands in the dirt? That will never be me.

-4-

FINAL EXAMS ARE next week. I should be paying attention, but I mostly daydream through social studies and English. After school lets out, I clatter down the high school steps and hurry along the gravel path leading into town. Madame Durant's ballet studio is only a few blocks away from Fairbury High, but the sooner I get there, the more time I'll get in the studio before class begins.

My Bass Weejuns are nothing like tap shoes. Still, once I reach the sidewalk, I start tapping away anyway, zigzagging in a traveling buffalo to the left, then the right, then back again. The marmalade cat from the barbershop trails behind me down the sidewalk, yowling. I doubt he's complimenting my dancing so much as objecting to the racket, but I give him a little extra flourish and a bow anyway. The cat promptly rolls onto his back, kicking his feet in protest.

The bell tinkles overhead as I push through the studio door. I head to the back, where I kick off my loafers and peel away my school clothes. I turn to the mirror and pull my thick hair up into a bun that, if I'm lucky, Mme Durant won't make me unpin and put up again before she'll so much as look at me. The leotard and tights don't do a thing for my complexion. They just make every bit of me—my skin, my lips, the freckles across the tops of my cheeks, even my strawberry blonde hair—look a dozen shades of pasty pink.

I don't have a prima ballerina's body, and I never will, even though I take lessons four days a week. Madame has informed me of that fact at least a thousand times. I know what she's saying—that I wouldn't make it in her world. That's okay. Much as I love it, I have no illusions about my future as a ballerina. I come from a long line of farmers, solid Nebraska stock. I don't have the elegant lines or willowy limbs folks write poems about. But I'm strong, and Mrs. Muth says that heft helps me project onstage. So I'll take it.

I face the mirror, lift my leg onto the barre, and slide into a good, long stretch. I round my spine, then arch back, my arm trailing a beat behind the tilt of my chin. I'm impatient to get going, but I slow down anyway. I've been working so long toward that big Broadway dream, no way am I going to let a torn muscle or rolled ankle stop me now.

When I'm good and limber, I pluck a record from my book bag and slide it out of the sleeve, careful not to scratch the vinyl. I cross to the record player in the corner cupboard. Mme Durant hates that she has to use the thing at all—a proper studio should have a pianist at all times, she says. But this is Fairbury. The best she can do is keep the player hidden from sight. If she paid Mr. Meeks for every solo lesson she gave, Madame would have to shutter her doors within the month.

When the edges of the record are balanced on the pads of my middle fingers, I let it drop carefully onto the slip mat. I flip the switch, and the yellow MGM lion begins to spin. I touch the needle down, then back into the center of the room, waiting for the static to swell into music.

I meet my own eyes in the floor-to-ceiling mirrors set into the far wall, tilt my chin, and bend one elbow, pretending I've got Gene Kelly on one side of me and Donald O'Connor on the other. And from the first giddy note that soars out of my mouth, I *am* Debbie Reynolds and oh, what a good morning it is.

The song starts out like a conversation, but then halfway through the second eight-count they're dancing up a storm. I taught myself to tap at the theater in town, the Bonham. It's not as fancy as the Paramount or the Brandeis in Omaha, but I can't imagine Fairbury without it. Jesse's little sister Nelly works there on the weekends, and she must have snuck me up to the projection room at least a hundred times last summer so I could block out every single step of this dance number.

I'm breathing hard even though this first part is just singing and striding across the stage, elbows bent as if I really did have a pair of fellas singing with me and tapping out the rhythm with their heels. Then things really pick up and I'm leaping onto the piano bench to hit the high note and doing my best at tap dancing in ballet slippers; Mme Durant would murder me if I actually touched a metal heel to her virgin floors. Even with the right shoes, though, anybody who knows what they're doing could tell I haven't had formal training—I'd have to go all the way to Lincoln for lessons, and we can't afford that sort of extravagance.

I hear the muted click of my teacher's dance shoes behind me, and my voice chokes off, mid-belt. My shoulders drop back out of instinct. I'm sucking in breaths now, my ribs flaring as Debbie seeps out, and all that's left is me—an imitation ballerina about as far from Broadway as you can get.

Class hasn't even started yet, but I know Mme Durant is already ticking down the lines, marking the curve of my neck, the tuck in my abdomen, and the turnout she's trained into my stubborn hips. Of course, that's not really her name. Momma went to Fairbury High School with her back when she was plain old Eunice, before she left to tour with a real company out of San Francisco. She only came home because her mother fell ill and needed somebody to care for her. My dream may be a bawdy knockoff of the real thing in her eyes, but we understand each other all the same. So I *Oui, Madame* and *Non, Madame* as if I never even heard of the name Eunice.

Madame has been my ballet teacher since I was four. I almost quit when I was sixteen, but then I read an article about how Broadway shows were beginning to combine their dancing chorus and singing chorus into one ensemble; that more and more, a performer was expected to be able to do both—and act, too. So I stuck with it. I'll never be the kind of dancer who can make every movement seem effortless. But I'm stubborn, and I work hard.

Madame taps her heel twice and sniffs as if my music is leaving a sour smell in the air. I scurry to the cupboard to switch out my record for one of hers: Debussy, as always, to begin. She gestures toward the barre as the arpeggios flutter like autumn leaves through the air.

"Let's begin with our usual barre. Second position and *grand plié*: one and two, three and four." She crosses behind me while I move through the four-count. "Reverse the arm into fifth, and reach. *Tendu* into first. Now, *demi, demi, grand plié*, forward and back. Down and up, then rise and balance."

Madame makes little noises of approval or disapproval while I work, reaching out every so often to tap my hip or press her palm between my shoulder blades. My bearing on the outside world slips away until it's just me and my breath, and the familiar cadence of her voice. Madame is by turns sharp and soft; sometimes I think she gets as lost in it as me.

After I've completed the center work to her satisfaction, Madame demonstrates a new combination. "*Relevé, attitude, pas de bourrée*, three and four. *Pique arabesque*, and again, *chaînés, pas de bourrée*."

She adds a few *pirouettes* at the end and I move through the steps at tempo. Mme claps her hands before I can launch into the other side. "No, no. Shoulders down when you turn."

So we drill the *pirouettes* until Madame is satisfied enough to put it all together again. If she's in a good mood, if her joints are being kind, she'll move through the gentler combinations with me, spinning at a diagonal across the floor for the sheer joy of it. By the end of class, my muscles are trembling, sweat soaking through my leotard. It feels so good to work my body this way. In the final *reverence*, I hold that lowest, deepest bow for an extra moment so Mme Durant knows how truly grateful I am for her.

A ballerina does not pant for breath, but my nostrils are flaring like a quarter horse as I cross to the record player and lift the needle to spare her the indignity. Then I slump to the ground, unlacing my slippers and peeling off my tights. I stink. If I hurry, I can grab a shower before my evening shift at the diner.

"*Merci*, Madame. I'll see you tomorrow."

"Will you?"

Without waiting for an answer, Mme Durant sweeps out the door, her skirts fluttering around her calves, still hard as a pair of river stones. It's the same question she gives me every time. She knows I'm set on Broadway—that if I had the money, I'd already be gone.

-5-

EVERY FRIDAY, JESSE'S mama has me over for supper. He raps on our front door promptly at six, freshly showered after helping his papa lay irrigation pipe, a sheen of Brylcreem parting his hair sharp enough to satisfy the military ways neither one of our fathers can seem to shake. He steps into our parlor, all Yes, *ma'am* and *No, sir*, trying so hard to be good it makes me want to kiss the proper right off his face.

"Give my regards to your mother," Momma says as she sees us to the door, while Nana waves from the parlor window.

We make a dash for the truck, laughing as a gust of warm wind rolling off the prairie flattens wisps of hair across my face. I stay on my side of the bench seat until we turn out of our long driveway, then I scoot over beside Jesse, take the stick shift out of his hand, and lean in as he drops his free arm around my waist.

He relaxes against me, clearly exhausted. It's hard for him, doing farm work in the morning before school, then more chores after school, homework, then driving me home each night after my shift is over at the diner. And probably more schoolwork after that. Nelly says he falls asleep at his desk most nights.

Jesse is flush with sisters. Lois, the oldest, still lives at home even though she was done with high school something like fifteen years ago. Never had a boyfriend and never seemed to want one. She's up before the sun every morning, working the farm alongside Papa Schmidt.

Jesse's sister Joy and the neighbor boy eloped back in '43, the day before he shipped out, and still live right down the road from her parents. Violet married a grocer over in Chester and has two kids in diapers. Then there's Rose, who's too smart for her own good. If she isn't at her job down at the law office, she's got her nose in books so thick and dry, they probably don't even keep them at the university library in Lincoln.

Nelly is the baby at thirteen and boy, do the rest of them spoil her. But it doesn't seem to have done her any harm—she's just about the sweetest girl you'll ever meet. So that's five sisters and no brothers, meaning there's only Jesse to take over the farm after his folks.

The war left Jesse's papa with a bum knee, and keeping up the farm hurts him far more than it should. The sooner Jesse can take over, the sooner his papa will get some relief. So Jesse doesn't get to have dreams of his own. His life is right here in Fairbury, for the rest of his days. But if he *did* get to dream? He'd go to college and stay there for a decade or so, picking up a degree or two in rocket science or astrophysics—whatever it takes to land a spot on one of those teams the government's got shooting space junk into the atmosphere.

It was hard enough to get his papa to agree to let him finish senior year, so Jesse makes the most of what schooling he's allowed.

Nobody takes a heavier load of coursework than him. All the other boys at school work their farm chores around basketball or baseball practice. But Jesse doesn't bother with any of that. By the time he graduates from Fairbury High and steps beside his papa full-time, he'll be the smartest damn farmer in Nebraska.

It's a waste, if you ask me.

He toes the clutch and I shift into third, leaving one hand dangling over the stick and running the other along his thigh. Patsy Cline is crooning on the radio, and the cab of the truck is cozy, rocking a little as a gust of wind blows up out of nowhere.

"Can we just keep on driving until we reach the ocean?"

Jesse chuckles. "Should I stash a getaway bag with a change of clothes and a toothbrush behind the seat?"

"Yes, please." I drop my head onto his shoulder. "I just wish there was nothing holding either one of us here."

He's quiet for a long moment. "Yeah. Me too."

We don't say any more about it, but the weight of those words hangs in the cab the rest of the drive. Jesse and I have known each other since before we could walk or talk—that's what you get when you grow up in a small town. I wonder sometimes what it would be like if I never came to know him as anything more than that brainy kid a couple farms down the road. It'd be a million times easier to leave this place. Even so, I can't bring myself to wish for a life without him at the heart of it.

The truck slows, I downshift, and Jesse spins the wheel, the tires bumping over the washboards that a winter flood cut into the driveway. Twin hedgeapple rows lead down the gravel drive, cutting up the wind and the view from the old farmhouse. I wait an extra moment before I lean over, drop a line of kisses along his jaw, and scoot away to the far side of the truck.

By the time Jesse cuts the engine, Nelly is already flying out the front door of the farmhouse. She yanks my door open and sweeps me up the porch steps while the wind tosses our hair around our heads. When we tumble inside, Mrs. Schmidt beckons from the living room.

"Mazie, *schatzie*, come sit." Her hair is drawn into a knot at the nape of her neck, shocks of gray like comet trails at each of her temples. Her face and neck are flushed, and she pats them with a corner of her apron.

Jesse blows through the door a minute later, leaning against the wind to get it closed again. He crosses to his mother's side and kisses her cheek, then hefts the ottoman and sets it on the braided rug in front of the sofa. Rose drops on one side of me, Nelly plops on the other, and the three of us kick up our feet all in a row. Mr. and Mrs. Schmidt settle into twin wingback chairs, and the barn cats who wheedled their way inside last winter—a portly tabby and a gray with half an ear missing—leap into their laps. The smell of borscht and dark bread wafts out of the kitchen, steam clouding the windows on the whole ground floor.

I love it here. I really do. It's just—everybody expects that any day I'll become another one of Mrs. Schmidt's daughters. And I'm not ready for that. Not even close.

After supper, my belly is full and my cheeks ache from smiling. It's still gusty outside, but no way am I missing the movie on account of a little wind. Jesse and I trip down to the truck, hand in hand, and I slide in from his side. Lois leaves when we do, pulling out of the driveway with a flick of her hand that's more like a salute than a wave.

"She's headed out of town?"

"Yeah. Going to see her army friends in Lincoln again."

Lois is a grown woman—can do what she wants, I suppose. But . . . "If that's where she wants to be all the time, why does she bother coming back?"

Jesse shrugs. "Sometimes I think it's for me—Papa needs help with the farm, and Lois knows how bad I want to finish high school. Maybe in June when I step in full-time she'll cut loose." He hesitates, chewing on a corner of his lower lip as he cranks the wheel.

"What?"

"It's just—I can't hardly imagine the farm without her on it. We never would have survived that drought a few years back without her knowing how to work the big machinery, punching holes all over the fields, looking for water. I just can't see it."

Jesse grabs my hand and laces his fingers between my own. "It'd be like you saying, *Ah—forget Broadway.*"

"Ha!" I lift our clasped hands up to my lips and kiss the tops of his fingers. I never thought about Lois that way—as someone with hopes and aspirations of her own. For all I know, she dreams about corn, and mathematically straight rows in the soil. Or busted-up diesel engines in desperate need of her attention.

"So, what's this picture we're seeing?" Jesse asks through a yawn.

"*Some Like It Hot* with Marilyn Monroe and Tony Curtis; Marilyn's got top billing this time. It's set in the twenties—a couple of jazz musicians witness a murder and dress up like dames to hide from the mob. It isn't a musical, but there's plenty of singing."

"Oh good, 'cause I was worried." A smile cheats across his face.

"No need. I'll be singing the songs on repeat for the next week, at least. Want to hear my best, breathiest Marilyn?"

That gets a chuckle out of him. "No, thanks. I like this Mazie just fine."

My Marilyn impression catches in my throat, and I swallow it down. I mean, I like myself well enough, too. I love my home and my family and what I come from. It's just—I know there's more to life than what's here in front of me. And I'd be a fool to think *this* me, the *right now* me won't change a little along the way. I'm only seventeen! Jesse doesn't mean he thinks it'll always be exactly like this between us, does he?

We take it slow getting to the drive-in at the next town over and find our usual parking spot in the eighth row back, dead center. The drive-in has only been open for three weeks this spring, and the lot is half-empty. Only the diehards come out in this kind of weather. When Rhonda and Billy pull in next to us, we all chuck blankets and pillows into the truck beds and climb on in.

Billy is vice president of the Fairbury High chapter of the Future Farmers of America; I think half the reason he and Jesse are even friends is that Jesse plans on wringing all that farming know-how out of him once school's finished. Though it's a fair enough trade since Billy never would have passed a single mathematics class without Jesse's help.

Rhonda has a knit hat pulled down almost over her eyes, with two blonde braids sticking out the bottom. No matter if she's milking cows on her family's dairy farm or whooping and hollering as captain of the pep club, she's always got that fuchsia lipstick painted across her lips.

"Can you believe we're almost done with high school?"

Rhonda's only parroting what everybody's saying, but I feel Jesse stiffen beside me. For most people, the end of high school means freedom, but for him, it's the opposite. I open my mouth to change the subject, but Rhonda's off again before I get the chance.

"And guess who was selected as chair of the reunion committee?"

Billy makes a show of rolling his eyes, while Rhonda preens like a peacock.

"For the five-year, we'll have a potluck in the afternoon so everybody can show off their babies, and a semiformal ball that evening that'll put the disaster that was our junior prom to shame. I've already narrowed down the theme to two options: *Summer Nights* or *Unforgettable*. What do you think, Mazie?"

I could be tactful—pretend I care. I *could*. "In five years, I'll be working as an actress in New York City, and I doubt I'll be able to make it back."

Rhonda stares at me, her jaw slack. I can see it in her eyes—she thinks I think I'm too good for here. Most of the girls at school do—it's always put some distance between them and me. They don't understand that it's not about escaping our small town for some big city. Staying here would mean fighting what's been in my bones as long as I can remember.

Rhonda purses her lips. "Can you believe this weather? It's going to rain *again*! I can smell it."

Billy tugs the blanket up under her chin. "Nah. You're nuts."

She wriggles down deeper. "Say what you want. I'm never wrong."

"No comment," Billy mumbles. He braces for impact, and sure enough, she whacks him on the arm.

"I don't mind a little rain," I say. I missed this movie when it premiered in March on account of spring musical rehearsals; I thought I wouldn't get the chance to see it.

When the projector flickers on, I quit talking. Music crackles out of the speaker box beside the truck, and I hunker down in the truck bed so nothing and nobody will distract me from the glory that is about to be. Movies aren't the same as a live production onstage, but they're as close as I can get in corn country on a Friday night.

Jesse scoots his arm around me so I can lean against him. I don't know how he can even think about sleeping, but the next thing I know, his head drops back against the cab and his breathing goes slow and warm on my neck.

The screen is all tones of gray and white as the names of the cast and crew flash on and off. Behind it, the sky above and all around is lit up in streaks of pink and purple as high winds yank the clouds around. I pull the blanket up under my chin and then—I don't know how to explain it except to say I stop being me and this stops being Nebraska and I don't even mind that my right leg is falling asleep and I'm going to have to pummel my thigh and calf muscles with my fists to wake them up again.

When I was little, I told anybody who would listen that I was going to sing and dance on a big stage when I grew up. As the years went by, people stopped nodding their heads along with me, and this pinched, pitying sort of look took its place. So I stopped talking about it. But this thing that's driving me—it's not something I want. It's not something I hope someday will happen. It *is* me. Without my big Broadway dream, I'm not sure I even know who I am.

-6-

SUNDAY MORNING, WE pull into church, Daddy, Momma, and Nana in the cab, with me bumping along in the bed of the truck. The brakes squeal to a stop, and I hop over the side so I can give Nana a hand getting out. She reaches up to steady the wide-brimmed straw hat perched over her silver curls, turning it so a cluster of bright tulle flowers stitched onto the brim are front and center.

"Save me a seat," I whisper.

"You bet." She pats my cheek with a white-gloved hand.

While they head to the foyer for coffee, biscuits, and the chance to catch up with old friends, I make for the back room with its dingy carpet, yellowing signs on the wall, and a coffee-maker purring away in the corner. As always, Mrs. Muth is seated at a pockmarked cabinet grand, running scales up and down the keyboard.

"Mornin'!"

She nods from her spot on the piano bench without missing a beat, her messy curls bobbing with alacrity. Not only is Mrs. Muth the church organist, she directs our school musical and conducts the choir, too. And she's coached me through a dozen audition songs. Any time one of the neighboring towns hires her to do the music for a community theatre production, she makes sure I'm the first to get the call for auditions, and she lets me ride along with her to all the rehearsals since Daddy and Otis need our truck at the farm.

When she finishes her own warm-up, Mrs. Muth gives me a look, and it's my turn. Her fingers prance over the ivories, leading me up and down, then through an array of leaps, sighs, and slides. My voice cracks on a couple of the trickier jumps, and I resist the temptation to clear my throat.

"Breathe through it," she commands. "No fear!"

That's right. No fear. I try to forget about the crowd gathering outside and just let go. I close my eyes, and the notes lie down like a star chart, my voice leaping from one pinprick of light to the next. If I think too hard about the intervals, everything tightens up, but when all I'm doing is hopping from star to star, it's easy.

Mrs. Muth slaps her hands onto her thighs. "See? Confidence, Mazie. You just gotta get out of your own head and let loose what the good Lord gave you."

I shuffle my feet while she gets the sheet music in place for this morning's duet. It's a classical piece I learned last year for the spring vocal showcase: the "Flower Duet" from the opera *Lakmé*. Reverend Mitchell doesn't mind secular music so long as it inspires piety in a general fashion. If you ask me, he's savvy enough to know that his livelihood is tied to the contentment of his congregation; if a little heavenly harmony puts a smile on folks' faces, so be it.

Mrs. Muth takes the mezzo part, and that leaves me with

the soprano. It's a stretch, especially considering that wide-open high B. Most of the piece is two voices in close harmony, so there's cover if I'm stretched a little thin in places. At least that's what I tell myself.

We run through the tricky patches a second time, then Mrs. Muth shuffles her stack of sheet music and, with a wink, leaves me alone in the back room while she takes her seat at the organ. I've seen the posters from Fairbury High School musicals back in her day, and yearbook pictures, too—Mrs. Muth was a real beauty. She still has a belt that could knock a person flat if they stood too close. Maybe she really could have done something with that voice of hers. But the difference between her and me is that she's happy as can be right here in Fairbury. She doesn't need to step outside of herself to find more.

I peek through a crack in the side door while wheezing chords call the congregation to their pews. My family sits in the second row: Momma, Daddy, Nana, Otis with his wife and kids, and Lucinda with her husband and kids. Us Butterfields take up the whole dang pew. Jesse and his family, except Lois, settle in the third.

Things were hard for them during the war. Daddy told me Mr. and Mrs. Schmidt did more for the war effort as translators than anybody else in Jefferson County. After the Nazis surrendered, the Schmidts tended their farm like they always had, regardless of the cold reception they got from some folks. You'd hardly know now that they were ever treated different for speaking with an accent and having a surname that called to mind the enemy. But it's not the kind of thing a person forgets. They never take down the Stars and Stripes hanging in the parlor window. And they always take care to be visibly, demonstrably American.

Reverend Mitchell steps out of the door opposite where I'm standing, and Mrs. Muth hammers a trio of warning chords. The sound of shuffling pages fills the air as everybody hurries to find their place in the hymnal.

I sing along from where I am. I don't need an old book to tell me the words or the chord progressions that are predictable as a trail of ants at a summer picnic. My voice fills the humble back room, glancing along the low ceiling and setting the thick windowpanes to humming. I let the melody slip away, then try a new harmony in syncopated echoes of the congregation's steadily marching phrases.

An extra dose of rustling fills the silence after the third hymn is over. Mrs. Muth blows a single note on her pitch pipe. *Crap*—I'm late. I fly out the door, trying to hide my scurrying beneath the long skirts Mama insists I wear on Sundays. I get a look from Mrs. Muth when I stumble to the spot beside her on the dais. Then we inhale together, and without any other warning, it begins.

Our voices are like swallows circling the beams of a lofty barn, dipping and swooping together. My neck stretches out, reaching for those high notes, and sure enough, ever so gently, Mrs. Muth jabs her elbow into my ribs. I drop my chin back where it belongs, try to relax and trust my training. I close my eyes; when the sound bounces back to me, I can feel it push against my breastbone and set my skin to tingling. My heels lift off the ground, begging the rest of me to take flight.

When the last note cuts to silence, the absence of that soul-stopping harmony jars me back to earth. Baring myself like that—I might as well be naked in front of the whole congregation. The almost silent reverberation of the last note stretches out unbearably long while I scurry down the steps and slap my behind onto the pew beside Nana. I peek over my shoulder to see the entire Schmidt family beaming at me.

Nana takes my hand in both of hers and squeezes. She's got her chin high, but the corners of her eyes are wet—the woman is so damn proud of me she can barely keep it in. Nana doesn't see anything wrong with my dreams being too big for this place. Hers were, too.

As Reverend Mitchell winds up and gets rolling, the rush of performing fizzles out of me, leaving me feeling dull and spent. I dip my head to peek sidelong at Momma. Her eyes are fixed on the pulpit, so my gaze slides back to my hands clenched in my lap. She'll never set foot in the Frosty Top to see me sing; still, I should know better than to look for a compliment after any of my performances in church—it wouldn't be Christian. Even if she'll never understand why I do the things I do or want the things I want, I wish she could find a way to be proud of me anyhow.

When the sermon is over, we take our time spilling out of the church and down the wide steps. Daddy stretches his arms over his head, leaning back to take in the sky, blue as a robin's egg.

"Radio says a storm's on its way, coming from southwest of here."

Momma flattens her hand and squints upward. "You wouldn't hardly know it."

May is a fickle month, sunny as can be or dumping enough rain for the whole year over the course of a single week.

Daddy grunts. "Summer's coming soon, just not until the last of these spring storms has had its say. Can't say as I mind—we could use a little moisture."

Jesse saunters over, shakes Daddy's hand, and dips his head to Momma. "Ma'am." He offers his arm to Nana, and she grabs hold of it with a cackle. I rise up on my tiptoes and kiss his cheek, no matter that everybody can see. I don't rightly care. Jesse's not just good to me, he's good to everybody that matters to me, and extra good to Nana.

"Be right back—I want to find Mrs. Muth." I weave through the clusters of families, some laughing, some whispering the week's gossip as if the morning's sermon wasn't all about hoeing your own row.

There's no more than a hundred people gathered, and Mrs. Muth was never one for blending into a crowd. Still, I don't see her anywhere. With a shrug, I head back to the impromptu Butterfield/Schmidt gathering when a familiar voice stops me still.

"That girl thinks she's better than the rest of us."

It's Rhonda—I don't have to see her bright pink lips forming the words to know it. Her voice drops low and sugar sweet. "The poor thing believes her singing will take her all the way to Broadway. I feel sorry for her, is what."

"She wouldn't leave—not when Jesse's right here!"

There's a collective gasp at that. "Oh, come now, Carol. You wouldn't mind consoling that sweet boy in her absence one bit." A flurry of giggles escapes from their tight circle.

I swallow and make for the back of the church, my cheeks stinging like I stuck my face into a hornet's nest. If New York is anything like the movies, auditions will be cutthroat—every actress for herself. I try to tell myself Rhonda's words don't hurt, that those girls are one less thing to miss when I go. But I was raised to tell the truth, even to myself.

-7-

WE SIT FOR our final exams Monday and Tuesday, and to celebrate us being released from school for good, the folks down at
the Legion are putting on a dance. Momma makes a pie to bring
along, and even though her peaches have been in jars for the better
part of a year, I swear each bite is like summer dripping down my
chin. Daddy comes in early from the barn to wash up. When he
trots down the stairs, the smile on Momma's face is surely worth
the extra effort he put into pulling on a freshly starched shirt and
combing out what hair he's got left. Anytime they go dancing,
those two are out there on the floor from the first song to the very
last, like a couple of teenagers. It's embarrassing, that's what it is.

I don't fuss too much getting ready. I'd just as well wear dusty
overalls, but I pull on the dress Momma made for me last summer
instead—it'll make her happy to see me in it. Jesse doesn't care what
I look like, so long as I show up. I grab my brush off the dresser and
swing into Nana's room, but she isn't there. When I clomp down
the stairs, I spy her sitting in front of the fire, a blanket drawn over
her knees.

"You're not coming?"

"Nah—not tonight."

I sit on the rug by her feet. "Are you feeling all right?"

She pats my hand absently. "Just a mite dizzy."

"Do you want me to stay with you?"

"Lord, no! You get out there and dance with that handsome fella of yours."

"I could ask Momma to tell Jesse I stayed behind—he'll understand. Or better yet, he'll head this way and we'll both keep you company. We'll play checkers, and you can help me cheat."

That gets a laugh out of her.

"Turn around." She takes the brush out of my hand and pulls out the ribbon and pins, one by one. "Now, you and I both know you'll need the practice. Partner dancing is all the rage in the new Broadway shows, that's what I hear."

"*Shush*," I say with a giggle. "You do not!"

"Maybe not, but dancing's good for you all the same." Nana twists and pins the sides behind my ears so the ends bob up at my shoulders. Then she shoos me away with a wink and a flap of her hand. I drop a kiss on her forehead, and we're off.

Inside the cab, Momma scoots over next to Daddy, and I hop in after. And just for a minute, I can see it—Jesse and me twenty years from now, driving our own kids to a dance, still every bit as head over heels as we are now. I jam my chin against my collarbone. Jesse and me twenty years from now—that doesn't scare me. Kids, though? That's flat-out terrifying. If there's one thing I've learned from watching Lucinda and her friends, it's that falling in love is great, but you better be right sure you're ready for babies before you go and get married.

It's chilly in the cab. I tap my toes against the floor mat until the blanket draped over my knees ripples like rapids after a hard rain. When the old truck bumps off the road and comes to a stop in the parking lot, Daddy goes around to offer Momma a hand down. The place is lit up by a couple dozen lanterns hung from stakes driven into the dirt. The moon is high and white as a bowl of sugar. A string band plucks away inside, and the sound of laughter floats like mist on the crisp night air.

The summer will be long and hot, with no end to work in sight. Everybody knows it, so we make sure to soak in all the easy we can now, even if that means staying out a little too late on a weeknight.

I take Momma's arm on one side and Daddy's on the other, and we walk together under the floodlight and through the double doors. Folding chairs have been arranged along the walls, and the floor is swept clean as any big-city dance hall. The guy on the standup bass used to play in the high school band, and the Nelson twins are playing dueling violins, like usual. Mr. Hanson will be up there half the night, plucking his guitar, I'm sure of it. I don't care what kind of music is playing, so long as Jesse's swinging me around the dance floor.

He spots us the minute we step inside, and pivots, twirling Nelly in our direction. She breaks off mid-spin and dives for me. Her arms cinch around me so tight I'll probably have a crick in my neck tomorrow morning. Jesse catches Nelly's elbow as she's about to drag me over to where her friends are all practicing some new dance move from *American Bandstand*. He sends her scurrying off and, with a nod to Daddy and Momma, leads me onto the dance floor.

The first time Jesse asked me to a school dance, he seemed surprised that I'd expect him to actually dance, much less keep at it the entire evening. Nelly told me that after that night, he spent half the summer begging dance lessons off his sisters. I would have guessed as much even if she hadn't spilled the beans—it's just like him to do whatever it takes to have a shot at making me happy.

Jesse maneuvers us into an open spot. He ducks his head, drawing the curls away from my neck. "Took you long enough."

I smirk, settling my arm across his shoulders. "Never knew you to wish for more time on the dance floor."

"You got me there." He laughs and pulls me closer.

When we first started seeing each other in the summer after ninth grade, we talked all the time about him going to college to study rocket science and me singing and dancing on Broadway. But as the years passed and things between us deepened, we stopped. I'm leaving. He can't. It's going to pull us apart eventually. So why keep bringing up the fact when there never was and never could be any solution? Still, it hangs there in the air between us, and we pretend we can't feel it coming in with every breath.

After the set break, Jesse asks Momma for a dance, and off they go. I find a space against the outer wall between dangling pennants and eagle-topped flag stands and lean back with a sigh, taking in the whole room. There's Nelly and her friends trying to make western swing moves work on an old-time song. There's Billy and Rhonda slow dancing in the middle of the floor, barely pretending what they're doing out there has anything to do with the music. She'd better not come over here—I don't aim to pick a fight, but I'm not gonna pretend we're friends when it's clear now we're not. And there's Jesse leading Momma around the dance floor like there's nothing he'd rather be doing. I'm so busy watching them, I don't notice Lois settle in on the other side of the state flag until she speaks.

"Evenin', Mazie. I've been meaning to talk to you."

"Oh! I didn't realize you were back from Lincoln."

Lois shrugs off my comment. "Look, if you're going to leave Fairbury, go already. Quit stringing my brother along."

"I—" I'm so shocked I can't think of a single thing to say.

Lois's face is half-hidden behind a ripple of midnight blue fabric. She's got the same big brown eyes as Jesse, though for the life of me, I don't see half the heart in hers.

"Oh, come on. It's about time somebody said something."

"I don't remember asking your opinion." Anger has finally come to my rescue, but it's too late—she's already got me on my heels. Lois is almost twice as old as Jesse, and she's tall, with arms and shoulders as big as any man's. Makes a solid girl like me seem puny.

"Look." Lois fixes me with a flat stare. "I've got no interest in hearing whatever sentimental nonsense you're about to lob my way. You know you're doing wrong by him. And you shouldn't need me to tell you so."

Across the room, Daddy cuts in to sweep away Momma, and Jesse spins in a slow circle, looking for me. His face lights up when he finds me, then clouds over when he glances between Lois and me. He weaves between twirling pairs and reaches out as soon as he's close enough to take my hand.

"Lois?"

She doesn't answer, only shoves off the wall and walks away. A notch crinkles up the skin between Jesse's eyebrows—I should say something to smooth things over. But I can't.

"I don't feel much like dancing," I finally mumble.

If I wanted to put him at ease, that's the last thing I should say. But right now, it's the only thing that doesn't feel like a lie.

-8-

WHEN WE GET home from the dance, I climb the stairs to the second-story landing, my palm gliding along the spindle railing as I pass my room, then Momma and Daddy's, circling to the back of the house. Nana always keeps her door cracked, says she likes the old house talking to her while she sleeps.

Nana never left Fairbury—she never had the chance. The War to End All Wars swept through the county and the country—and the whole world, for that matter. Then came the Depression, and the Butterfields had to fight the very earth to hold on to this farm. So there was no time for her to find any other life than this one.

But Nana had dreams, big ones. When I was little, she wouldn't spin fairy tales or read nursery rhymes by my bedside. Instead, she'd send me to sleep with excerpts from Osa Johnson's memoir or stories about the travels of Isabella Bird or Gertrude Bell. Nana wanted to see faraway places, to learn languages with no ties to our own. She dreamed of adventure. She's probably dreaming right this minute.

I peek inside. The room is quiet except for the soft whistle of her breath and the chorus of insects buzzing outside her open window. Nana snores something awful when she's really out—I don't want to wake her if she's just dozing off. I'm about to back into the hallway and tiptoe to my own room when, without cracking an eyelid, she pats the bed beside her.

"Tell me all about it."

The veins across the backs of her hands are dark against her moonlit skin. Her pulse flutters at her collarbone, intersected by her long yellow-white braid. When she lies in bed like this, straight as a board, the quilt barely ripples over her small frame.

I sit on the edge of her bed, running my fingertips over the freeform stitches of her cherry tree quilt. "Lois let me have it."

Nana opens one eye like a bullfrog. "Oh, really?"

I twitch my shoulders, sort of a shrug. "She thinks I'm doing wrong by Jesse."

"Because you're planning to leave?"

I nod, picking at a loose seam. "While he has to stay."

Maybe Lois is right. It's just—I can't bring myself to break both our hearts until it's absolutely necessary.

Nana is quiet. There's a rattle in her chest when she sighs. "Does he aim to wait for you?"

"I couldn't ask him to." I stare at my hands.

"Good."

That gets my attention. "Why would you say that?"

Nana's got both eyes open now, watching me closely. "There's nothing wrong in loving a good man. And yours is on his way to being a very good one. But there is a whole hell of a lot wrong with stuffing who you are, and who you could become, deep down inside to make room for the kind of life that loving him would hand you."

My eyes drift to the open window and the darkness beyond. "So I have to pick?"

Nana's mouth turns up at the edge. "That's life, honey. You gotta pick the one thing you can't survive without and wring every last bit of joy out of it."

I see it in Nana's eyes sometimes—longing for what her life might have been. I see it in the way she's looking at me right now.

Everybody I tell about my big dream thinks I'm going to chicken out, that it's just something to run my mouth about, that I'll give up when something else comes along. They assume that once reality sets in, once my head dips down below the clouds, I'll have a change of heart real quick. But they couldn't be more wrong. I may as well try to stop a tornado in its tracks.

Nana's the only one who believes I can do this, truly. Sometimes I wonder if without her, I would have stopped believing by now, too.

-9-

THURSDAY EVENING, WORK is dull as nails hammered into hard wood. Me and the other carhops watch the minutes tick by, begging the hands on the clock to move faster.

We slink outside to deliver our trays to the cars parked in neat chevrons, grumbling about unappreciative audiences that don't deserve us. The crowd stares while we dance, their eyes glazed, slurping on their straws as if that's exactly the accompaniment we always dreamed of. I may be the only one of us carhops who's in this *for* the song and dance, but a performance is a performance, and we've all earned at least a little respect.

When the group number is over, I decide to switch up my solo. I was all ready to sing "Leaning on a Lamp-post," but nothing that low-key is going to work tonight, when the crowd is half-asleep. Instead, I sub in "A Wonderful Guy" from *South Pacific*. See if they can nod off during that one.

I start out by clacking my roller skates like tap shoes between the first few verses. That wakes them up good. The customers sit up in those vinyl red booths, the ladies dipping the toes of their shoes like a chorus of conductors keeping time for me.

Edna busts though the kitchen door then, the telephone pressed against her bosom, her eyes wide as saucers. Something's wrong. Mrs. Muth trained me well, so I don't break the high note I'm holding, but if I had hackles they'd be spiky as porcupine quills all up and down my spine.

I keep singing, but the back of my throat goes dry. She mouths something I can't quite make out. I shrug and turn my back to the audience, like it's all part of the choreography.

What?

She tries again, but it's no good. I cut out the last verse and end on the chorus, flapping my hands in the air to make the finale seem more, well, final, then hightail it to the kitchen door.

"What?" I whisper.

She shakes her head, shoving the phone into my hands like it's diseased. I lift the receiver to my ear and duck into the kitchen, plugging my other ear against the noise of clattering dishes and blasts of wash water.

"Hello?"

"Oh, Mazie, honey."

"Momma?"

"You need to come home, right now. It's your grandmother."

The receiver slips from my hand and smacks against the linoleum, the yellow plastic splitting along the seam. I sag against the wall. The noise from the kitchen roars like a combine slicing through the chaff, spitting grit and dirt and cornstalks over everyone and everything in its way.

-10-

BEHIND THE BARN, just east of the fields, there's a low rise—what passes for a hill around here—with an old oak tree at the top. It's survived floods and twisters and countless wet spring blizzards. It's here we lay our family to rest.

We stand stiff in our Sunday best, huddled together while Reverend Mitchell clasps his hands over the good book, talking about some passage in Ecclesiastes and the virtue of a life spent tending the earth. I keep thinking that if Nana were here, she'd be poking fun at our crestfallen faces and snorting at the picture the reverend is painting of her as a sweet, obedient farmwife.

Our neighbors from across the county fan out behind us in a semicircle. The uneven ground gives away their nervous shuffling; I don't have to turn around to know they're glancing at the heavy clouds overhead, debating whether they'll make it home before it starts to rain.

I'm trying to say goodbye here and now since I didn't get the chance before Nana passed. But thinking of her body down there, abandoned to the frigid earth—it saps every last bit of strength I've got. I knew she wouldn't live forever, of course I did. But knowing a thing like that is about as helpful as when you hit a big old pothole in the road, and the next person to drive by leans out the window to say, "That pothole put a hole in your tire. It's flat." Well, thank you very much for stating the obvious. But the hole's still there, and nothing anyone can say will knit it back together again.

Nana would like that bit about the pothole more than anything the reverend's got to say about planting and watching the winds or whatever. At some point he quits talking, and the remaining Butterfields let the dark clouds herd us back inside. Our neighbors head around to the front of the house like they're guests at a party we're throwing, but my feet stutter to a stop halfway there.

Nana's peonies lining the east side of the house went and got carried away by the warm April we had—those green balls of unfurled petals are set to open any day now. A heavy rain will snap the stems if I don't tie them back. I fall to my knees, scrabbling through the hay for the lattice brought down by winter's heavy snows.

Jesse drops to the ground in front of me, his knees to either side of mine. He draws my hands under his jacket and pulls me close, holding tight until I let go and sag against him. "Leave it. You go on inside. I'll get some string from the barn and prop them up good."

My head falls onto his chest. I should have known Nana was failing. I should have seen it. I should have dragged the doctor over when she stayed home from the barn dance and made him mend whatever was wrong.

Jesse's shirt has been worn soft, the seams beginning to fray. And that's all it takes to pry the ache loose—a soft patch of cotton and a warm triangle of skin when the whole world seems lost to heartbreak. I weep silently, soaking through his shirt until the sky begins to darken and we're both shivering.

At length, he gets me up and moving again, and I head inside. Daddy has retreated to the back of the house, so Momma stands steady in the entryway to receive the crowd ambling through the place. All anybody has to say is how sorry they are, over and over again, as if that could make it any better. I should go help Momma bear the weight of all those people fumbling for the right words. Instead, I make myself busy, avoiding eye contact whenever possible.

At some point Jesse comes back inside to follow me from room to room, picking up plates I leave behind or napkins that slip from my grip halfway to the laundry bin, and holding my elbow when I start trembling so bad I nearly drop one of Momma's china teacups. When I pass Daddy seated at the small table in the corner of the kitchen, he hands me an envelope with my name written on the front in Nana's handwriting.

"Found this among her things."

The chatter in the living room is suddenly deafening; I abandon the reception, make my way upstairs, and circle the landing to Nana's room. It still smells like her inside, and the room is unaccountably warm. I perch on the mattress, my heels brushing against the unruly edges of the maps stored beneath her bed. When I tear open the envelope, a parcel of cash with a letter folded around it slides into my lap. The stationery is a faded cream, with apricot mallows stenciled around the edges. Nana didn't write much, but I can't read a darn word between my shaking hands and the water pooling in my eyes. A soft knock sounds at the door, and Nelly peeks in, her brown braids swinging loose.

"Did Jesse send you up to check on me?" My voice is flat.

She sits beside me, burrowing under my arm and tucking her head beneath my chin. "Yeah. But I was worried, too."

My face is hot. I can't remember how to swallow.

"That's from your grandmother?"

"A graduation present, I think." It doesn't seem right reading it without Nana when she must have planned to give me the letter in person. "I can't seem to . . ."

I stretch the folded paper toward Nelly, who searches my face before taking the page out of my hands. "You want me to read the letter out to you?"

I nod.

Nelly slides off the bed and stands opposite me, like she's delivering a report for school or something. "Congratulations, dearest Mazie. Now, I know graduating from high school was never the dream you pinned all your hopes on, but you stuck with it to the end, and that's something to be proud of, if you ask me." Nelly pauses, checking my face to see if she should go on.

I nod a second time.

"I see no reason why you should hang around here a moment longer now that's behind you. We both know it will take you half a lifetime to save enough money working at that confounded diner, so this is for you. By my calculations, this should buy you six weeks in New York City."

I look down at my hand—there's roughly two hundred dollars here . . . and a pair of train tickets, one from here to Chicago and a second on to New York City.

"There are a hundred reasons to stay. But we both know you only need one good reason to go. You leave your folks to me—they'll come around. So get out there and show that big old world what you've got." Nelly's barely whispering by the end. "Yours, Nana."

Her glance flickers from the money in my hand back to the letter. "You're leaving?"

I'm too numb to answer. The bills slip out of my fingers. The train tickets, too. I skitter to my feet and brush past Nelly, around the landing, down the stairs, and out the back door. My breath is coming fast and hard as I cut through Momma's kitchen garden, still buried under a blanket of hay.

I start running, my breath ragged, my long skirts tugging at my knees, trying to slow me down. I glance up at the low-hanging clouds just as a few fat raindrops hit the ground. At first it's only scattered showers blurring the ruts in front of me and soaking into my clothing. I keep running until my lungs are burning so bad I can't feel the chill. I should feel it—I should feel something. Instead, there's nothing where my heart should be. Just an empty space collecting stray raindrops.

It's really coming down now. I must have gone a half mile at least—the farmhouse is little more than a gray shadow in the distance. I squint to keep the sheets of water out of my eyes. I slip in the mud and fall to the ground, a rock the plow dug up tearing at the skin on my knees. I'm trembling. I should turn back. Nana did not say: *Go, be a first-class fool and catch pneumonia in the first storm to blow past.*

What she said was: *Go, follow your dreams.*

How can I say no to that?

I drag myself to my feet. It's no use trudging through the muck. I lean into the falling rain and cut toward the road. A chill nips at me through the thin cotton. I cinch my arms across my chest and tuck my fingers under my armpits.

An old pickup barrels down the road, swerving and skidding in a stretch of standing water. I yell—like that'll do any good—then throw myself out of the way, into the ditch, as it careens past. I sit up, my bare legs stinging, my breath coming in rapid-fire bursts of panic.

A second set of headlights bears down on me. I stand up, shivering so bad I can't even get a single shout past my lips. I can just make out a bright green bumper, the wipers clearing the way for a face I know all too well.

Oh, Jesse. This is going to hurt.

I climb up the embankment, wave my arms over my head, and sure enough, he skids to a stop.

"Mazie?" Jesse jerks open the truck door and splashes across the road toward me. "What are you doing out here? You're soaked through!"

My whole body starts trembling—shock setting in, I guess.

"Come on, let's get you home." He takes my hand and starts to walk me over to the truck, but I can't seem to make my legs move.

Worry rolls off him, but all I can do is stand there.

Jesse holds me at arm's length so I have to look him in the eyes. "Did somebody back there say something?"

I open my mouth, but nothing comes out.

"Mazie, talk to me."

I shake my head and then—it all spills out of me. Right there, standing in the middle of the road. The letter. The money. The train tickets. My nose is running. My hands are balled into fists. I'm a mess, but I have to finish. I have to tell him.

"It's time." It comes out like a bleating calf. "I have to go."

"Go?" He looks so confused. Wounded, like he's not sure where the hurt is going to come from, but he knows it's on its way. "What do you mean? Mazie, you're going to have to give me more than that."

"You know I've been putting aside money for train fare to New York City and a room to rent once I get there. For auditions." He's looking at me like I'm speaking Swedish or something. "I don't have enough saved—at least I didn't before Nana . . ."

He just stands there, stunned, his hands gripping my shoulders, like if he holds on tight enough, I can't actually leave.

"There's no reason for me to stay anymore."

He flinches like I struck him, his arms dropping to his sides like dead things. "No reason?" The fear is beginning to thaw, and anger's taking its place. "Nothing. Really?"

"I mean—" I reach out to grab his shirt and pull him back, but I stop myself short. "The way I see it, I'll only ever get to be half-happy. Either I stay with you, but I'm gut-shot, knowing I gave up on myself. Or I get to chase my dreams, but I have to break my own heart to get the chance. The first—I just know, no matter how I might try, being a farmwife can't make me happy, no matter how much we love each other. I'd only make both of us miserable. The second—at least you'll be free to find somebody else and have a chance at a real life, a full one."

"Dammit, Mazie, I'm not going to up and find someone else. Look around you. You think what your parents have is normal? Well, it's not. Joy got married on account of the war, and Violet has only been with Gary for five years and *already* she can't stand him. You think Rhonda and Billy have anything like we do? Look"— he kicks at a hunk of mud, the edges weeping into the standing water—"I'm not trying to stop you. Go, if you need to. I'll wait."

I fling my arms into the air. "Mary Martin has been on Broadway for twenty years already. And Ethel Merman has been going for—what—thirty? So you're hoping I'll fail. Is that it?"

"Come on, Mazie, of course that's not—"

"You *knew* this was my dream, Jesse." Rain streams down both our faces, whole rivers of water. The world has gone dim.

Jesse plants his hands on his hips. "I hoped you'd find a way to make that dream happen here."

"What—doing some community theatre production once a year? I've done that already, a dozen times. And, yeah, sure, I could do it again. That is, *if* I can squeeze in rehearsals between birthing babies; canning jams, jellies, pickles, and hams; then milking; keeping the books; handling the paperwork; and the thousand other things that go along with farmwifing. But, Jesse, I want *more*."

Shock washes over his face, and hurt, too.

I cross my arms over my chest. He doesn't understand. I thought he understood?

"You can't tell me I'll be able to spend my days how I want if I stay. Nobody around here gets that kind of freedom."

"I thought you loved me. I thought you and me—" His voice is choked when he continues, broken. "I thought we were forever."

"I *do* love you. But everybody around here gets married right out of high school and pregnant five seconds later. I'm not ready for that. Not for any of it."

"*Christ*, Mazie, who said anything about having babies?"

"Jesse . . ."

"Get in the truck. I'm not going to leave you out here. Just—" He rips the hat off his head and turns away from me. "Get in the truck."

I climb into the cab and lean against the window as he turns the truck around. I stare at the empty fields streaming past. He cranks up the heater, but I don't stop shivering all the way home. Jesse swerves into the driveway, hits the brakes, and knocks the stick into neutral. He doesn't get out. He won't even look at me. When I stumble outside, he reaches over to yank the door shut before I can say one more word. Then the truck skids on the loose gravel, and he's gone.

I run up the porch steps and inside, past the crowd of people. I hold it together until I get upstairs, then lock myself in the bathroom, plug the drain, and turn the faucet on all the way so nobody can hear the ugly sobs rattling out of me.

-11-

PEOPLE DIE ALL the time. And the folks left behind grieve, make their peace with it, and resume their lives. I've seen it happen dozens of times. But Nana dying—I don't know how I'm supposed to get over this.

Once the neighbors are all gone, I tiptoe downstairs to the kitchen, where the telephone hangs from a nail beside the pantry. I dial the operator, praying that just this once nobody down at Jorgensen's is listening in on the party line.

"Operator."

"The depot, please."

"I'll connect you." There's more than a little question in Verna's voice, but I'm not offering anything by way of explanation. That's one thing I won't miss about small-town living—everybody in your business all the time.

"Rock Island Depot."

"Hello, Mr. Gill. I've got an open ticket to Chicago and another one on to New York."

"That you, Mazie?

"Yeah."

I can tell he's trying to give me room to say whatever it is I've called for, but eventually the silence stretches too long. "I'm real sorry about your grandmother."

I swallow and try to answer, but I just can't.

"She came in two weeks ago, just tickled at the thought of surprising you with a trip out east."

"I want to go as soon as I can. Tonight, if possible."

"Are you sure, now? Might you want to wait? I can hold the reservation awhile, until you're ready."

"I need to go, Mr. Gill. Now." My voice crumples on that last word, which I guess convinces him, because I hear a shuffling of papers and a clunk before he's back on the line.

"I've got a seat on the Rocky Mountain Rocket leaving tonight at nine twenty, but that one isn't a sleeper. Then a transfer onto the 20th Century Limited tomorrow afternoon, straight on to Grand Central."

"I'll take it."

I hang up; the silence in the kitchen is deafening. There are more calls to make—to the boardinghouse in New York to secure a room, and to Otis to see if he'll drive me to the train station. But it's going to be a minute before I can manage anything more than remembering how to hold myself upright, and how to breathe, and how to *be* in a world without Nana.

Back upstairs, I yank my suitcase out from under the bed and flick the stout latches, letting it drop open on the quilt. The old thing's banged up and shabby; only one of the latches really works, but it'll have to do. I grip the headboard and glance around my room, taking it all in: The narrow bed shoved against the wall to leave a section of exposed floorboards for a makeshift stage. A worn block quilt draped over the back of a chair Daddy fixed twice when I kept busting it trying out some new dance I saw in the movies. The low gabled window looking out over the fields where I would sit and dream for hours when I was supposed to be doing schoolwork.

I don't know where to begin—how to leave this place I've lived my whole life. But I'm sure that if I don't go right now, Jesse and I will patch things up and this gaping hole in my chest that Nana's passing ripped open will fill in with everyday nothings, bit by bit, until leaving becomes flat-out impossible.

I pull together the sheet music for my audition songs, then kneel in front of my dresser, reaching into the very back of the bottom drawer, beneath a lumpy wool sweater, for the shoe-box where I've been storing my stack of theatrical pictures and résumés. Last summer I talked the guy running the photo booth at the county fair into coming to work an hour early to shoot a bunch of stock poses. It was a bargain at ten dollars for the sitting and five for a stack of reproductions. They may not be up to big-city standards, but they're a start.

There isn't much on the résumé. Singer-dancer. Height, weight, hair color, eye color, vocal range—the usual. Experience: a couple of singing competitions, four straight plays in high school and four musicals, a dozen community theatre shows, and one regional theatre production, the lone professional gig on the entire page. Skills: ballet, assorted line dances, and every single square dance known to mankind. Special talents: Um, bucking hay?

Mucking stalls? Milking cows? I figured it was better to leave that one blank.

I peek into my closet, snag my hatbox, and toss it onto the bed along with Lucinda's hand-me-down purse, a quilted brown leather bag that's only a little cracked at the edges with a brass snap closure and a loop handle. There's no point in packing my filthy overalls and work boots. I take my three newest dresses off their hangers and fold them in the bottom of the suitcase, then tuck the scarf Nana knitted for me last Christmas, two pairs of nylons, and a sheaf of stationery for writing home into the side pocket. I pick a pair of dress gloves from the top dresser drawer and the pearl earrings Momma gave me on my sixteenth birthday. I throw in my housecoat, a set of warm pajamas, and my ballet slippers and dancing shoes, tights, and two leotards. At the last minute I dig under my pillow and pull out the ratty T-shirt of Jesse's I sleep in most nights and toss it in with the rest. I sweep the frames off my dresser last, tucking them facedown so I don't lose my nerve looking into my family's faces.

Before I know it, the suitcase is full. I sit on the lid to snap everything in and cinch a strap around the middle to make up for the busted latch. I tuck the tickets and cash into my purse and carry it all downstairs, set my luggage in the entryway, drape my coat over the top, and peer into the dining room. I check my wristwatch; I've got a couple of hours before I need to leave for the station. Momma and Daddy are seated, heads bowed and hands clasped together. My heart sinks clear to my toes.

"Mazie, honey," Momma says when she sees me standing in the doorway. "Come sit."

I can hardly look at the pair of them. "Nana left me a letter. Train tickets and some money. She wants—she wanted me to use it to get to New York City, so I can audition."

Daddy looks up at that. His eyes are red and puffy.

I draw in a ragged breath. "I called the station and reserved a seat for tonight."

The air goes out of the room, the candles on the sideboard sputtering and dancing sideways. "You did what?"

I slide into the empty chair across from them. "I have to give it a shot. You know how long I've been wanting this. It's what Nana wanted, too." I push the letter across the tabletop. "See for yourselves."

The table has stood in this dining room for as long as the Butterfields have held this land. The planks are stout, but every so often the dark walnut grain buckles and crimps, signs of a hard winter or scorching summer that bit deep into the tree. My fingers trace a long steady line in the burnished wood, then a jagged section before they drop off the edge.

Momma grips Daddy's arm, their heads hanging low.

"Daddy, say something. Please."

Finally, he looks up from the letter, shadows staining his cheeks. "Us Butterfields don't run away when things get tough, Mazie." He shoves back from the table. "I've raised you better than that." His chair catches on the rug and topples as he stamps out of the room. Daddy's boots scrape against the kitchen floor, and the back door slams behind him.

"Momma?" I can't keep the wobble out of my voice.

"How can you be so selfish? Mazie, your family needs you right now."

Her words are like a slap across the face. "I know it must seem like—"

"Your father is grieving. He just lost his mother!" She plants her hands on the tabletop and pushes away, bustling into the kitchen. I trail after her as she draws an apron over her shoulders, knots the strings around her waist, and reaches for a drying towel. Momma plunges her arms into the wash water and scrubs as if the dishes are coated in day-old gravy and not merely dusted with crumbs from the reception.

"Momma, come on, let me do that."

She keeps her head down, eyes fixed on the suds frothing out of her way. "What's the hurry? You haven't even graduated yet."

"My exams are all finished. It's just waiting for the ceremony at this point. I don't need to walk across that stage for a piece of paper. I don't even want to without Nana in the audience."

"So stay for the summer. Give your family a chance to grieve together. You can go to New York in the fall maybe, after the harvest is in. Once you're eighteen."

"I can't wait. Momma, I can't stay here and pretend this is the life I want, not if I have the chance to go."

"Your nana wouldn't want you abandoning your family."

"Nana knew it would be hard to leave. That's why she insisted—"

"It's only a few months more! Mazie, be reasonable."

I shake my head. I know it has to be now—before the clean break has a chance to knit back together, before I lose my nerve. Mama hands me a saucer, water sliding along the curved rim. I reach out to take it, but as she whips back to the sink, the china slips through my fingers and shatters on the floor. Momma's eyes go dull and her jaw ticks to the side, drips of soapy water sliding from her elbow to the tip of her pinkie.

"I'm sorry," I whisper. I drop to my knees and begin gathering the pieces, trying to refit the circlet of painted roses together, but the brittle edges only flake away the more I try to force it. Momma steps around the shards and away from me, her footsteps heavy on the stairs.

I finish the dishes alone, sit through a wordless supper, then shut myself in my bedroom. It's dark outside, except beneath the floodlight over the barn doors, where a hard rain falls through that triangle of light. The longer I stare, the more the pummeling rain seems to shift and change color, from silver to yellow to flickers of orange at the tips, until I could swear it isn't water but fire falling from the sky. Sparks leaping out of a campfire. Comets burning trails of stardust.

The ground is hopelessly wet—by morning it'll be a muddy, slippery mess out there. I close my eyes, the falling sparks searing my eyelids. It's all such a mess.

-12-

DADDY ISN'T SPEAKING to me, and Momma refuses to drive me to the station. Just as well—I wouldn't want them out in this. Otis pulls into the drive while Momma watches balefully from the dining room.

"Please don't go," she whispers.

I swear, one more blow and my heart will crack wide open. "Momma, I . . ."

"We're all sad. But that's no reason to upend your whole life."

She turns her back, shoulders hunched against whatever new excuse I've thought up. Daddy doesn't come out from the barn to see me off when I trudge down the steps to where the truck is idling. I pull the door closed, and Otis wheels away, taking it slow and dodging puddles in the road, eyes straight forward so both of us can pretend that whimpering sound is coming from some squeaky wheel bearing and not from me.

When we pull up to the broad brick building, I give Otis a quick hug.

"Take care of them, okay?"

"Yeah." He's never been one to waste words. "You take care of you, too."

"Thanks." I try to smile. "I will."

I hurry inside the station, my shoes clicking along the cold tile. I check the clock on the wall and duck into a phone booth in the corner, pulling the wooden privacy screen closed. I dial the code to the Schmidt farmhouse. I shouldn't be calling this late, but I can't leave without saying goodbye. Nelly answers after three rings, out of breath.

"Nelly—it's Mazie."

"Oh. Hi. I'm real sorry, again, about your nana."

"Thanks. Can I speak to your brother? It's important."

"He's out in the barn. I could run and get him if you'll hang on for just a minute?"

"No—there isn't time. Just give him a message for me?"

"I'm sure he'll come in before long, and you can tell him—"

"I'll be on the train soon, and I won't be able to call."

"You're leaving now?"

I swallow, hard, glancing outside as the silver train pulls into the station. "Tell Jesse I'm so sorry we fought, and that things between us ended the way they did."

"Ended? Mazie, I don't think I should . . ."

A porter walks the length of the train, calling the passengers on board. "I have to go. Tell him I'm sorry, Nelly. *Please.*"

I hang up the phone and grab my luggage, my suitcase digging into my ankle and my hatbox leashed to my wrist as I hurry out onto the platform. Gripping the handrail, I climb up the short flight of steps and start down the aisle. I spy an open seat by the window, tuck my luggage into the metal racks overhead, and settle in.

I must have dreamed of this day a million times—I imagined it would be the most exciting journey of my life. Now Nana is gone, Jesse and me are busted beyond repair, and my whole family is mad at me. It wasn't supposed to feel like this.

A mother with a whole passel of kids settles into the seat opposite me. She's got a boy in knee-high socks, twin girls that look to be school-aged, and two more in diapers. Dark smudges punch into the skin beneath the woman's eyes and cheekbones. Her head hangs forward slightly, like she can hardly be bothered to hold up its weight any longer.

I turn away and press my forehead against the glass as the horn blares, the engine chugs to life, and the platform slides away. Chin in hand, I stare as the buildings blur together—the grocer, the bank, the shoe repair shop, the high school in the distance, and the ballet studio, lit by a few lonesome streetlights.

At the end of class Wednesday, when I finished my *reverence* and said my goodbyes, Mme Durant had answered with her usual question, whether I'd really be back. Tomorrow she is going to walk into her studio, expecting to cringe away from the racket of my latest show tune. Only, I won't be there.

Town thins out, and soon we're in the thick of farmland, puddles filling in the rows and shimmering as we pass. There's the Bucketts' farm. And the Davises'. The rain has started up again, streaking across the windows and pinging against the rounded metal roof. The train slows a mite as it chugs around a bend to sidle up along Cub Creek. The river is black, moving fast, cutting into the banks on either side. I look up, craning my neck to see across the aisle and out the opposite windows. Beyond the tracks is a rocky beach with the best swimming hole in Jefferson County.

I shoot out of my seat. A green Chevy is parked in the pullout, the headlights barely piercing the dark, exhaust coughing out of the tailpipe. My heart is banging like it's gonna jump clear out of my chest.

The train picks up speed as it rounds the curve and stretches out along the straightaway. I stumble down the aisle, hurrying toward the back of the train, to the gap between cars where a single window looks out over the water.

He's there. Standing on that beach soaking wet, hands in his pockets, watching the train pass by.

"Jesse!" I bang my palm against the glass, but his eyes never find anything to land on. He doesn't see me. "Jesse!"

Of course he can't hear me. A moan slips past my lips. The train is flying now; the lonely beach is nothing more than a pair of distant headlights.

I slide to the floor and drop my head into my hands. The last time we went to Cub Creek was the Saturday before senior year started. A late-summer heat wave had made the long days spent prepping the soil for winter pure torture. I remember it as clear as if it were yesterday.

I had a kerchief tied over my braids, mud boots, and short shorts on the bottom with one of Daddy's old button-down shirts on top, the sleeves cut off at the shoulder with the tails knotted around my ribs. I was covered in dirt and sweat, and Jesse was no better. We smelled like pig slop, the pair of us.

So we stripped down to our underwear and ran into the river. As the water swirled up to our necks, he pulled me toward him, his brown eyes shining. "If it was up to me, I would've married you yesterday."

Another day I would have laughed him off and changed the subject, pretended I didn't know how serious he was. Instead, I looked him straight in the eyes and kissed him slow, and long. When we came back up for air, I wrapped my arms around his neck and countered with, "If it was up to me, I'd steal you away with me to New York City tomorrow."

A shadow fell over his face. "You know I can't go."

"You know I have to."

Jesse dropped his forehead onto mine, so our noses touched and our breath mingled. I wrapped my legs around his waist, and he spun us in slow circle after slow circle, the dust from the fields that coated the top of the water twirling around us. Finally he came to a stop, and his hands wandered up the back of my neck and into my hair.

"Just come back to me," he whispered. "When it's all over, come back to me."

I held on to him tight as I could, but I didn't answer. We hardly said anything else, though we stayed down by the river well past my curfew, lying side by side in the back of his truck, watching the sun set, bright red from all the corn dust kicked up into the air, the moon rise, and the stars flare up one by one.

The night seemed every bit as hot as noon had been, and

before he drove me home, we went back down to the water one last time. This time we left every last stitch of clothing on the rocks, letting the water wash us and everything between us clean. I hadn't promised him, not in so many words. But the moon on the water and the flicker of lightning bugs, the way our bodies rose and fell together—that was as sacred as anything I've ever known.

Daddy hadn't even scolded me when I stumbled down to breakfast late the following morning. I think in everybody's eyes Jesse and me already belonged to each other; it was only a matter of time before the reverend made things official. But really, only he and I knew just how fragile was the thread that stitched us together.

A shiver scatters the memories, calling me back to the moment; trains are drafty, uncomfortable creations. The gap between the floor and the wall whistles as the last gasp of Jefferson County air squeezes into the car.

Come back to me. I know that's what he's saying right now, out there on the soggy riverbank. It splits me straight down the middle.

The woman across the aisle watches me stumble back to my seat. "Do you need some help, miss?" But the way she asks, if I was going to say yes, I'd better be nearabout dying to make her day one pinch more difficult than it already is.

I shake my head. I let the words blubber out of me, 'cause if I try to hold them in, I think it might actually kill me. "I'm leaving home. I've hardly set foot outside Fairbury, and I think maybe I just made the biggest mistake of my whole life."

"You got somewhere you're headed? Somewhere safe?"

I nod, blowing my nose in the handkerchief Momma pressed into my coat pocket at the last minute.

"Good for you," the woman says, her chin thrust out and her voice hard. "Don't you ever look back."

I toss my head up and sniff. "No, ma'am." I blink the last of the water out of my eyes. I will not.

-13-

I CAN'T SEEM to get warm—it's as if my blood quit circulating the minute I left Nebraska. The train wheezes along, empty plots of farmland flitting by out the window, the wheels rattling and whining against the tracks, scolding me with every passing mile. I had to take this chance. I had to leave. So why do I feel so miserable?

Whenever I couldn't wrap my head around a thing and Nana would find me sunk in the mopes, she'd say: *Aren't you a Sarah Bernhardt?* Then, with an exaggerated sigh, she'd drape a hand across her brow or pretend to faint or something. That would get me laughing, and more often than not, we'd figure it out together. Without Nana, I'm like a weather vane that can't decide which direction to point, yanked this way and that by fretful winds.

Or, if I couldn't talk to Nana, I'd tell Jesse. We could sit for hours in the cab of his truck, fogging up the windows doing nothing more than talking. He'd find some parallel in the science of jet propulsion or rocket theory, and somehow my troubles would seem perfectly manageable after a while.

What if I can't do this without him—without both of them?

I change trains in Chicago with a five-hour stretch break in the waiting room at the LaSalle Street Station. I mostly keep to myself, huddled into the wing of a double-sided bench, shrinking away from the daylight streaming in the half-moon windows, all the while contemplating the ways that leaving when I did, the way I did, was a mistake. It wasn't only Daddy who needed family around him to heal from Nana's passing—it was me, too. Instead, I took off the minute things got hard, leaving everybody who loves me behind. I grit my teeth and hug my knees to keep from trading my ticket in for one that'll take me straight home again. Because I'm absolutely certain that if I turn around now, I'll never get up the nerve to make the trip again. And I can't bear that thought.

When it's finally time to board the shiny bullet of a train that will take me to New York City, I can hardly move my jaw from clenching it so long, so hard. I don't know how many times I perched on Daddy's armchair while he read the paper, admiring the full-page ads for the 20th Century Limited and its famed Water Level Route, imagining myself in the stately dining car or watching the scenery float by from the observation car. Used to be movie stars and moguls frequented this route, waltzing in on a red carpet, sipping elegant cocktails and eating caviar. But passenger trains are not what they once were—the rich and famous all travel by air now.

Forget caviar, I can't afford to eat anything other than the sack lunch I packed. I settle my things in my sleeping berth and wander the length of the train. In the ladies' room, I splash water over my face, leaning awkwardly over the tiny sink so the water draining off me doesn't spill onto the front of my dress. I won't be changing into a new one until tomorrow, and already this one feels stiff and travel-worn. My eyes skitter away from my reflection—everything is blotchy and puffy and pulled down by too much sadness. Instead, I focus on a slender vase clipped to the wall behind me with a single peony dropped into the water. The bloom is halfway open, crepey petals peeling away from the bud.

My head drops like a stone in a dry well, and I hold my arms rigid, elbows locked, gripping the cold ceramic to keep from sliding onto the floor. I close my eyes and I'm right back there, kneeling in the mud beside Nana's peonies, grief drenching me like a bucketful of icy water, the cold cutting clear to the bone. Only Jesse isn't here this time to hang on while it shudders through me, to chafe my arms and lend me his warmth until the worst of it releases me.

I lurch upright and back into the hallway to find a seat away from the crowd. I gaze out the window as we roll through Toledo, then Cleveland, then Buffalo. When I can't watch another dirty railyard or industrial town of grays and browns and coughing smokestacks slide by, I retreat to the sleeping car, where at least if I close my eyes I can see the wide-open sky and the steady-on roll of the prairie.

After tossing and turning through the early-morning hours, replaying the fight with Jesse over and over in my mind, and the hurt etched into Momma's and Daddy's faces, I give up and throw back the privacy curtain. There's a sour taste at the back of my mouth and a grimy film over my skin. I clamber out of my bunk and make for the dining car.

All that's been left out from the night before is a carafe of lukewarm water and a jar of Sanka. I dump in two heaping spoonfuls and stir, grimacing at the oily sheen on the surface as I gulp the almost-coffee down quickly to cut the bitter aftertaste.

I grip the railing, peering out the window as the train barrels south now, sloughing off the silt from the long cross-country slog. *Almost there.* This is all I've wanted—to finally make it to Broadway and see if I really have what it takes. But now that I'm nearly there, it's all wrong. Whenever I pictured my triumphant arrival, it wasn't with Momma hardly speaking to me and Daddy not at all. And it certainly wasn't with things between Jesse and me over, and Nana gone. This was a mistake, pure and simple.

I need a bath and maybe one of Mme Durant's lectures. Something from home to make me feel like myself. I glance over my shoulder. I'm all alone in the car, so I flick off my loafers and roll my toes. It's not like anyone will see. I grip the railing, turn my feet out, and lift my chest. I close my eyes and, swaying with the screeching train, glide through a warm-up and into one of Madame's regular barre routines until my blood is moving and the familiar motions chase the worst of the jitters away.

A smattering of applause filters through the dining car, and my eyes startle open. A porter and one other passenger who apparently couldn't sleep either have collected at the opposite end of the corridor. I take an impromptu bow, my nostrils flaring as my heart hammers in my chest.

The thrill of being seen courses through me. *This* is why I tore the heart out of my own chest. For *this* feeling, no matter how much I long to run right back to Jesse and Momma and Daddy and *home*. Every second on this train is bringing me closer to the life I've always wished for. I guess I'm going to have to get used to heart-ache hunkering down beside joy and wrapping itself tight enough so I can't ever forget it.

-14-

AS WE CAREEN through the lush bends of the Hudson River Valley, I make my way back to the observation car, where windows look out on the early-morning darkness; shadows cloak the dogwoods, slender reeds, and bowed cattails along the opposite riverbank. The porter, a Negro man with a shuffle to his step, sets a glass of water on the narrow table beside my elbow. I offer a sheepish smile and thank him—just because I'm too fitful to sleep shouldn't mean anyone else has to be up. I rest my chin on my hand and watch the tracks slide away behind us, twin trails of moonlight.

In a matter of hours, this train is going to come to a stop, depositing me in the middle of Manhattan, ready or not. All I know about the city is what I've read in the show papers and seen in the movies. In my mind, Mrs. Cooper's boardinghouse is exactly like the set of *Stage Door*, down to the last detail. But for all I know, it's a crummy rat-infested hovel. And New York City will pummel me for thinking I can make it on my own at seventeen.

When the train finally pulls into Grand Central Terminal, the hiss of the brakes and buzz of people everywhere slaps me out of my gloom. I step through the steam onto the platform while the busy station whirls around me. With a firm grip on my luggage and my purse cinched under my arm, I let the wave of people carry me into the main terminal. The ceiling is impossibly high, like some medieval church, and *oh*—it's bright turquoise, with star charts painted in gold. Jesse would love this. He'd probably spend half the day staring at that painted sky while the city waited outside.

I tell myself to quit gawking like the tourist I am—but I keep spinning in slow, starstruck circles, my gaze roving from the enormous Big Ben clock to the illuminated ticket booths and the mass of people, their paths crisscrossing the polished stone floor like choreography. Sunlight streams through a row of high windows, pooling on the floor like stage lights. I've half a mind to drop my bags and start singing right here and now.

But Mrs. Cooper is expecting me soon at the boardinghouse. The address and telephone number are tucked into my purse, and though I can't afford it, I'm sorely tempted to give the address, 323 West 84th Street, to an obliging taxi driver and get someplace I can call home as quick as I can.

New York City is unlike anything I've ever seen. And it's suddenly abundantly clear that in leaving Fairbury, I wasn't only giving up our house and farm and familiar small town, but the whole idea of *home*. I'm a stranger here, surrounded by strangers. I square my shoulders and pick up my chin. I'll be taking the subway every time I go to Midtown for auditions, so I might as well get used to it. With a last longing look toward the street and the line of waiting taxis, I step into the crowd heading down the wide stairway.

There's a smell to the world belowground, like that year the Little Blue flooded its banks and damp clung to everything for weeks. I wind through the moving crowd to study the colorful transit map on the wall. The subway lines are red and blue arteries pumping people in and out of Manhattan. I trace up the North River with my finger, to the Hudson, then down the Harlem, then the East River, back to where I started. I swallow, hard. Nebraska has water, sure, but the state is good and landlocked. Why did it never occur to me that Manhattan is an island?

I clear my throat, tamping down the rising panic. My finger finds Grand Central, then follows the stations north. The Lexington Ave. line looks like a straight shot to the 86th St. station, with no transfers—that should be easy enough. I glance around the crowded platform. If this were Lincoln or Omaha, I'd ask somebody, just to be sure. But no one makes eye contact down here, not on the subway platform, not while we elbow our way into the cars, and not when we're standing inches apart, holding on as we speed north. I thought the train was noisy, but the subway has it beat by miles. It clangs and screeches, the air out there in the darkness whooshing past. Each time the subway jolts to a stop, I peer outside at the station numbers, doing the best I can to reassure myself that as long as the numbers keep climbing, I'm headed in the right direction.

When I finally make my way back up into the flat daylight, I take a deep breath, then regret that decision immediately. It's nowhere near fresh Nebraska air, but it's leagues better than that stale stuff below the city. I check the address one more time, then step into the stream of people on the sidewalk. Even though I'm bleary and travel-stained, I can't stop a jubilant smile from spreading across my face.

The breeze has a bite to it, damp with the threat of coming rain—apparently summer hasn't arrived here yet either. I can't see much of the skyscrapers I've read so much about, or even the sky, for that matter. The streets are narrow, and the several-story buildings loom overhead.

But there's plenty to see on the street level—the swerving, honking traffic; the bumping, jostling crowds; the frenetic energy that seems to pulse up from the concrete. I've never seen so many people in one place! A newsstand attendant barks out headlines as a passing city bus flutters his papers stacked on the sidewalk. A traffic cop in white gloves blasts his whistle, halting the cars and waving the pedestrians across. I sidle around a cluster of ladies, their handbags dangling mid-forearm and swaying like pendulums, ticktock ticktock with every step. I swerve too late to miss the mail carrier's cart and bang my shin on the exposed metal. As I double over, hopping on one leg, a suit in a top hat elbows past me, knocking my hatbox into a puddle.

"Hey!" I yell.

A passing taxi burps a cloud of exhaust in my face. I collect my hatbox, grit my teeth, and put my shoulders back just in time for the sky to sneeze all over me. The wind picks up speed between buildings, blowing sideways and spraying gusts of rain all down my front. I cinch my coat tighter around my waist and turn off the busy street. Since my hatbox is already soaked, I hold it over my head to keep off the worst of the rain and hurry down the sidewalk, my suitcase banging against my leg.

The corner sign reads 84TH ST., so I'm nearly there. Finally. But when I turn and walk down the street, there's no 323. That can't be right! It isn't until I've circled the same city block three times, panic rising until it feels like every single one of my internal organs is trying to squeeze through my throat, that I realize I've made a serious miscalculation.

I heft my suitcase, praying the straps hold the blasted thing together—if it were to bust right now on the sidewalk, I might give up entirely. I bite down on my lower lip to keep it from trembling and head back to the corner, my footsteps quickening. If you get lost out in a blizzard on the prairie, the very worst thing you can do is panic, so I try to tamp it down. This is a big city. There are plenty of people around—someone will help me, surely? The butcher shop and the restaurant are both closed, so I cross the street, making for the German bakery.

A bell tinkles overhead as I step inside. "Excuse me?"

The round woman behind the counter looks me up and down, grimacing at the puddle forming around my shoes. I let the door fall closed behind me. It's warm inside, so blessedly warm.

"I seem to be lost." This woman doesn't know me, so maybe she wouldn't know that a wobble of desperation isn't usually part of my speaking voice. I stretch my hand out and turn the paper so she can see Mrs. Cooper's address. The baker squints at the writing.

"West." Her accent is thick, like Mama Schmidt's.

"Pardon?"

"*West.*"

"I don't understand."

She steps around the counter and points down the street. "You want West Eighty-Fourth Street. This is East Eighty-Fourth Street. You need to go that way. West."

"*Oh.*" I tuck the paper back inside my purse. "Back home, a street is a street. I didn't think to . . . *well*. Do I need to get on a different subway?"

"They don't run east to west. You walk."

"Is it far?"

"Yes, far. West." She points again, her eyebrows meeting over her nose.

"Thank you." The last thing I want is to go back out there in the cold, but I'd better not waste any more of her time. "*Vielen dank.*"

Her face softens a little at the German courtesy, and I back out of the bakery. The rain has stopped, but the air is chilly. I put my shoulders back—nothing like a brisk walk to warm the blood. I tromp west until I come upon a startling row of trees instead of buildings and grass instead of concrete. Of course I've read about Central Park, but still, a sob breaks from my lips at the sight of all that green. I'd imagined strolling beneath the trees on a sunny afternoon, not lugging my suitcase, sore and tired and so hungry I could eat one of those pigeons bobbing along the sidewalk.

I pick up my pace, hunching away from the gray sky as I follow the winding paths through the park. It's *huge*. Never-ending. Why did I think I could do this? A man in a disheveled suit rolls off a park bench, lumbering toward me, and I don't even wait to see if he's offering help or harm—I start running and I don't stop until

I'm out from under the trees and hit once again with the blare of traffic and the glare of streetlights.

After a few blocks, the traffic thins again. Rows of brownstones, some stately, some crumbling, rise on either side of the narrow street. Lines of cars are parked along both sidewalks, their chrome bumpers so close I can barely imagine the maneuvering it would take to slide one of those long sedans in without knocking the headlights clean off. Children perch on the bricks surrounding a tree planted in the sidewalk, digging at the dirt, spoon and pail in hand. *Lord*, is that all the space they have to play?

I nearly collapse in relief when I reach the broad stairs leading up to Mrs. Cooper's front stoop. Maybe it's a rite of passage: the city throws its worst at you and if you don't blink, well, then you get to stick around.

If you're lucky.

I heft my bags one final time and walk up the steps.

-15-

MRS. COOPER'S BOARDINGHOUSE for theatrical young ladies is a narrow row house with a red stone facade and a dark cornice zippered across the top. Stout columns frame wide steps leading to a recessed front door. It takes everything I've got to make it up those steps. My feet are killing me. I'm thirsty and my empty stomach is making itself heard. I set my suitcase down on the front stoop and flex my fingers. After lugging the thing halfway across the city, angry welts slash the undersides of my fingers on both hands. I thought all those years of farm work built up calluses that could take any manner of abuse, but the handle rubs in an altogether different spot. I ring the buzzer, then clasp my hands behind my back. The door is promptly whisked open by a slim young woman in a red pantsuit with matching crimson lipstick. She's got sleek black hair cut short like a flapper and loads of black pencil lining her eyelids. I know I look a state—I was greasy and travel-worn before I got rained on, then lost and flat-out terrified.

"You're the new girl, Mazie?" She smiles, blinking those dark lashes at me and checking her wristwatch. "You're late! I was beginning to wonder if we'd lost you."

I nod, though I can't quite laugh off the truth behind her words.

"Well, I'm Nat. Come on in!" She grabs my suitcase, and I've never been so happy to see a thing taken out of my hands.

I follow her into the entryway, where framed playbills from *St. Louis Woman*, *Stormy Weather*, and a half dozen other Broadway shows line the walls.

"Those are Mrs. Cooper's," Nat says with another smile. "She was a dancer on Broadway in the years after the war. There was a flurry of shows with parts for Negro actors—people thought things had changed for good. But those parts dried up after a time, so she switched to working as a costume mistress until her eyes got so bad she couldn't see the stitches beneath her fingertips."

Nat hauls my suitcase up the narrow stairs, chattering the whole time. "I guess she figured there was money to be made off all us starry-eyed girls from the sticks trying to make it in the big city."

She's being kind with the "us." Or maybe that's what happens to a person after being here awhile—rough edges are polished up and country ways spit-shined. I follow her up the stairs, taking the narrow length of the place in—we don't have row houses in Fairbury, not even in the middle of town. Back home, there's plenty of room for everybody to stretch out.

Nat pauses on the second-floor landing and raps softly on a wooden doorframe surrounding frosted glass panels. "Mrs. Cooper has the whole second floor to herself, while us girls live either on the third floor or below the main level in the old servants' quarters."

Before I can ask Nat where I'll fit in all that, a woman with soft brown skin and a chin-length gray bob steps out onto the landing. She must be nearly sixty, but her back is straight as a rod. Her gaze ticks over the turnout trained into my hips, the bulk in my arms and legs, and the eagerness that surely shines through my soaked and sorry appearance. I'm tempted to clasp her hands and gush with thanks for making room for me at such late notice, but clearly this is not a woman who suffers fools.

"Mrs. Cooper, this is our new girl, Mazie."

She gives me a pert nod. "You are most welcome here. Nat will show you to your room and fill you in on the way we do things."

"Yes, ma'am."

"You will follow the rules or you will find another place to lay your head. Understood?"

"Of course. Thank you, ma'am."

Mrs. Cooper closes the door again, and I turn, a little wide-eyed, back to Nat.

"She's strict, but you're going to love her. We all do." Nat continues up the stairs to the next floor, rattling off the house rules all the while. "No boys allowed beyond the first-floor parlor, absolutely no liquor on the premises, and no phone calls during the day—we need to keep the line free for casting agents. Mrs. Cooper insists on a nine o'clock curfew with the exception of evenings spent at the theatre."

A night at the theatre! I get tingles up and down my arms just thinking about it. I can't spare eight dollars for a ticket, at least not now. But once I book a show of my own? I bite down on my lip to keep a giddy smile from spreading across my face.

"There's a regular rotation of household chores, and we're

all expected to pitch in," Nat continues. "Anything from prepping meals and cleaning bathrooms to picking up the weekly show papers in the wee hours of the morning or answering the telephone in the hallway and taking down messages. Or showing a newcomer the ropes." This girl is all smiles. "Sure, you can trade with somebody else to work around an audition, but the work gets done or you'll soon find yourself back on that stoop."

"Understood. I'm no stranger to hard work."

"Good. We sleep four to a room. You'll be sharing with Peggy from upstate, Marsha from Tennessee, and Evie from Long Island. You'll share the bathroom with all twelve girls on this floor. There's a daily sign-up sheet outside the door, and if you don't keep your bath quick, by golly, you'll get an earful. I took the liberty of penciling you in for a slot after lunch."

Nat opens the door to what will be my bedroom and plops my suitcase on the floor beside an empty narrow bed against the far wall. "We have family dinner every evening, and if you're here, you are expected to attend. Mrs. Cooper believes that for actors, good food and a good night's sleep is every bit as important as God-given talent."

Momma would agree, at least about needing a full stomach to get on with your day. I sidle along the wall, taking in the room around me. There are three other narrow beds, neatly made, with shoes, hatboxes, and suitcases tucked beneath and a side table by each headboard covered in an assortment of picture frames and mementos. There's a closet in the corner, for coats and dresses, I suppose.

Nat backs toward the hallway, checking her wristwatch again.

"In fact, lunch will be laid out in the dining room in fifteen minutes. See you downstairs?"

"Yes. Thank you—for everything."

Nat closes the door behind her with yet another smile.

I peel off my wet coat and slump on the bed. With a click, I open my suitcase so it lies flat on the floor and dig around for my picture frames. I prop them on the little table beside my bed. There's my whole life laid out in a neat row: Momma and Daddy on their wedding day. Nana in her rocking chair on the front porch. The third photo is one Rhonda took of Jesse and me last summer during her short-lived obsession with photography. We're sitting in the bed of his truck, our legs swinging free, his arm slung over my shoulder. Jesse's looking right at the camera with a wry smile on his face, while my head's thrown back, cackling at something he just said.

I haven't felt that kind of happy since before Nana died. Before my awful fight with Jesse. I trail my finger along the tin frame. I miss him so much I think my ribs might cave in. And picturing him now, that smile gone, aching every bit as much as me, makes me want to scrub away my skin until I've left my wretched self behind.

I check my time on the sign-up sheet outside the bathroom, then splash some water on my cheeks before heading down for lunch. The last thing I feel like doing is making small talk with a bunch of strangers, but I grit my teeth through the noon meal and even manage a real smile or two. I meet my roommates just getting back from morning auditions. Marsha is sweet as can be, if a little dim. Evie doesn't seem all that friendly. And Peggy is a looker—she's got blonde hair set in sleek waves, wide brown eyes, and a wry little mouth—the kind of face that's sure to make a casting director sit up and pick her out of a lineup of a hundred girls. I press my arms against my ribs, my elbows digging into my waist. What if, because I don't look like *that*, I never get the chance to open my mouth? What if nobody sees past my freckles and strawberry hair? I try to push the thought away, but it cinches around my midsection like a corset, leaving little room for the meatloaf and scalloped potatoes in front of me.

The minute we're excused, I peer into the hallway to see if anyone's using the telephone. The hall leads clear to the front door, both sides papered in gold and pale blue damask stripes. Walking through that narrow hallway is as close to wandering through a field of tasseled cornstalks as I'm liable to get in this city.

I know I'm not supposed to use the telephone except evenings and weekends, but surely they'll make an exception so I can let Momma know I've made it here safe and sound. I'll only be able to afford a minute or two on the line anyhow. So while the others are in the parlor staging an impromptu sing-along of *Kiss Me, Kate*, I drop two quarters in the jar, lift the receiver to my ear, and dial the long-distance operator.

"How may I help you?" A pert voice crackles on the line. I give the operator the code to the farmhouse, and she says, "Okay, I'll ring you through."

The clock on the sideboard, rounded over the face and curving down like a mustache at the edges, ticks steadily while I wait, the sound unnervingly loud in the empty hall. A slender vase of cut daisies sits beside the clock, doing its best to cheer the place up.

Momma answers on the first ring. "Mazie?"

"Yeah. It's me." My voice cracks. I've gotta keep this short.

"Oh, thank heavens. You're at the boardinghouse?"

"Safe and sound." And I'll never tell her any different.

"Was the train ride all right? Are they feeding you?"

"Yes, of course. But nothing close to your cooking."

"*Humph.* You warm enough?"

"Yes, Momma."

The line goes quiet. "And are you happy, honey?"

A pained gasp escapes me, though I hurry to cover it with a cough. "I will be. Please don't worry about me, Momma."

"You've always been as stubborn as a mule." There's a long sigh on the other end of the line. "Just like your nana, I suppose."

It's all I can do to keep from breaking down right then and there. I know there's a tiny part of Momma that understands. And that's really something, considering. But is it too much to wish she'd be proud of me? That she and Daddy might see my setting out into the unknown as even fifty percent bravery and fifty percent foolishness?

"I need you to promise me something." I'd know that severe turn of Momma's voice anywhere. "Go on, give that dream of yours a shot. But if you don't get cast, you come straight home. I cannot abide a daughter of mine lost to that city. You think I didn't read those show papers you always had lying about? I know how it is—actors chasing auditions for years, working in some seedy nightclub or worse; hungry, broke, and too far from the people who love them."

I swallow, hard. "Okay, Momma. I promise."

"You never let your savings dip a penny lower than it will cost to hop the train back home, you hear?"

"Yes, ma'am."

"Six weeks, then."

"Six weeks."

I twirl the telephone cord around my finger until the tip is nearly purple. I have to swallow a few times before I can get another word out. "Where's Daddy?"

"You know your father. If it isn't one thing around here that needs attention, it's another." A stranger would be able to tell she's forcing that bit of cheer into her voice—Momma never was any good at lying.

"He's still angry with me for leaving?"

The static on the line stretches out, clicking and crunching. Momma doesn't answer.

"I love you all." My throat chokes off, but I keep going, no matter that she can hear me struggling. "Tell Daddy I'm sorry, will you?" I rush to finish, before I break down completely. "I shouldn't talk any longer. I left my number here at Mrs. Cooper's on the sideboard; I'll wait for your call Sunday after church."

"You take care, Mazie, you hear?"

"Yes, Momma." I want to ask about Jesse, but it doesn't feel right—like I don't deserve to know the answer to that question anymore. "I miss you all so much. I miss . . . everybody."

I hang up the phone, dragging my sleeve against the daisies by accident and knocking half the petals off. They litter the sideboard, tiny crescent moons. I sweep them into my palm and drop them into the waste bin.

When I turn back to the stairs, Evie is watching me, arms crossed over her chest. "You're not supposed to use the telephone during the day. It's against the rules."

"I know, but . . . I had to tell my family I arrived safely. I was only on the line for a minute." She doesn't look like she cares one bit.

"What if a casting director tried to get through and couldn't? What if you just cost me a show?"

"Look, I'm sorry." The last thing I wanted was to get into a squabble with one of my roommates on my first day.

"Rules are rules. I'll have to inform Mrs. Cooper." Evie spins on her heel and glides upstairs.

Fantastic. I trudge up the stairs after her. When I get to my room, I set aside my pajamas, a clean set of clothes for the afternoon, and toiletries. I shove my suitcase under the bed and out of sight—I'll deal with the rest later. Then I lock myself in the bathroom, draw the hottest bath I can stand to boil away the grime, and sink into the water, hissing. As the steam washes over my cheeks, everything goes limp. I can't believe I'm never going to have another late-night talk with Nana. I can't believe I'm hundreds of miles away from Jesse. I can't believe I left when Momma and Daddy are hurting and angry with me.

I miss the privacy of my own room. I miss the sound of my family rattling around the old farmhouse. I miss the singular quiet of a small town. I miss not having to say a single word if I don't care to. I even miss the goddamn cornfields.

When I get back to our room, the girls don't pry, though I

know my eyes are red and whatever grin I summon is fake as a ten-point jackalope. It doesn't matter that it's the middle of the day, that the lights are on and Peggy is helping Marsha run lines for a callback she has in the morning. The second my head hits that pillow, I'm out.

-16-

THE NEXT MORNING, a siren on the street below startles me awake, and I'm nearabout climbing the wall before I remember where I am and what on earth could make such an unholy racket outside my bedroom window.

I glance around the room, blinking and starting to unwind the Spoolies from my hair. Evie is already gone. Peggy must be in the bathroom—her purse is still draped over the foot of her bed. Marsha mentioned last night that she'd be in the kitchen all morning, peeling carrots and chopping onions, prepping for dinner.

There's no chance I'll be able to go back to sleep now, but I don't know if I feel ready to take on the city yet, either. I drag my stationery box out from under the bed and settle back beneath the sheets. I need to write Jesse a letter—I owe him that much after the way I left. I need to try and explain one more time why I had to go in such a hurry, and why he shouldn't waste his time waiting around for me. The only way the two of us stand a chance is if New York City chews me up and spits me back out again, and I refuse to let that happen. So this is the end for us. It has to be.

But writing those words—getting them to lie down on the

page—is like slicing myself open and dipping into my own veins for ink. I've started and stopped a dozen times when Peggy plops down at the foot of my bed and slaps a folded rectangle of newsprint onto the quilt.

"So, who are we going to be today?"

"Pardon?"

"Auditions, silly." Peggy turns the paper so we can both read down the column of announcements, smoothing the edges with her fingers. "We've got high drama, experimental one-act stuff, *ooh*—will you look at that?—a movie production is looking for extras! It says here they're interviewing at an agent's office from ten until noon at 545 Fifth Avenue."

"We can go to anything we want?" I bite my lower lip. I've waited years to get within spitting distance of a real Broadway audition, but now that I'm here, I'm having a hard time getting out of bed.

"Course we can. Well, anything that's an open call. It's your first day, so you get to pick."

"But . . . why are you being so nice?"

Peggy laughs, throwing back her head like Greta Garbo. "Honey, you've been watching too many movies. Listen, this business is rough. If we tried to go it on our own, we'd all be scurrying home with our tail between our legs after a week of rejections."

She tilts her head to the side. "That, and I came to Manhattan with my best friend since we were both in diapers. That's her bed you're sleeping in."

"Oh!" I draw my elbows in close to my sides. "Sorry?"

"Don't apologize—that lucky broad is touring with the

company of *The Music Man* this very second. We toughed it out together for a year before she left, and I wouldn't have lasted half as long without her. Anyhow, she made me promise to be nice to the new girl when she arrived, so"—Peggy sighs, floating her eyes upward as if even the idea of being kind is exhausting—"you're stuck with me."

A year? I don't have that long—not even close.

Ten minutes later, we make our way downstairs. The sideboard in the hallway has a coffee pot warming on a burner just like the one we had back in the diner, plus a hot plate with a pot of clumpy oatmeal. We help ourselves, dumping a healthy amount of sugar and cream in each. Peggy eyes the crowd in the dining room, saying in a low voice, "Some of the girls are standoffish—you've met Evie?"

I nod.

"Others look at everything that walks as competition. But I figure, if she's going to get the part instead of me, she's going to get it whether I'm glaring daggers into her back or rooting her on."

Peggy heads into the dining room, but I'm stuck out in the hall, staring at the mush, sadness suddenly pulling down the grin I'd called up. That's the thing about homesickness—there's no logic to when it hits. All I know is I'd give anything for one of Momma's farm breakfasts right about now.

The dining room is one long table down the middle filled with women, a few as young as me but most a good deal older. Some are laughing and chatting, while others have their noses buried in scripts, cramming till the last possible second. Peggy scoots in at one end of the long bench and nudges until there's room for me, too. She introduces me to the girls opposite us, then tucks in, with nothing to say for the first time this morning. She's halfway through her bowl of oatmeal before I've even taken a bite.

How is a person supposed to go onstage with nothing but a little horse feed in her belly? And then it gets me, right in the gut. I'm going to an audition today. This isn't singing in front of the diner's milkshake bar. Or in church. Or the high school auditorium. Or some community theatre production. I shovel a big bite of oatmeal into my mouth. Right. Maybe bland is best. Anything stronger probably wouldn't stay down.

In an undertone, Peggy points out a few of the girls on the other side of the room. "See the one in the beret like she's Brigitte Bardot or something? Keep your distance. And the one with the blonde ringlets? She's nice enough, but a five-minute conversation will turn into three hours of her yakking your head off if you're not careful. That group over there by the window holding court—they recently booked shows."

The coffee has cooled enough for me to take a few big gulps. "But they still live here?"

"Yeah. It's a bargain if you don't mind the subway. Phyllis—the one in the green pantsuit with that lily-white complexion and long ginger hair—she booked a one-act off-Broadway. And Velma—the one with dark skin, bright red nails, and an even brighter yellow jumper—she's in a brand-new show at the Ethel Barrymore. *A Raisin in the Sun*, I think it's called?"

Holding court is right—Phyllis and Velma can hardly get a bite down between all the girls huddled around and peppering them with questions. Soon enough, Peggy and I make our excuses, throw our coats over our shoulders, and check our reflections in the hall mirror. I redo a bobby pin or two and am all set to call that good when Peggy rolls her eyes and yanks me back beside her.

She uncaps a bronze tube and twists until a wedge of cherry red lipstick appears. "Pucker up."

"But I don't wear—"

"You do now." And with that, she smears it along my lips, dabbing at the edges. "Smack."

I start a little at my reflection. That's my dress and my hair and my big hazel eyes. Still, with those bright red lips, it hardly looks like me.

-17-

PEGGY AND I march arm in arm down the sidewalks and deep underground to the subway. The theatre district is a straight shot on the Broadway line, thank goodness, so I think I'll be able to manage the subway on my own tomorrow if I keep my wits about me. When we climb up again into the brisk city air, I press my free hand under my nose and step around a puddle on the ground— someone, or several someones, have relieved themselves right there on the sidewalk. Peggy looks at the ground, then up at me, and smiles as if to say, *That's New York for you.*

I'd take the ripe smell of a barn that needs cleaning over this any day.

Midtown is LOUD, like every single person on the sidewalk is wearing tap shoes. Back home, everybody's bound to be going about their business. Farmers crunching numbers, prepping for planting, farmwives looking through their thinning winter stores to plan for the week, and storefronts downtown just beginning to open their doors. The busiest spot in Fairbury at this time of day is the high school, and even that—the rush of people moving between classes, hollering after their friends and slamming lockers—isn't half as chaotic as this one city block.

I start to wonder how many streets there are just like this one in Manhattan, and probably some that are even noisier, but then my head starts to swim and I have to clap my hands over my ears and focus on the back of Peggy's head for a few steps while I think about nothing more than breathing in and out, in and out, no matter how foul it smells.

We pass a deli with a line out the door and around the block, and a flower shop with tin buckets filled with long sprigs of forsythia, quince branches, and the biggest hydrangea clusters I've ever seen. We skirt around a café with metal tables covered in red-and-white checkerboard cloth and people dressed all in black sipping coffee out of tiny porcelain cups.

Except for a dozen or so people, everybody in Fairbury is white. And you only ever hear English unless you're at the Schmidts', or if the farrier is visiting—Bob only uses enough English words to say hello and secure payment when the job's done. But here, there's folk of all colors and sizes and ways of dressing, speaking languages I've never heard—I wouldn't even be able to guess at what corner of the world they hail from. Nana would love it. And that thought's like taking a tack to the plump balloon that is my growing delight at the city. Nana should have used her money to see the world while she still could. And all over again, I'm holding my head in my hands, trying to keep it together.

Peggy weaves in and out of the masses ahead of us like she's doing a dance of her own invention. But every time I think I'm getting the hang of moving through the flow of people charging down the sidewalks like it's a race or something, I misjudge and get clipped on the shoulder. I'm gonna have new bruises to go with the ones my suitcase banged into my shins yesterday. Peggy chatters away as if the chaos doesn't bother her one bit. If I hunch over and lean in, I can just about make out what she's saying.

"The minute I step outside Mrs. Cooper's door, I become somebody else—I like to think of it as cultivating a mystique. Every leading lady has one." She tips her sunglasses down, cutting her eyes at me. "And you need one, Nebraska."

I drag my bottom lip between my teeth. *Oh, crap!* I forgot about the lipstick—it's probably all over my teeth now. "So who are you today?" I cover my mouth with one hand and scrub my teeth with the other. Some mystique.

"Marlene Dietrich, the most glamorous actress of them all." She narrows her eyes, going for the signature smolder, then laughs it off again. "It's all just acting practice. But try it—see if people don't treat you differently when you act like the spotlight's where you belong."

She turns down a side street. The road is jammed with cars double-parked on one side and a delivery truck with its ramp down taking up the other half. Drivers stuck in the bottleneck lay on their horns, darting one at a time between the narrow gap, then honking again, just for good measure. The racket makes me want to turn around and go straight back to Mrs. Cooper's, squash a pillow over my head, and disappear under the sheets for an hour at least, until my head has cleared enough so I can hear myself think. But I didn't come all this way to chicken out.

"You got to the city at a great time," Peggy shouts above the racket.

Really? I dart a glance at the pigeons bobbing between bits of trash that last night's rain plastered against the curb.

"Gals I know who have been auditioning for years are finally booking shows. Producers here are casting for television and movie jobs in L.A., Broadway shows, and all the regular traveling gigs: out-of-town tryouts, touring companies, industrials, you name it."

"Industrials?" A car backfires inches away from us, and I leap like a startled cat, clinging to Peggy's arm.

"Oh yeah—they're big business. Companies with a new product coming on the market sweep in, grab up some of the best Broadway writers, directors, and talent, then take the show on the road or put on a performance at their annual sales meeting."

"I didn't come all the way to New York City to sing about cosmetics, or cars, or . . ."

"Toilets?" Peggy snorts. "Believe me, if it's good enough for Florence Henderson and Chita Rivera, it's good enough for you. Doesn't matter what kind of show you book, you'll find yourself working alongside castmates who become colleagues and friends, and with dance captains or technical directors who'll be moving on to another show once that one closes. Who knows? If you impress them, they just might bring you along. Besides, industrials pay good money. Every one of us has a ticking clock—a time when we run out of money or energy or hope that our big break is right around the corner. There's no shame in taking a job that winds that clock back a bit."

"Oh. I never thought about it that way."

I trail a step behind Peggy as she turns down a greasy alley and throws open an unmarked side door. My breath wheezes out of me like a pipe organ in desperate need of cleaning as we step into a narrow hallway lined with about fifty actresses. Every one of them looks like someone out of a Macy's catalog: hair pressed and rolled, lips pinked, dresses pert and stylish. They look like pros, and next to them I feel like a kid with skinned knees and grubby hands playing dress-up in her mother's closet. But Peggy is all confidence. She grabs my hand, cutting a path through the crowd to the opposite end of the hallway, where a woman in a blue felt cap guards the producer's office from behind a metal desk.

"Names on the line. Have your sixty-second monologue ready." She glances up at us, but only to make sure we heard that last part. "Not a beat longer."

Peggy nudges me forward, so I lean over and print my name beneath hers.

"Butterfield?" Peggy whispers. "Oh, honey. We've got to change more than your lipstick."

"*What?* I'm not changing my name!" The Butterfields are good, strong people. Our name means something—to folks back home, anyway.

I can tell Peggy is taken aback by my outburst, but she shrugs with a *suit yourself* as we wind back to the end of the line.

Without Peggy, I probably would have waited by the door for far too long before I even figured out there was a sign-up sheet at the front. I'd thank her, but she's already focused on a slender notebook no bigger than her palms, and the tiny script filling the pages inside. Right. I should be prepping, too. I'm going to do "What a

Pretty Girl Wants" from *The Seven Year Itch*. I've had the monologue memorized since the spring talent show junior year. My lips move silently over the familiar phrases. I've practiced it a hundred times, but suddenly, in line with all these other actresses, it seems silly. I should have picked something more serious, or dramatic, or—I don't know—*something*.

I scrape at a snag on my fingernail. I'm not accustomed to second-guessing myself—what I wear, how I do my hair, or whether I wear lipstick or not, for crying out loud! No matter how much Momma tried to convince me of the virtues of humility, I was never one to lack confidence. I always thought that's just who I am—it never occurred to me that while it might be who I am back home, take away Nana backing me up at every turn, and Jesse there to swat away the doubts, and that confidence would wither right quick.

I knew leaving Jesse would be the hardest thing I ever did. But I thought I'd miss him most in the evenings or first thing in the morning, when we'd normally be driving to and from school or work. Or on the weekends, when we might be on a date at the movies or at his folks' house. I never imagined I'd wake in the middle of the night, my cheeks wet and all of me just aching for him. Or in line for an audition, for Pete's sake!

And I never thought I'd lose him and Nana both in the same breath.

I'm glad Peggy is so absorbed in her little notebook—it's going to take everything I've got to put a brave face on this. I slap my cheeks and, blinking a little too quickly, try out my monologue again.

The line inches forward, the aisle down the center constantly flowing with new people making their way to the front and others leaving after their audition is over. As we draw closer to the office door, I watch the people coming and going. Some girls are inside for ten minutes, while others seem to come scurrying back out again before the door can fully swing closed behind them in the first place. It seems rude to peer into their faces drenched with emotion: relief, embarrassment, anger—or, somehow worst of all, hope. But I can't seem to look away. Besides, no one makes eye contact with me anyway. Not a one of them. Have they already sized me up and decided I'm not competition? Just the thought sends me right back to the whole *grubby kid playing where she doesn't belong* feeling.

I close my eyes and try to block everything out. If I can get my head in the right place, I know I can nail this audition. I run through the monologue another time, but I keep tripping up over lines I know cold. The more I try to practice, the worse it gets, until I'm convinced I'll be lucky if I can remember my own name in there.

After nearly two hours of waiting, the woman behind the desk calls Peggy's name. When she sidles inside with a wink, I'm tempted to forget the whole thing and make a dash for the alley. But I grit my teeth, and when Peggy comes sailing back out again and it's my turn, I lurch upright and make momentum do the hard work of carrying me inside. I smile like Mrs. Muth taught me, and I hold my chin so high even Mme Durant would approve. Somehow, I make it through that door and across the office to the X taped on the floor.

I dart a look at the folks behind the table: two men in sharp suits—one pinstriped and the other a lemon yellow—and a woman in a tweed pantsuit, her sleek blonde hair pulled into a knot behind one ear. That table's much closer than I'd imagined, and the room is smaller, too, like I haven't waltzed in for an audition so much as I've been summoned to the principal's office. I try to swallow, but my throat's gone dry, and instead this croaking sound comes out, like a frog with the hiccups.

"Name?"

"Mazie Butterfield."

The woman snickers.

"Go on," the guy in the pinstripes says, tapping his toe against the table leg. But it's clear as a jug of spring water he doesn't really mean it.

I lick my lips. They've already written me off. Because of my name? My *hot off the prairie* skirt? Anger burns straight through the rest: the nerves, the dread, and the insecurity, like a steady simmer cooking off the brandy for Momma's Christmas fruitcakes. That heat settles in my belly, and it reminds me who I am; that it's gonna take more than a little scorn to make a Butterfield back down.

I launch into the monologue, and it rolls out of me like the words are my very own, no thanks to the lather I worked myself into back in the hallway. I get maybe halfway through when the man in the yellow suit waves a hand toward the door. "That'll be all, thank you."

I swallow the words about to spill off my tongue, blinking, reeling the character back, and swaying a little at the recoil.

"I . . . thank you for the opportunity." I can do better. I know

I can. Anyway, Daddy says behind every closed door is a chance to learn something. "Do you have any notes for me?"

The guy in the pinstripes groans, rolling his eyes to the ceiling.

"Don't take it personally," the one in the yellow suit offers. "We're after a different . . ." He swirls his fingers in my general direction. "*Look.*"

"Next?" The woman hollers so loudly everyone in the hallway can surely hear it.

I scurry out of there as fast as I can. I knew this wouldn't be as easy as auditioning back in Nebraska—I wasn't such an idiot that I thought Broadway would welcome me with open arms. But I thought those people would listen. I assumed they'd want to see what I might bring to a role.

When I get into the hallway, Peggy is waiting for me.

"You did it!" she crows, clapping me on the back. "The first one's always the hardest."

I grimace. "Promise? Because that was pretty awful."

"Cross my heart. Now, I've got to dash. I've got an appointment in an agent's office in—*oh!*—thirty minutes."

An appointment? No wonder whatever I picked this morning was a lark to her. She was only hanging around until it came time for the real thing she had lined up later on in the day. Peggy wiggles her fingers in a cheery wave and pushes through the door.

I gather my coat around my waist, feeling a dozen kinds of foolish. Of course she wasn't going to babysit the new girl all day long. Of course she had other things to do. I thrust my hands into my coat pockets, my purse dangling off my wrist as I head out the door.

Those people behind the table weren't interested in anything I had to say. I was just one name, one face out of hundreds. Back home, I may have been a daydreaming loon to everyone else, but when they looked in my eyes (and they did look in my eyes, not through me or past me) they saw Mazie Butterfield, the biggest voice in Jefferson County. They saw *me*.

Well, I'm not in Nebraska anymore. I'm just going to have to find a way to make these city folks sit up and see me, too.

When I step into the entryway at Mrs. Cooper's, I sag against the door in sheer relief. I should get a medal or something for successfully navigating the New York City subway system all by myself, and without mishap. Everybody out there is in such a dang hurry! I drag myself upstairs. After lunch, I want to get a good look at the weekly show papers to find an open call tomorrow. I learned a thing or two today, so my next audition will be better. I know it.

-18-

I'M HALFWAY THROUGH breakfast the following morning when I notice the date printed at the top of the newspaper resting on the table next to me. The girl sitting to my right (who's been ignoring me the entire time) rolls her eyes and snatches it away, but not before the date registers. Yesterday, the Fairbury High graduating class—*my* class—walked across the stage, shook hands with Principal Echter, and said goodbye to high school for good.

And I missed it.

I missed seeing the proud look on my parents' faces. I missed seeing Jesse's face when he got to hold that diploma in his hands after pulling double duty for so long to make it happen. I should have been there to celebrate with him. And I should be there to deal with the fallout now that he has to put it all aside for a life no bigger than the borders of the Schmidt family acreage.

I always thought Jesse and I would at least cross that stage together. I slide my half-full bowl of oatmeal away, push back from the table, and climb the stairs to my room. I've been lonely pretty much since I left home, but go figure, the one day I'm hoping to have some time to myself to collect my thoughts and reckon with my grief so I can make the most of the day's audition, every single one of my roommates is inside. I guess everybody has their eye on auditions later in the day.

Evie is leaning against the window frame, lips pursed, one eyebrow cocked, while Marsha pulls dresses out of the wardrobe one by one and slaps them down on her bed.

"Oh good. We're all here," Peggy says when I walk through the door.

"What's going on?"

"We're raising our game."

I shrug out of my sweater. "What do you mean?"

"We're going to pool our clothes," Peggy explains. "I've been wearing the same two tired dresses to auditions going on three months now, no matter if the part was for a frontier granny or a boarding school brat."

Marsha jumps in. "When I first started auditioning, I went as me, and I got in character a couple of seconds before I began reading or singing or whatever. But good gravy, you can tell some of the girls prep for that one part; they come in looking like they've already booked it and it's the first day of dress rehearsals. Makeup, clothes, swagger, the whole thing."

I pull my shoes out of the closet and line them up beside Marsha's bed. "You're going to dress for every single part you go out for? But what if you've got two different auditions in one day?"

Peggy shrugs. She takes a step back, dropping my pale pink pillbox hat over her circle dress with the Peter Pan collar. "Not every time. But it's good to know what you've got at your disposal."

I glance at Evie, perched on the sill, filing her already perfect nails and gazing out the window. "You too?"

"Gosh, no. I don't want to be owing any favors when I'm standing in an audition line next to one of you."

Marsha rolls her eyes skyward. "Here." She lifts her cherry red sheath dress up, pinching the shoulders between her fingertips and holding it against me. "You should try this one. It would look amazing with those strawberry curls of yours. So long as you don't need to dance—it narrows a little severely at the knees."

I look down at my front and then at Marsha's tiny figure. "There's no way it'll fit me. You're half my size!"

"Fiddlesticks. I knitted it myself, so I know it's got plenty of stretch."

We spend the next hour mixing and matching, dressing up a plain frock with a knotted scarf and dressing down a tea-length skirt with a pair of flats. Who knows if all this will do any good. But I guess it's worth a shot.

Two hours later, I trip down the boardinghouse front steps. I'm wearing one of Peggy's outfits, a simple enough pencil skirt with a scoop-neck blouse. The audition is for a straight play, so there's no dancing or even singing needed. It's a good thing, 'cause I can't take more than half a step in the dang skirt. But I figured if I didn't have my singing voice to impress them with, I'd need a little something extra. So I let the girls talk me into wearing a pair of bright red heels and matching lipstick.

I feel squished and squeezed into Peggy's clothes. The part is a vampy secretary, so a too-tight skirt seems right, but halfway to the office building where they're holding the auditions, my shoes are beginning to rub at the heels and pinch my toes. By the time I find my place at the back of the audition line, they're throbbing. I shuck the heels and examine my toes—blisters are already bubbling up.

The rest of the women in line wait in their pert business suits and heels as if they'd never been more comfortable. I'm an actress, right? I can pretend any clothes fit like a second skin. And I'm a dancer—I'm used to performing through pain. I can do this.

When I'm next in line to go inside, I try to wedge my feet into Peggy's heels, only I think they've started to swell because the fit is even worse now. Walking two steps forward feels like clogging on an anthill.

I smile big, hoping it doesn't look like a snarl, and trade the assistant my picture for a sheet detailing my lines and cues. I scan the page: shuffle papers, walk across the room, say line, flirt, end scene. It all looks simple enough, except for the walking part. But no way am I going to let some stupid blisters ruin this for me.

The folks behind the table don't look up when I enter the room, so I head opposite the guy standing behind a lectern—I'm guessing he's my scene partner. When he gives me a nod, I bend one knee, tilting my hips and lifting one shoulder to get into character. I rap the paper against a chairback and set out across the room.

I figure if I can get them to focus north of my waistline, maybe they won't notice a hitch in my step. I blink a few times when I reach the table, hoping it looks more like a doe-eyed ingenue and less like I'm trying to hold back tears.

"I've got those reports you ask—"

"Stop." The casting director's head is tilted at a wincing angle. "Is that supposed to be flirting? Looks more like gas pain."

"Oh!" A trilling laugh I've never once heard come out of my mouth before floats through the room. "Let me try that again."

I clench my teeth and cross back to the chair. *Remember the first day in pointe shoes? This is nothing.*

I flip back my hair and cross the room a second time. If I walk mostly on my toes, it feels almost like dancing, and that makes the pain more bearable somehow. I drop my chin and bat my eyes slowly, drawing a finger along the lectern. I make my voice a touch breathier than normal.

"I've got those reports you asked for, sir."

I lock eyes with my scene partner and lean in, draping my forearms over the lectern and reaching up to pinch the edge of his polka-dot bow tie. He's smiling dreamily back at me while he says his line, so I take that as a good sign and lean the smallest fraction farther forward. A god-awful ripping sound jolts me upright. I clap the paper behind my back. Maybe they didn't hear that? Maybe they don't all know the damn skirt split straight down my rear?

"That'll be all," says the director, still wincing. "Thank you."

The instant I close the door behind me, the room erupts with laughter.

"I'll just hold on to this paper, thanks." I grimace at the assistant and sidle around the wall to the office door. That's the last time I squeeze myself into some skinny girl's clothes to get a part.

I trudge home with that single piece of paper covering my derriere the whole way. I'm gonna need a long soak to get over this one. And another lifetime before I can even think of laughing about it.

-19-

AFTER BREAKFAST, I pull Marsha's wrap dress over my leotard and tights and head out to an open call for dancers. When I arrive, I swap my name for a square of paper with a number on it. I'm so nervous, I nearly stab myself a half dozen times trying to pin the dang thing onto the stretchy fabric over my belly. I wait in a cavernous room filled with dancers while the casting director walks briskly down one line, then the next.

He looks me up and down, and I get cut with a crisp *no* before I get to dance a single step.

Chin up, Nana would say. Lord, I wish I could hear her voice one more time. Even if all I got was a tongue-lashing for getting down on myself so quickly, I'd take it. I miss her so much.

I pull the dress back on, swap my ballet slippers for a pair of flats, and grab a cheese sandwich at the Howard Johnson's, then screw up my courage to make the rounds at the William Morris offices, introducing myself to agents and producers. It's a bruising day, all told, but there's something about walking 46th Street, surrounded by people like me—theatre people—that has me grinning ear to ear nonetheless, spinning clear out of orbit.

I'm on cleanup after dinner, even though I'm likely to nod off standing up, using that stack of dinner plates for a pillow. Who would have thought one audition, a dozen introductions, then battling the crowds on the city streets would knock me flatter than a day spent haying from sunup to sundown?

The kitchen at Mrs. Cooper's is homey enough—the cabinets are painted butter yellow, and the gas stove and oven door are trimmed in pea green. There's a Hoosier cabinet against the back wall for storing dishes, and a butcher block table in the center of the room for meal prep. Kitchens back home look out over the fields, but there's no window here, not with the row houses sharing walls on both sides.

A lot of the girls grumble about the chores, say they should spend that time in the dance studio or working with a voice coach, but I don't mind. The work is like a tether to who I am and how I was raised. Don't get me wrong—what an actor does on the stage day in and day out is hard work, but there's a difference between making art and making soup.

There's a humility to sinking your hands into the soil or a sink full of suds or whatever it may be—it's something that goes unspoken at home, something Nebraska folk take so much for granted they don't even see the beauty in their own hands. I want to meet my dreams head-on, I want to make the kind of art that will drop people to their knees, but I want to hold on to that other kind of beauty, too, for as long as I can.

Mrs. Cooper joins me in the kitchen.

"Evenin'," she says softly. She peers over my shoulder to inspect my work and nods once in approval.

"I'm always happy to have you young women from the country stay awhile. You seem to know how to do a job right."

"Thank you, Mrs. Cooper. It's my pleasure."

She reaches into the cupboard to pull down a couple of unmarked tins. "Evie informed me of your ill-timed phone call."

My hands still. She isn't going to kick me out, is she?

"See that it doesn't happen again."

"No, ma'am. It won't."

Mrs. Cooper twists the knob on the radio, switching from a news report on a couple of monkeys the army launched into orbit inside a Jupiter missile, to static, to a dreamy jazz number that floats through the kitchen not unlike those poor monkeys once they hit zero gravity. I dunk my arms into the dishwater, fishing for a handful of soup spoons. I bet that launch is all Jesse can talk about right now. I bite down on the inside of my cheek, blinking away the tears suddenly threatening to spill over.

Mrs. Cooper's mixing up the roux for dinner two nights from now. It's her grandmother's recipe, and she won't let me so much as peek at the spices arranged on the counter while she stirs and sips and stirs again. She hums while she works, just like Momma, only you can tell Mrs. Cooper's got one heck of a voice.

When I'm finished, I push through the kitchen door, the oiled wood squeaking on its hinges, and trudge upstairs. The hallway is empty, and the bedroom, too. I sit on the edge of the bed, my fingers digging into the coarse blanket. I could try writing Jesse again. I could lay out my outfit for tomorrow and practice introducing myself to the folks on the other side of the table. I could call Momma and beg her to put Daddy on the phone. Instead, I only sit there, staring at the daisy chain wallpaper and hugging my arms over my stomach.

At harvesttime, when the combine winds through the fields, down and up the rows, slicing through the stalks, separating the corn, and spitting chaff over the soil in its wake, what was a rolling sea of green turns flat as a wasteland in the course of a single day. But by some mathematical improbability, every so often a single stalk of corn escapes the blades and is left, bewildered, to reckon with the winter winds alone.

Who knew a city full of people could feel like the loneliest place in the world?

-20-

SATURDAY AFTERNOON, WHEN I get back from an informal tap lesson Marsha led in the parlor downstairs, there's an envelope waiting for me on my pillow. My eyes focus on the tidy letters written in ruler-straight lines while the rest of me flares like a dying star, popping and crackling as it devours itself from the inside out. Even from the doorway, I recognize his handwriting. I slide to the floor beside my bed, break open the seal, and pull out a single page of notebook paper, folded in thirds. I don't register that my breath is trapped inside my lungs until it whistles out of me in one long, mournful note.

Mazie—

Don't be mad at your momma for passing along your address in the city. And don't worry—I'm not writing to ask you to turn around and come back home. I wouldn't do that.

I'm real mad at myself for how I acted when you said you were leaving. I was shocked mostly, I think. I didn't expect it—not for a long while, since we both knew you didn't have the money saved up yet. I thought we had months, maybe even a couple years, before you left. Maybe I was stalling all along, lying to myself because I didn't like the truth. But I was grieving that night, too, you know? Your grandma always was real good to me.

I know you think it's impossible for us, what with me here and you there. But let me tell you something about impossible. Robert Goddard's theories of spaceflight were mocked and derided for years—that is, until he launched the first liquid-fueled rocket and pretty much single-handedly ushered in the age of space exploration. Copernicus theorized the heliocentric model of our solar system over a hundred years before it could be proven— everyone thought the idea of the earth moving around the sun and not the other way around was utterly ridiculous. John Couch Adams studied planetary orbits for years on the hunch that an eighth, yet-to-be-discovered planet existed in our solar system, only to be scooped by a French scientist when he was on the verge of discovery. Everybody wrote him off as a failure. But because of all those years of study, he discovered that meteor showers are caused by cometary debris trails, which may not sound like much, but it was huge at the time.

Remember back in November when we drove out to the Sandhills to watch the Leonids? We fell asleep in the bed of my truck under a ton of blankets and blazing white streaks shooting across the sky—I thought your daddy *was going to murder me when I finally got you home well after the sun had come up. Anyhow, the only reason we know when to look up is because J. C. Adams believed in something when nobody else did.*

Well, I believe in us. I know you're trying to push me away because you think it'll go easier for me if there's a clean break. Well, I don't want it easy. I want you.

Just don't give up on us. Please.

—Jesse

I squeeze my eyes shut. Everybody's always talking about hope like it's so lightweight, the thing with feathers or whatever. But letting myself hope that it might all work out for me and Jesse feels like all those meteors burning through the atmosphere with the sole purpose of crushing me. I kick off my shoes and slide under the covers, drawing them over my head and shutting out the rest of the world the best I can.

Hope is the thing that hurts most.

-21-

MONDAY MORNING I head out on my own. This time it's a call for
vocalists, so I figure I've got as good a shot as anybody. I leave Mrs.
Cooper's early, but even so, the city's up before me, laundry strung
high in the alleys between buildings and flocks of pigeons scour-
ing the rain-soaked pavement in front of the pastry shop. I've got
plenty of time before the audition—I want to gawk at those theatres
and let my dreams swell big enough to fill all of Times Square, big
enough to shove my constant longing for home out of my mind. I
head over a block and a half and up to the subway station at the
intersection of Broadway and West 86th. I clatter down the stairs
and underground, where the walls are covered in pale tile with
mosaic detail heralding the station number, and more cast ceramic
tiles run along the ceiling.

I purchase a token for fifteen cents and make my way to
the platform, rocking onto my toes and back to my heels again.
A half dozen people mill between the columns, and I resist the
urge to check over my shoulder every time I hear a scuff of feet.
Can they tell I'm new here? I must have read a dozen articles
about how you can't let anything crack your confidence on the

way to an audition, but I haven't got so much a shell around me as a sponge.

When the southbound train arrives with a whoosh of stale air, I hurry inside and grab the overhead bar, leaning into my arm and staring out the smudged windows as we get moving. The whole way to Midtown, memory is playing like a movie overlaying the dark subway tunnel rushing by out the window, from a time when I was five years old and sitting on my daddy's shoulders while he sauntered through the state fair. We went from fortune-tellers to prize-winning Herefords, pies, and jams, from strongman competitions to blue-ribbon rosebushes.

Then Daddy wandered into the music tent where, instead of the usual plucky string band or crooning country singer, a stripped-down traveling production of *Carousel* had taken to the stage. They hardly had any props, just a couple of chairs, some crates, and a banner, but I felt the energy rolling off that stage like a gust of wind. I'd never even heard the term *musical theatre*—all I knew was, I wanted more of whatever I'd just seen.

The brakes squeal as the subway slides to a stop, and I take the stairs up with a throng of others. It takes me a moment to get my bearings aboveground—how does anybody know what way is what when you can't see the sun and nearly every building looks the same at ground level? It should be simple enough to find my way to the theatres.

I get moving. The tops of the skyscrapers are sparkling, all that glass winking down at me like we're in on the same joke. I've come to Midtown for a few auditions already, but I haven't had the chance to really *see* it yet. So this morning I take my time, zigzagging down side streets to get a look at the Winter Garden Theatre, where *West Side Story* is playing; the Mark Hellinger, where *My Fair Lady* is on; then the 46th Street Theatre, where *Redhead* is up, starring Gwen Verdon.

The Times Tower rises skyward, splitting the traffic at its base, with the Bond Clothing Store next door, its roof topped with enormous Pepsi-Cola bottles to either side of a giant bottle cap. Seems like there are theatres everywhere I turn. I fling my arms wide and spin, no matter that there must be a thousand people on this one city block. I can't believe I'm actually here!

As an afterthought, I check my wristwatch. I'm going to have to save all the rest for another day. I turn on my heel and hurry two blocks east to a set of offices in a gray high-rise.

I check the address twice to be sure—the building doesn't look especially theatrical from the outside. But when I climb the stairs to the third floor, there's already a line out the producer's door, snaking through the hallway past insurance and law offices, and an unlabeled door with dozens of women in bright primary-colored suits clattering away at rows of typewriters.

I step to the back of the line. The woman in front of me is twice my age at least, propping a folded newspaper in front of her and a pencil between her teeth, working away at a crossword puzzle. I peer down the line. They may not all have twice as much experience, but every single one of them has at least five years on me.

That's okay—they haven't got my voice.

But all those actresses look so polished. I glance down at my dress. Momma worked late into the evenings last winter to stitch the pleats by hand, lining up the pinstripes I was set on, no matter that it took twice as long to pattern and pin in place. At the time, I thought the dress looked sharp, but as I take in all the others in their smart collars and perfectly positioned caps, suddenly the shoulders seem too puffy and the hem unfashionably long.

I've never been ashamed of a single thing Momma's done, and that feeling hits my belly like too much bacon grease. Maybe the outfit just needs dressing up. I snap open my purse and root around for my tin mirror and the tube of lipstick Peggy lent me. I didn't put any on this morning—I wanted to step out for my first vocal audition feeling comfortable in my own skin. But comfortable is the last thing I feel right now, so I hold the mirror with one hand and paint my lips bright red. I rub them together, then remember I didn't bring anything to blot them with.

What was I thinking? I take one wincing look in the mirror. That lipstick is wearing me, not the other way around. I should run back downstairs, find the ladies room, scrub my face clean, and start again fresh. I peek over my shoulder. The line is down the stairs now, while I've only taken a few steps forward.

The morning started off with me buzzing with excitement, and now all I can summon is dread. I'm *not* going to the back of that line. I'm here to sing, so maybe they won't care how I look. Or maybe *this* look is the one they want. I close my eyes and try to picture Mrs. Muth in front of me, messy curls bobbing as she pounds up and down the scales. *Nothing will dry up those vocal cords like fear. No fear, you hear me? No fear!*

Okay, Mrs. Muth. No fear.

I start humming scales deep in my throat, slow at first, then gradually faster. Arpeggios next, hopping at intervals and rising steadily upward. Before long, my shoulders have dropped back and my lungs are filling with air, my jaw softening. The mirror stays in the purse. Perhaps, if the universe is kind, the lipstick will have worn off by the time I get to the front of the line.

Now that I know how long the wait before an audition can be, I came prepared with my sheaf of stationery. While I know better than to sink myself before the audition by trying to write Jesse about our breakup again, it'll do me good to write to Momma and Daddy to let them know I'm doing okay and to make sure they know how much I miss them.

It's noon before I make it through the office door. I have to pee, and my stomach is rumbling so loud, they probably won't be able to hear me sing after all. I hand my résumé and picture to the man with the clipboard and flash my best smile when he nods me through.

Inside is a cramped office, with three people in suits on the other side of the table. I hand the sheet music to the man behind the piano in bright red suspenders with an orange mustache curling up at the edges. *No fear.* I turn to face the table with a big smile.

"I'm Mazie Butterfield, and today I'm going to sing 'Somewhere Over the Rainbow.'"

There's a groan from the guy on the left. "Another one?" he whispers loud enough so everyone in the room hears.

My smile cracks, then shatters as the man in the middle tries to smother a laugh behind a cough. The accompanist gives me a four-beat lead-in, and I'm off. The first note is solid, even if the acoustics in the room are a little thin. That's okay, I can build from here. But when the man in the middle waves a hand after the first line, my voice chokes off.

"Mezzo?"

"Yes, but my range is—"

"That's all."

I clap my mouth shut. I'm supposed to thank them for their time. It's the polite thing to do, but I can't bring myself to say the words. I stumble over my own feet trying to get to the piano to reclaim my sheet music and scoot out the door as fast as I can. The assistant is already calling out the next name as he hands my résumé back. The pages slip through my fingers, and I scramble to trap them against my thighs before they float to the floor.

I hurry past the other actresses in line, avoiding eye contact. I pause at the stairs to collect myself, feigning nonchalance as I pull out the mirror and pretend to brush a few stray hairs out of my face. The lipstick did fade a bit, and no, it doesn't make me look like a clown. The bright red lips make my skin seem extra pale, and I suppose on someone accustomed to the look, that could be a nice effect. It's just—it doesn't look like me.

I try to shake off what happened back there and rethink the audition songs I have prepared. If those people aren't even going to give me one verse to prove myself, I'll need to find a song with a flashier beginning that'll really show what I can do right from the start. I snap the mirror shut and get myself moving again. When I've almost made it back outside, where every single person doesn't *know* I just got rejected, I spot a girl near the end of the line who looks every bit as young and green as me. Seriously green—she looks like she might lose her breakfast on the stairs any second.

I take one step toward her, to make sure she glances up, and whisper, "Give 'em hell."

I get a timid smile in return, and she seems to put her shoulders back, just a bit. There—now the day wasn't a complete waste.

-22-

WHEN I SHUFFLE out of the bathroom after dinner, Peggy takes one look at my face and says, "Get changed. We're going out."

"You've got to be joking." I glance down at myself. I've just slipped into my pajamas, resigned to spending the rest of the evening sulking. "I can't afford a night out!"

"Who says we're spending any money?" Peggy winks and flings the closet door open. "Second-acting is one of the essential rites of passage for us starving artists."

"Second-what?"

"You'll see. Now get dressed. Nothing too flashy, mind."

Well, that shouldn't be a problem considering my wardrobe. Forty-five minutes later we're coming up for air in Midtown, leaving the rumbling subway beneath us. The night is warm, a preview of the steamy summer on the way. Yellow taxis with checkerboard pinstripes and chrome-tipped sedans motor by. I gasp, grabbing Peggy's hand when a row of theatres comes into view. I just saw them this morning, and that was magical enough, but now, with the lights—*Oh, the lights!*—blaring above and rippling beneath the marquees. Tourists flit around the shimmering theatre entrances like moths to a flame, the lights blazing down the Great White Way, proclaiming this the merriest street in the whole world. And it really, truly is.

Peggy rummages in her purse as we approach the St. James Theatre, drawing out a stack of playbills.

I dart a look behind me. "What are you doing with all those?"

"They're our ticket inside."

"But . . . how?"

She links her arm through mine. "We're sneaking in! Ushers don't check tickets for the second act. All we have to do is hang around with the crowds at intermission out for a cigarette break and then slide back indoors when they do. Well, that and look for all the world like we belong there."

I can't decide if this is genius, or criminal, or both.

Peggy slaps my hands. "Quit fidgeting! You look guilty as a hound with a hen in its teeth. You're going to give us away for sure."

"Is this another one of your acting lessons?"

She snickers and hands me a playbill, stuffing the extras back into her purse. "You're in luck. We're seeing *Flower Drum Song* tonight."

I tuck the playbill under my arm where it's plainly visible and shove my hands into my pockets, trying to pull off nonchalant as we mingle with the crowd standing beneath the glowing marquee.

"Haven't you always wanted to see a show in a real Broadway theatre?"

I don't have to say a word; the answer is surely plain as day on my face.

"It's not like we're stealing," Peggy whispers. "It's a Monday, so odds are they didn't come anywhere close to selling out that theatre. Think of it this way: We're adding to the love the actors will feel from the crowd." She nods emphatically, slaps her playbill against my chest, then slips through the door and sets out across the lobby for the stairs, passing by an usher without missing a beat.

It *is* a little like an acting lesson, telling small-town Mazie to hush and pretending to belong here, with the rest of the tourists and socialites. But much as I try to pep-talk myself into following Peggy up those stairs, my feet won't move, not one step.

A chime sounds from inside. Five minutes until intermission is over. *Just pick a character and step into it, dang it!* The cigarette crowd hustles through the theatre doors, sweeping me up with them. I resist the urge to gape at the expansive lobby, though the chandeliers dropping out of the coffered ceiling are making it mighty difficult. Instead, I pick someone out of the crowd, an elderly woman piled in furs despite the warm evening, with jewels dripping across her collarbone and pinned into the circle hat on her head. I mimic her walk and the smug set of her jaw, and instead of stumbling up the plush stair runners I manage to glide upstairs, hardly noticing the uniformed ushers scanning the crowd. When I pass through the doors into the theatre, Peggy draws me into an alcove.

I prance in place, giddy. "I can't believe that worked!"

More chandeliers decorate the ceiling beside a track of stage lights. Murals line the walls above the descending rows of crimson seats. We wait until the house lights dim, then slip into two empty seats at the back of the balcony. It's all I can do not to check over my shoulder every five seconds to make sure the usher hasn't spotted us. But then the orchestra swells, the curtain rises, and all my nerves are forgotten.

The evening started with me trying to remember why I ever wanted to put myself through all this rejection when I could be home, where people love and appreciate me. But it's ending with me in the audience for my very first Broadway show—and a Rodgers and Hammerstein at that!

I check the playbill at least a dozen times, squinting in the dark trying to figure out what's going on. All I know about the story is it's a love triangle or two set in Chinatown. The "Ballet" dream sequence is by turns lovely and intense. And the "Wedding Parade" is spectacular. That Ta needs a smack upside the head for thinking he can take a girl like Mei Li for granted, though.

I can barely see the actors' faces from so high up, but the emotion they're sending out to us feels more real than the floor beneath my feet. When the finale is over and the actors make their curtain call, we leap to our feet, cheering. Peggy thrusts her fingers between her teeth and whistles, loud.

My cheeks are wet, my palms stinging from clapping so hard. I've never seen anything like it, *felt* anything close. I'm covered, head to toe, in goose bumps. That's going to be me onstage, and soon. There's no way I can come this close and *not* make it.

As we stroll back to the subway station, Peggy waltzes along the sidewalk, humming the refrain. The ending was a happy one—but why does a happy ending so often look like a wedding?

I pick up my pace, my feet too tired for waltzing. Much as being apart from Jesse has split me down the middle, I have a different kind of happy ending in mind for myself. And I'm going to do everything in my power to make it come true.

-23-

SEEMS LIKE I blinked and the six weeks Nana's money bought me is down to five.

On Tuesday I don't see any auditions that seem like a good fit for my particular skills, so I tag along after Marsha, who is spending the day visiting agents' offices. But all those *no's* in rapid fire are maybe even more demoralizing than waiting in an audition line for half the day only to be cut after being seen for all of twenty seconds.

So on Wednesday I decide to try the buckshot approach and jot down every single available audition that day, hitting as many as I can. And I have to say, I get to know Midtown a lot better by running from one rejection to another all damn day. Thursday I try for a straight play off-Broadway, then Friday I go for a summer stock revival of *The Pirates of Penzance*, and before I know it, there's two weeks gone.

If my life were a Broadway show, this would be the scene where the leading lady is running around a revolving stage like a gerbil in a wheel, knocking on doors that only slam in her face one after another after another. The days blur into weeks—three, four, five—so many auditions, so many rejections. I suppose it's like anything else—the more I do it, the better I get. But better isn't good enough, and as the weeks fly past, I'm beginning to worry if that *yes* is ever going to come.

It doesn't seem to matter whether the show is a punchy musical or a *dry as bones* one-act—the director and the assistant director, the casting director and the choreographer—they all look at you with that same glazed look, *if* they even look your way. We're all here for the art, for our love of the theatre. I want to hop off the stage, flick their disinterested foreheads, and tell them to have some respect, for mercy's sake.

I know my voice is my biggest strength—if I can keep my nerves from choking off the high notes like a rat snake coiling around a field mouse. I'm a decent dancer, and I'm not afraid of hard work to make myself better. It's just—how many of us are here chasing this same dream? All of us girls sitting in a never-ending audition lineup, legs crossed at the ankles, hair brushed to a sheen, dancing shoes just waiting for a reason to get going.

Three evenings a week, we clear all the furniture out of Mrs. Cooper's parlor for dance practice. We take turns playing dance captain while the others get a lesson in for free. All those years of ballet can only take me so far, and a person can only learn so much by copying what she sees on the big screen. There was no one in Fairbury to teach me jazz, vaudeville, or tap, so I'm doing my best now to make up for lost time.

Lessons at a real studio aren't in the budget, so I haven't missed a single practice at the house since I moved in. I spend the days after each lesson going over and over what I learn—basic things

I should have been taught as a kid. It's embarrassing, everything I *don't* know. If I'm honest, I thought all that love of the stage, and my big voice, and my bigger dreams would be enough, at least to get my foot in the door. And they are, I suppose. But they're not getting me cast. And now, after weeks of auditions, and weeks of rejections, the money Nana left me is getting low. I counted out what I have left last night, and I can only afford another ten days before I have to buy a train ticket back home.

What I keep hearing when I'm shown the door is that I'm not the right look, that if they were casting for *Annie Get Your Gun* it'd be one thing. They all see me as big-boned, clearly from someplace in the middle of the country they can't find on a map, and far too green to be taken seriously. But the only way to fix green is to get some experience. And the only way to bust out of that niche is to practice, and maybe to change my appearance to come a little closer to whatever "look" they're going for. I suppose I'll dip into Marsha's or Peggy's wardrobe again for the next audition—something with plenty of stretch this time.

When Patricia steps up to the bank of street-side windows for an introduction to mambo, I'm warmed up, limber, and ready to learn. Nat sets the needle on the record, and the room fills with bright music. All I can say is I am glad we're not in an actual dance studio with floor-to-ceiling mirrors on every wall. I know for a fact my hips are not gyrating like Patricia's. She is like a mermaid or something, her limbs fluid and graceful and so sultry. I'm pretty sure that I, on the other hand, look like a newborn calf, legs buckling every which way. But by the time we're done, my feet are sore, my heart is light, and my head is spinning.

I barely make it through the bedroom door when Marsha grabs my hands, drawing me inside. "Evie booked a show! She leaves next week for a national tour—can you believe it?"

My heart sinks. I can. Evie is a gorgeous dancer. She may not be the friendliest person in the house, but she's got the most expressive eyes I've ever seen. Of course she'd be snatched up. But—*I* want to be the one they pick. I *need* this. And soon.

What if the hard truth is that I'm simply not good enough? I get swept into the huddle of girls congratulating Evie. She's glowing, her cheeks wet and her eyes a little too bright. I step in and give her a quick hug. It's ridiculous to think her success is taking some opportunity from me. Still, as soon as I can, I slip away.

I let my clothes lie on the floor where they fall and pull on my pajama pants and Jesse's ratty old shirt, though it doesn't even smell like him anymore. There's a long line for the bathroom, so I grab a cardigan from my closet, draw it over my shoulders, and head upstairs. There's a door at the end of the hall that leads to the attic and a pull-down window that opens to the sky. I climb out onto the flat roof, the tar still warm from the sun's heat, and tuck my knees up to my chest, shivering while the sweat dries on my skin.

Low clouds hold in the city's glow, so nights here sometimes seem like never-ending dusk. I can't see the stars. Hell, I can't even see the moon, and that makes me feel so far away from Jesse I can hardly breathe. I lie back, my hands propped behind my head as I stare at the starless sky, my gaze losing focus, shifting inward.

Jesse and I went to the same school since we were kids, but it wasn't until ninth grade that I actually *saw* him. The harvest had just come in, and the church picnic that was supposed to be a light supper celebration had stretched late into the night, folks giddy at the end of all that grueling work and the end of worrying, for this season at least, that flood or drought, tornadoes or pests, could destroy the crops where they stood.

At some point that evening, the sun went down, the stars peeked out, and I found myself stumbling into the meadow surrounding the church, seduced by the chirping blackness and the dusty light from a half-full moon. I thought I was all alone out there—otherwise I would have kept my mouth shut. But the naked cornfields and the crickets and that dreamy moon seemed to want something from me. So I gave them "Hey There" from *The Pajama Game*, delighting in the sound of my own voice winging through that wide-open space. The Rosemary Clooney version was all over the radio at the time, so I knew every word by heart. It wasn't until the song was done and I turned back toward the church that I noticed Jesse leaning against an old walnut tree, some handheld contraption resting on his knee.

"Criminy!"

He scrambled to his feet, arms outstretched. "I didn't mean to startle you. I would have said something sooner, but—" He dropped his arms back to his sides, and his head dipped down, just enough so a curtain of sandy brown hair fell across his eyes. "I didn't know you could sing, not like that."

I thrust my chin out, glad for the low light. I had every bit as much right to be out there as he did.

"Really, I didn't mean to intrude. But I'm glad I got to hear it, all the same."

I'd never heard so many words come out of that boy's mouth. It startled the truth right out of me. "Someday I'm going to sing for more than cornfields. I am going to be a big star on a big stage."

I expected him to laugh, but Jesse only nodded, as if my dreams were the most natural thing in the world. "Someday I'm going to build a rocket that'll shoot clear to the moon."

And he lifted the contraption up to his eye like that was that. I had every intention of heading back inside but found myself drifting toward him instead, wanting a look at whatever was so fascinating about the plain old moon. Jesse must have felt me come alongside him; he set the thing in my hands, adjusted my grip, then dropped his arms once I had it right. I lifted it up to one eye, like a camera or something, but all I saw was dark. I pulled away, turning the thing over in my hands.

"What is it?"

"An old bubble sextant from the war. Pilots used them for navigation, but if you turn it on the night sky, you can chart a whole different course. Try again. See if you can spot one of those stars, then twist the drum on the side until that star and the bubble are lined up."

"Okay? Then what?" All I could see through the viewfinder was darkness.

"Well, now you know the altitude of that star."

Clearly that was supposed to mean something to me, but I didn't so much listen during science class as daydream.

"Now you can figure out where you are, or how to get where you want to go. They make better ones these days, but Papa says it's foolishness looking up at the sky all the time . . ." Jesse trailed off.

"Nobody says it to my face, but I know they all think being set on a life on the stage is foolish, too."

It was too dark for me to notice something like the color of his eyes, but I do remember how they fixed on me then, like he had all the time in the world to listen to what I had to say. Things were different between us after that. He was no longer the soft-spoken farm boy at the back of the room with his nose in a book. He was a dreamer, just like me. And now it seems the cruelest thing in the world that those dreams that first brought us together are what drove us apart in the end.

-24-

BY MORNING, I'VE got a new plan. Rather than waiting for who-ever's chore it is to pick up a copy of the weekly show papers and bring them back to the boardinghouse for everybody to pick over, I wake up at the crack of dawn to get my own copy. On the one hand, I can't afford the extra thirty-five cents to buy my own paper. On the other hand, I can't afford *not* to do something different.

I want enough time to scout out my own schedule, dash back home, dress for the part, and prep as much as I can before the audition. I don't take a bath, and I don't bother doing anything more with my hair than tucking it under the green Juliet cap Momma crocheted and sent in the mail last week. It's just like one Nana wore when she was my age.

I hit the sidewalk while it's still dark, the steam from the bakeries and coffee roasters billowing out of the grates and bathing my cheeks. The city is never really quiet, but the dark casts a hush over everything, dampening the squeal of brakes and quickening the feet of anyone caught outdoors so early. I hurry to Times Square, and without even spinning once in an enchanted circle to take in its glory, I swap my pocket change for a copy of *Show Business*, tuck it inside my coat for safekeeping, and scurry toward the Automat, where a cup of coffee is only a nickel and I can sit and drink lemon water with sugar as long as I please.

At the next table over, a pair of businessmen are eating Danishes and drinking cup after cup of black coffee, arguing with relish about the state of the space race. The man in a gray trilby hat insists that now that the fourth *Discoverer* failed to achieve orbit, that's it, it's over. The air force should just give up and admit the Soviets have us beat. Then he leans back, hiding a grin behind his coffee cup while his friend launches into what's surely not his first speech on the eminence of the Stars and Stripes in space. I'm pretty sure the first guy only said what he did to get the other one foaming at the mouth.

I relocate to a quiet table near the window. Forty-five minutes later, the coffee has started a good buzz, and though I haven't even looked at next week, I know what I'm going for today. It's an off-Broadway revue looking for singers with a little dance experience. I tip the cup back, swallow the last dregs of my coffee with a grimace, and check the time on the wall clock. I'd better get moving.

The whole way back to Mrs. Cooper's, I plan my outfit. Tight bun, clean enough to satisfy Mme Durant. Dancing heels tucked into my purse. Flesh-colored tights and a leotard beneath Marsha's wrap dress, if she can spare it.

Mrs. Muth always said you can never start warming up too early. So I tug Momma's cap over my ears and start humming as I step out onto the sidewalk again. I don't know yet what I'm going to sing, but I've got ninety minutes until the first group is seen.

I'm thinking something cheerful. Something the table can't help but love. A café door swings out in front of me, nearly clipping my shoulder before I scoot out of the way. The bell hanging over the door chimes: *ding, ding, ding*. Three times, clear as a—well, as a bell.

Tell me that's not a sign. "The Trolley Song" it is!

Later that afternoon, when the door to the audition room closes behind me, I have a good feeling about what happened in there. It was a dance studio, rented for the morning, with a folding table and four chairs backing up to the mirrors. The room was cold when I first got inside, but it reminded me of Mme Durant's studio back home, so I hung on to that feeling of familiarity as tight as I could. The folks behind the table warmed to me the longer I sang; rather than cutting me off mid-song like so many others have done, they leaned in, took some notes, and even asked me to read from a few different sides. They didn't jump out of their seats and beg me to take the part when I was finished, but when they thanked me for coming, they meant it, I could tell.

I'm almost to the door when the woman behind the reception desk calls out, "Butterfield? M. Butterfield?"

I freeze, my hand curled around the door handle, and pivot, my heart in my throat. "Yes?"

She holds out a slip of paper. "Come back tomorrow, eleven a.m. sharp."

I take the paper, slipping it into my breast pocket before she can change her mind. "Same place?"

"Yes." She meets my eyes then, her expression softening a

little. "They'll want to see you dancing with a partner tomorrow. Waltzes, lifts, that sort of thing."

"Thank you." It comes out in a squeak. I make my way back down the narrow hallway. Some of the girls look away and down, regret plain on their features. But one meets my eyes and offers a tight smile.

After that, the streets don't seem so lonely anymore. *A callback!* It isn't enough to beat back the worry about the dwindling savings tucked under my pillow, but it's not a no either. And that's a start.

-25-

BACK AT MRS. Cooper's I hurry through the entryway, past a flock of girls huddled around the television for a glimpse of Queen Elizabeth and President Eisenhower on the royal yacht, opening a seaway to the Great Lakes. Another day, I'd be right there with them, but there's no way I can sit on news like this. I've got a callback tomorrow. *A callback!* I barely crack the bedroom door open when Peggy tosses Marsha's sheath dress at me.

"Hurry, get changed!"

"Okay . . ." How did she know I had something to celebrate?

I start pulling the dress over my head while Peggy stands in front of the mirror, lifting first one foot, then the other, her mouth puckered, her head tilted to the side. "What do you think—green or brown?"

I can't see a thing. I've got my shoulders crammed through the neck opening, shimmying upward, trying to get the narrow waist over my shoulders. I duck back out of the dress. Her green shoes are kitten heels with a bow at the toe while the brown ones are a high-heeled oxford. The first is demure, the second sensible. Neither one is particularly . . . Peggy.

"Depends," I say, my voice muffled by the dress I'm trying to slide over my shoulders for the second time. "Where are we going?"

"You'll see." She chucks both pairs back into the closet, slips a pair of ballet flats on her feet and stilettos into her handbag. Then she whirls around just as I shimmy the fabric over my hips.

I don't own a stitch of clothing this cherry red—I would have thought it'd wash me out, but it does the opposite: it makes my skin look pale as whipped cream and my hair like something out of a confectioner's display case. My hands fly up to cover my cheeks. I do not look like Mazie from the farm. And it isn't only the dress; it's how it fits me. I've changed a little, without even noticing. It makes sense, I suppose—I'm pounding the sidewalk instead of hauling water and pig slop. And while Mrs. Cooper's dinners are plenty filling, I haven't had a good farm breakfast since I got here. I haven't had a proper ballet class where my legs are quivering so bad afterward I can barely walk. Of course my muscles would thin, and my waistline, too.

I'm not sure what to think—I figured the city would change me, I just didn't think it would be something I could *see*. I pull my coat over my shoulders and cinch the belt around my waist to hide the figure this dress is so hell-bent on revealing. I feel dizzy, like I'm standing on the roofline and the smallest nudge will send me tumbling one direction or another. I don't want to go back to where I was, always wishing for something out of reach. But what if being here means I become someone I don't recognize anymore? Am I still even me?

We tromp downstairs and onto the sidewalk. Peggy's walking

so fast I practically have to run to catch up. "Okay, you have to tell me where we're going."

"The Hotel Astor on Broadway and 44th. The gay half of the bar, to be specific. Then dinner and a trip to the rooftop garden after."

I stop dead in my tracks. "The *what* half?"

"Gay." Peggy stops, too, watching my face with a puzzled expression.

"You mean, *homosexual*?" That last part comes out as a whisper.

She's looking at me like I've lost it. "Nobody uses that word. Nobody kind, anyway. It's too . . . clinical or disapproving or something."

"Oh. Sorry. It's just, I've never met anyone like that before."

Peggy walks back to grab my arm and drag me with her. "Of course you have."

I don't know what to say. Obviously my face is as red as the stupid dress that seems to keep creeping lower, baring more of my cleavage with each step. "What do you mean?"

She rolls her eyes skyward. "Half the boys in theatre are gay, Mazie."

"They are?"

"Most definitely."

"It's just—we don't have that sort of thing in Nebraska."

She gives me a look, and I know I've said the wrong thing again. "Look, you may not have gay bars, but people are people. There are all kinds in all places. If you don't know any, all that means is they're underground. Well, that, and you haven't earned their trust."

That's not true. Is it? We clatter down the steps to the subway station. "But how do I—I mean, I wouldn't know how to begin . . ."

"They're people, Mazie. Treat them like people. Truth is, it's loads better being in a room full of gay men than straight ones. No one's ogling your ass the minute you turn your back or your breasts when you're trying to have a conversation."

I knew when I came to this city that I'd have a lot to learn about auditions and theatre etiquette and standing on my own two feet. But I had no idea how much I had to learn about just plain life.

"So, who are we meeting? A friend of yours?"

Peggy peeks down the yawning tunnel mouth. "Yeah. Arlo. He and I did summer stock together up in Maine two summers ago. We both moved to New York that fall and have been friends ever since."

The subway pulls into the station and squeals to a stop, fluttering the edges of our skirts and tossing our hair. The doors sweep open, and we hop on board.

"His folks come down from Rhode Island to visit twice a year, and I go out to dinner with them. It's a lovely evening—the fanciest dinner I'll never afford on my own. Arlo's *gorgeous*, and I don't mind pretending to be madly in love with him for an evening if it means he gets to stay in his parents' good graces for another season."

"They don't know?"

She shrugs. "Maybe they will someday. I guess you never really outgrow wanting your parents to be proud of you, do you? If it's between a lie and that kind of loss, well, it's no easy choice."

We get off the train, come up for air, and head straight for the hotel. It seems like everybody in the city has the same idea we do—or, at least, some version of it. The sidewalks are teeming with people, ladies in heels and sleek skirts with fluttering capes draped over their shoulders, hanging on the arms of gentlemen in tailored suits. Everybody is on their way to a show or to go dancing or simply to be out in the city at night, where the air is thrumming with energy.

I cast a longing look at Henry Miller's Theatre as we pass by, but Peggy only tugs me onward. "We're going to be late!"

"But you still haven't told me what *I'm* doing here."

"Well." She leans in conspiratorially. "Arlo has met someone. He wants Walter to meet his parents, so you're going as Walter's girl."

"Wait, you want me to lie, too?"

Peggy's lips draw into a thin line. "I thought you'd enjoy the chance to do something nice for somebody. To see a side of the city us starving artists never would otherwise. Was I wrong?"

I stare at the pavement passing beneath my shoes, stained with discarded chewing gum, spilled drinks, and bird droppings. She's asking me to go along with a lie. But this lie sure seems like it's for a good and true reason, even if it isn't, strictly, the truth.

"Mazie." Peggy snaps her fingers beneath my nose. "Was I wrong? If that's the case, tell me now. Arlo and Walter will be nervous enough as it is—I'm not bringing somebody along who can't put aside her own stupid judgments about a thing she doesn't know beans about."

Her words smart, and I'm tempted to snap right back. But Daddy raised me to face things I didn't understand head-on. And Momma raised me to be kind. I'm not about to forget that now.

"You're right—I don't understand. But I'd like to. Of course I'd be happy to help your friend."

"That's my girl." Peggy whips out her compact, checks her lipstick in the mirror, then snaps it shut again. "We're here," she announces with a wink, yanking the glass door open with a little bow.

When I left Nebraska, I thought my life was small because of opportunity: farmworking for the boys and farmwifing for the girls. But maybe it was more than that. Maybe it was about ways of thinking, too—of being, loving, and living that are different from anything I've ever known.

Well, if what I wanted was to live surrounded only by things I understood, I never would have left home. But I wanted to step into the wider world. Hell, I wanted to leap.

-26-

I DON'T SO much leap as trip over the threshold, my mouth open as wide as a hooked catfish. I have never seen anything half as elegant as the entryway of the Hotel Astor. Massive marble pillars rise to meet an inlaid ceiling with murals lining the walls below. Two bronze-and-marble staircases lead upward to what I can only guess is more of the same. While I'm busy staring, Peggy swaps her flats for the heels in her purse and shrugs out of her coat. I reluctantly peel mine away, drape it over my arm, and hug it against my midsection.

Peggy's face lights up, and she waves high over her head, grabbing my hand and pulling us toward the crowd around the hotel's circular bar. She runs the last few steps to grab the outstretched hands of a man who looks to be in his late twenties, with dark hair slicked at an angle and a lopsided smile. They kiss each other on the cheek *one-two* like we're in Paris. Then she pulls back, nodding her head at the other young man beaming beside Arlo. He's tall, with bright red hair trimmed short like a soldier, and the posture to match. "This is him?"

A slow smile spreads across Arlo's face. Peggy places one hand along his cheek. "Of course it is."

I almost back away—who am I to interrupt such an intimate moment?—when Arlo peers over Peggy's shoulder. "And this must be Mazie."

I step forward. "Pleased to meet you."

They chuckle at that, and heat rises in my cheeks. "No need to stand on ceremony with us," Arlo says with a wink. "You're doing us a kindness tonight, and we're grateful."

"So," Walter announces with a clap of his hands. "What are you drinking?"

"I'll have the midnight blonde, of course," Peggy says, plumping her silky waves, though they need nothing of the sort.

"Just a lemonade for me, thanks."

"You got it."

When the drinks arrive, Arlo lifts his glass and sucks a breath through his teeth. "To family?"

"To family," we all agree, and tip our glasses back.

I trace a fingernail along the deep etching in the glass. I still haven't heard from Daddy, even though I've sent a dozen letters, some forcing a cheerfulness I don't feel, some running down the day so he can picture me here, in a place utterly unlike anything he's ever known, and some begging him to forgive me for leaving when I did. It's never taken him this long to cool off before.

"What else are we celebrating today?"

Peggy strikes a pose. "This gorgeous hat that makes me every bit as charming as Judy Garland, of course!"

"To the hat!"

That gets a laugh all around and another clink of glasses.

"What about you, Mazie darling?"

I can't hold back a smile—this glittering place is leagues above where I imagined celebrating my news today. "I got a callback."

"Hell yeah, you did!" Peggy exclaims.

Arlo clinks glasses with mine. "And you're wearing that dress for it—say you are!"

"No!" Nervous laughter spills out of me. I cross my arms over my waist, as if there's a thing I could do to hide my figure now. "This dress was a mistake."

"Honey," Arlo says, "if that dress is a mistake, who would ever want to do the right thing?"

The four of us are huddled together, laughing, when Arlo suddenly straightens, his eyes focused on a middle-aged couple waiting in the lobby. He reaches out and takes Walter's hand beneath the bar. They exchange a long look before letting go, then we turn together and settle into the roles we've adopted for the evening.

Mr. Cartwright orders for us all, and the courses arrive promptly, one after another. First a platter of oysters for the table, followed by a cold, green soup and a wilted salad almost too bitter to eat, and some tiny roasted bird that I have no idea how to get at with a fork and knife. Finally, an assortment of cheeses and a dessert of strawberries and cream.

Throughout the whole meal, Arlo never stops talking about his role in the ensemble for Ethel Merman's new show, *Gypsy*, in the first month of its run at the Broadway Theatre. He's talking a mile a minute, and he can't seem to stop mimicking the choreography with his hands. But the Cartwrights sit stiff and aloof, lips pursed, jewels clustered at his mother's ears, an enamel pocket watch in his father's hand as if he's counting each minute as it passes until the dinner is over.

I steal a peek at Walter's face—he isn't an actor like the rest of us. He's sitting ramrod straight, his manners impeccable, his face tight. Momma may not understand this world that pulls me so far away, but she can't help but be caught up in my own enthusiasm, no matter how she wishes she could keep me close. And Daddy—well, I know he loves me even if he is still angry about how I left. Jesse's family welcomed me from the first day I stepped through their front door. Walter's never gonna have that—not with these two.

It makes me steaming mad. So what if he's not who the Cartwrights imagined their son would end up with? Arlo's in love. And they're lovely together. What more could a parent want for their son?

The heat of my own anger surprises me. I reach out and curl my hand around Walter's elbow. He lays his hand on top of mine, and though he doesn't look at me, his shoulders drop a little, his jaw unclenching a bit.

When dinner is over, we walk arm in arm up to the rooftop. A ten-piece band is playing, the music fading into the night the farther it floats away from the stage. A string of lights swoops between flagpoles around the perimeter, ferns and flowing vines stretching from column to column. Walter takes my hand and leads me to an open space on the dance floor.

I could get used to going out for an evening with friends and dancing under a wide-open sky. I didn't know what to expect from this night—not the gay bar or the fancy dinner. But I never would have guessed that spinning around the dance floor in another man's arms would slice open the ache of being without Jesse.

I clear my throat, dropping my gaze to the ground and blinking madly, trying to distract myself. "Where'd you learn to waltz?"

Walter grins. "I couldn't escape it, what with all those cotillion classes."

I laugh at that, and ease into his arms. "Jesse wouldn't know a waltz from a fox-trot."

"Who?"

"Oh. I've got somebody back home—or I did." I haven't told anyone here about Jesse. I suppose I figured if I didn't talk about it, the hurt would ebb quicker.

"You left him behind?"

I nod, the ache spiking through me like spilled ink on a damp cloth. "Back in Nebraska. I broke both our hearts to get here."

Talking about home is like an incantation. My eyes flutter closed, and it's right there: A pale blue sky stretching from horizon to horizon. Blanched peaches bobbing in the kitchen sink. The smell of fresh cut hay and dark soil crumbling in my palm. Rain falling like campfire sparks. Corn stalks rustling in the breeze. A feather-light pulse. The back of a wrinkled hand smoothing her cherry tree quilt. A big orange harvest moon hunkered down on the horizon. Biscuits browning in the oven. Thick, sandy brown hair between my fingers and flannel beneath my cheek, rising and falling with shallow breath. Warmth, in and out and all around me.

Walter's voice drags me back to the rooftop garden, and the

glowing lights, and the strangers on all sides. "You're an actress, like Peggy?"

I swallow, reluctantly blinking the memories away. "I hope to be."

Walter nods, and his eyes travel across the room until they find Arlo. "Life doesn't always offer up the choices we want to make. I figure it's what we do with the choices we *can* make that matters."

"Yeah." I drop my head against Walter's chest, and he folds our hands at his collarbone in a surprisingly tender gesture.

"You're still hung up on that Nebraska fella?"

"Yeah." My voice cracks. "More than the day I left, if that's even possible."

Walter whirls me in a slow circle, my head drops back, and I drink in the warm air and the darkness above. It's a clear night, but still, I can hardly see the stars. Back home, the sky would be smothered with them, so many and so bright you'd think if you only stretched up a little farther you might touch them. A piece of me has been hoping that, in spite of everything, Jesse would find a way here. That we could live out our dreams side by side in this crazy place. Only now, looking up at this starless sky, I'm not even sure he'd want to.

-27-

I'M STILL CAUGHT up in the dream and ache of last night, lounging between the sheets longer than Momma would ever allow, when Peggy bursts through the bedroom door. She jumps onto my bed, shaking me awake.

"I got it! I got the part!"

"What?" I push her back, and she spills onto the floor, cackling and kicking her legs in the air. "What part?"

"The audition was weeks ago—I'd given up on it completely. It's a small role, but it's *mine*."

"Wait—does this mean you're leaving?" I should be thrilled for her, but it feels like a betrayal, her leaving me all alone here. What would I have done without Peggy? How long would I have hemmed and hawed, shaking in my boots, too scared to get out the door and go to my first audition?

"I'm headed home to see my folks today—as soon as I can pack up my things. We start rehearsals in two weeks in Chicago, where the show is doing an out-of-town tryout." She searches my face. "Mazie, you don't need me to hold your hand. You've got a callback today! You're going to nail it, and you'll be off on a show of your own before you know it."

Peggy squeals once more for good measure and hops up. "I have to tell Mrs. Cooper!"

She darts out of the room, and I'm left hugging my knees, the glow of last night scrubbed away completely. I wish I didn't feel even a twinge of resentment or jealousy. I run my fingers over the scratchy wool blanket draped across my feet. Maybe Peggy and I weren't friends, not really. Roommates. Co-conspirators once in a while. But not friends.

Sometimes it seems like nothing in this city is real.

I arrive ready for the callback a good ninety minutes early and limber up in the narrow hallway, trying to stretch without calling too much attention to myself. I watch the other girls go in and come back out, sometimes after five minutes, sometimes after much longer. I can't read too much from their faces, but their bodies say enough about how hope shatters when it hits the ground.

Finally, my name is called. I follow the choreography easily enough, and I spin through the lifts even though partnering isn't something I've done much of. They have some sides for me, and they ask me to sing again. But I can't feel any connection with the people on the other side of the table, and though I know I did well, I also know I am not going to book this job—even before the casting director walks me out and tells me so.

"You're a capable dancer, and that voice is a thing of beauty. They're just after a different . . . look. You understand."

She's being kind, telling me even that much, but it stings all the same. Still, I'm an actor, aren't I? So I smile, blinking a little too fast. "Thanks," I manage. I toss Nana's scarf over my shoulder and push through the studio door like it didn't just kill me to do that much.

-28-

I WRITE A letter to Jesse when I get home. I tell him all about the city and Mrs. Cooper, about Peggy leaving and all those auditions. How when it's in the back room of some producer's office, and you can see the people judging you, their reaction can knock you off course in a blink if you aren't ready for it. How one time the production assistant passed a note to the table letting them know she'd just brewed a fresh pot of coffee and they didn't even pretend my reading was cut short for any other reason. How when it's in a theatre with only the audition light on and the house is pitch black, sometimes that's even worse—a disembodied voice interrupting halfway through your song like the angel of judgment himself.

I tell Jesse about the long walk back to Mrs. Cooper's after the callback, my brain whirring with all I did well and all I could have done better. I tell him how at night I lie in bed, my feet cramping from walking across the city, my ears ringing from the sheer noise of the place, but my brain empty, too tired to think. I tell him how it stops my breath sometimes how much I miss him.

I write that last part and know that I'll never send the letter—I can't. It was me who did this to us, and I've got no right to expect sympathy from him. So I let myself say it all. I beg him to forget the farm and follow me here. I tell him how we'd move into a shoebox apartment on West 45th Street where the boiler would run too hot in the summer and freeze us out in the winter. How we'd eat beans on toast like paupers and read day-old newspapers. How I'd spend my evenings at the theatre and he'd spend his studying the sky. How we'd wake each morning tangled up in each other and we'd stay there until the hunger to be inside the other's skin was sated, until our throats were parched, sweat sticking our bodies together. I write until it's all down on paper, what I want so bad my body throbs with it. I can't even cry, though my eyes are hot and itching.

The following morning, my head is pounding and my pillow is wet. I open my fist and the letter is still there, crumpled in my hand. I tiptoe to the bathroom, rip it into pieces, and let them fall into the waste bin.

-29-

BEFORE BREAKFAST MONDAY morning, one of the girls across the hall leaves Mrs. Cooper's for good. I don't even remember her name, but I've watched her dance, and she's good. We all come into the hallway to see her off, in our housecoats and bare faces. She's crying silently, tears rolling down her cheeks like they'll never stop.

Marsha leans over my shoulder and whispers, "She's been here three years. Worked in a ticket booth on the weekends and auditioned during the week. Never booked a single show."

"Three years?" It's like a punch in the stomach.

"Yeah. And *West Side Story* closed over the weekend. After a run of seven hundred and thirty-two performances." Marsha shakes her head, her eyes wide. "Sure seems like a sign or something."

I duck back into the bedroom, determined to forget the scene in the hallway and focus on getting ready. I glance at Peggy's empty bed. And Evie's. Money's running out. I paid my weekly rent to Mrs. Cooper yesterday—all I had left, except for the train fare back home.

There's a part of me that thinks it'd be a whole heck of a lot easier to go back to Nebraska—at least at first. I'd get to see Momma and Daddy. And I'd have no reason to push Jesse away if my big dream had fizzled into nothing. But things between us would be different even so—worse than if I'd never left, because at least before, I had hope to cling to. If I go back now, if I have nothing to show for all this rejection and heartache, I'm pretty sure I'd sour everything I touched.

They're after a different look.

That's what the casting director said yesterday, and I've heard it enough by now to know exactly what she meant. Well, I don't have three years to wait. I've got one week. Back home, you'd rather lose your house and your land if you only got to keep your integrity. But I can't shake the feeling that if I don't change who I am, at least on the surface, it'll be me going home next.

So what is it about me, exactly, that's so *unacceptable*? The freckles, for one. And the home-sewn dresses, I suppose. My bare lips. Would it be so awful to put forward a lacquered-up, slimmed-down, spit-shined version of myself if it means I get to stay here?

Marsha sweeps in, unwrapping a towel from her head.

"Marsha?"

"Hmmmm?" She runs a comb through her wet hair, leaning out over the rug.

"If you wouldn't mind . . . I've had my eye on that tea-length dress of yours, if you're not wearing it today."

"You know, Viola across the hall has a felt hat that'll really make the look."

"Oh—thanks! And could you show me how to use that face powder? I want to hide my freckles before setting out."

Marsha flicks her hair out of the way and tosses a pale pink compact my way. "Sure thing!"

My stomach is rioting, even though there's nothing in there yet. My freckles have been a part of me since I was a kid—every time I looked in the mirror, every time I belted out a song for an audience of milking cows and plow horses, every time I threw my head back and laughed at something Nana said. I lift the sponge up to my cheek and, bit by bit, wipe away any trace of that sun-kissed country girl.

Thirty minutes later, I hit the pavement in Marsha's dress with Viola's hat set at a jaunty angle on top of my curls. Viola sent a hairpiece along with the hat, and I made her show me three times how to pin the thing in right. Her hair is more red than strawberry blonde, but it does add this delightful bounce when I dance. I worry the casting director will be able to tell, that I might look ridiculous in the glam hat and the hair that isn't all mine, but being myself hasn't gotten me anywhere so far, so maybe this will.

My lips are painted red, and my fingernails, too. This one's a cattle call for vocalists, but I tucked my dancing shoes into my purse just in case. There will be hundreds of hopefuls lined up around the block; I'll probably stand on the sidewalk for hours just to get in the door.

But this is what I came here to do. I'm determined to make this audition count. I prepared "Get Happy" from *Summer Stock*, and, keeping in mind what Peggy said about using the trip to the theatre to get into character, I put on a smile as I click down the sidewalk past the fish market, the Chinese restaurant, and the beauty salon with the jewelry store on the second story. But the smile feels hollow, and the people I pass seem to take it for weakness, bumping and jostling me even more than normal.

From half a block away, I can see that the audition line stretches down the street and around the corner. I settle in and pull out the miniature guide to New York City I nabbed from Mrs. Cooper's borrowing bookshelf. I flip to the section on the theatre district. The librarian back home brought in a book like this for me once, but it's different to read about the Lunt-Fontanne when I just passed it yesterday on the way to an audition, or the Broadhurst with its curving brick and pale cameos, directly across the street from me this very second. How anyone could stand in the shadow of those old buildings and *not* be bowled over by the story and glitz of it all is beyond me.

The hours pass slowly, and the fog that's hung around my head ever since Peggy left dissipates a little. Seems like every five seconds I'm having to swat away some stray thought or another about how if I wasn't good enough for the last thirty-odd auditions, there's no reason to think today will be any different. It's like I've got my own personal cloud of doubts following me all through the long wait.

The line moves inch by inch until the sun is high overhead, beating down on us all. At nearly three o'clock, the person in front of me makes it inside, and then, finally, so do I. My last audition was in some beat-up rehearsal studio, but this one is in a theatre. The same production company putting out the call has a different show running in this space, so I guess they figure why not use it during the day for auditions.

I drop my picture and résumé in the pile with the rest and sign in. The assistant stage manager groups ten of us together and tells us to wait while she peeks around the curtain and checks the time on her wristwatch. I peel off my extra layers and prance in place, trying to get the blood flowing. It feels like my stomach is eating me from the inside out, and I'm kicking myself now for skipping breakfast.

Finally, our group of ten gets the go-ahead. "Stay in this exact order. Drop your sheet music on the piano and cross to the red X downstage. They aren't letting anyone sing more than a few bars, so don't be thrown when they cut you off. They *will* cut you off."

When she shoves us into the wings, I can't seem to get my lungs to work right, much less my feet. I can't sing if I can't breathe, so I focus on that. Just breathe. Breathe. *Breathe.* And it must work, because by the time the girl in front of me is done and I drop my sheet music on the piano with a tight smile for the accompanist, at the very least, there's air in my lungs.

The empty theatre is cold. I cross to the mark, stepping into the glow of the rehearsal light. I can't see anyone out there, only the dim outlines of the first few empty rows beyond the orchestra pit. When a shortened intro nods to my entrance, I breathe into the opening note. My voice gets going without a squeak, and I send a silent thanks to Mrs. Muth that it does what it's been trained to, no matter that my brain has turned to pudding. They cut me off before I can swing into the second verse, and even though I was warned, it's still jarring. I scuttle over to the piano, collect my sheet music, and go wait with the others backstage. When the last girl has finished the few bars they allow her, the stage manager strolls down the aisle to the front of the stage.

He clears his throat. "If I lay your picture on the stage, that is all, and we thank you for your time. If you do not see your picture, please exit stage left, collect your belongings, and proceed to the rehearsal studio, where you will be taught the choreography for the dance portion of the audition."

He turns on his heel and marches up the aisle into the darkness again. We cross to the scattering of photos on the stage floor, and I nearly trip I'm so shocked—mine isn't there! Eight photos litter the stage floor, so two of us are through to the next round.

I back away, clapping a hand over my mouth to keep it together. This isn't over yet—there could still be a hundred people vying for one part. I shrug into my cardigan to try and warm my body as much as I can while another assistant leads us to the rehearsal studio.

"Drop your belongings in the hallway; there won't be room inside."

I roll my clothes into a tidy knot, plop Viola's hat on top, shuck the flats I sang in, and pull on my dance shoes. There are at least a hundred people in the studio, pressed against the walls, stretching and pretending not to watch the choreographer, casting director, and dance captain conferring behind a folding table at the front of the room. Mirrors line every wall from the high ceiling down to the well-worn floor. I let out a sigh of relief—it's a real studio. I hurry to grab the last open spot at the barre and begin a hasty warm-up. Well, as much as I can. I'd kick no fewer than three people if I tried a *grand battement* right now.

But the room is warm from all the bodies crammed inside, and the familiar movements bring me back into my body. Besides,

I can't help glancing around, and what I see are people who'd look right as rain strolling through downtown Fairbury. Stocky builds and wide-open, honest faces. Hair straight as straw and sun-bleached at the tips. Maybe I've stumbled upon an audition where the "type" they're looking for is me? Maybe, *finally*, they'll take the time to see what I can do. By the time the stage manager sweeps in and slaps a stack of pictures on the tabletop, I'm feeling good.

The dance captain steps into the middle of the room and claps his hands for attention. "We're going to repeat the same eight bars until this group is down to twenty." He pretends not to hear the groan that wavers through the room. "Then those twenty will head back out onstage so the director and producer can get a look at you, and we'll cut another dozen."

He spins to face the mirrors. "Watch, now. It's one-two-three-four, five-six-seven-eight."

Adrenaline spikes through me. I can do this—it's a jazz number with a little soft-shoe thrown in. The dance captain breaks down each eight-count, first slow, then at tempo. They give each group of ten twice through to get the steps right before the cuts begin.

The accompanist bangs out the music, and each time my group slides to the side, the next one kick-steps on like the dance floor is a massive conveyor belt. By some miracle, I don't get that tap on the shoulder telling me I've been cut. The clock ticks by—ten minutes. Twenty. Thirty. Everybody's sweating, breathing heavy. I glance to either side of me. There are only two groups of a dozen each left.

The piano transitions from the end of the stanza right back to the beginning again, and all around me, the girls snap to attention, lipsticked smiles plastered on their faces as they shimmy and whip through the steps. They're good. They're all so good.

A wiggle of unease gets under my skin. I've got to do something more with this round—make up for my lack of experience with a big dose of heart. So I give everything just a little *more*. I kick and shuffle, leap and spin, and arch back so far I think I might snap in half, then whip my head forward.

I feel an odd tug at my scalp. And then a rip.

Out of the corner of my eye I see Viola's hairpiece flying end over end, arcing above me. My legs keep up their box stepping and my hands are still jazzy as ever, but time slows as the pertly curled mop cartwheels over the line of dancers in front of me, landing like a splayed mop on the floor. My feet stutter to a stop, and the dancer next to me bumps me out of her way.

The dance captain taps my shoulder. "Sorry, honey," he whispers.

I go limp as a marionette with its strings cut. I'd rather never see the damn thing again, but while the rest of my group is still dancing away, I force myself to walk to the front of the studio, bend over, and pick up Viola's hairpiece. It feels like a wet fur in my palm. Probably smells like one, too.

From outside the studio, the piano sounds like something out of a cheap carnival. I don't even have the energy to cry. I got *so* close. I peel off my dancing shoes and slide back into my flats. My feet are killing me.

The day is warm and sunny when the stage door slams shut behind me, but I start shivering right away. Tourists mill around beneath the marquee, no clue as to the hearts breaking inside that theatre at this very minute. I blink away my disappointment—I made it through some deep cuts in there. They responded to my voice. And my dancing was almost good enough. Almost.

I coax my aching feet to get moving. Halfway home I remember that Claire is giving a tap lesson tonight in the parlor. Tired and frustrated as I am, I know I'll be in the front row, ready to learn. I didn't come all this way only to fail.

-30-

IT'S MY TURN to scrub toilets, and after a morning audition that was a complete waste of my time, I can't say as I mind. On the farm, all those hours doing chores was really time spent dreaming. But I'm here now, where my dreams are supposed to be coming true. Only they're not, so what's the point of daydreams?

Instead, I take advantage of the time and those generous acoustics to work on a new number I'm prepping for auditions. I prop the sheet music on the sink while I scrub, going over and over that tricky spot in the bridge with all those little stair-step jumps and then the high note, long and too exposed to get away with being breathy.

By the time the second- and third-floor bathrooms are done, I figure out how to sneak a breath into the previous line so I can push through the intervals and into a sustained vibrato. Mrs. Muth would be proud, I think. I run it a few times to be sure I've got it, then lean back, roll out my neck, and let myself imagine that tomorrow will be my last audition, that somebody will see I'm exactly what they've been looking for.

The minute the chores are done, I get out of there. I could be running lines or practicing choreography, but it's beginning to feel like if I don't get outside for a few hours to clear my head, the twitchy feeling behind my eyes will never go away. It's so humid outside I'm sweating by the time I clatter down the front stoop.

I head straight east under a gray sky, past rows of apartments and brownstones, street vendors, and droves of churchgoers in their Sunday best. I pass a man in a tattered and filthy suit slumped in the shade of an iron-barred bank window, looking every bit as desperate as I feel.

I change course abruptly and make for the park at the heart of Manhattan. When I cross under the shade of a grove of towering trees, a breath sighs out of me. It's nothing like home—not even close. I can still hear the rattle and hiss of the city, and I can smell it, too. But there are birds in the branches, and squirrels, and everyone is moving slower, breathing easier here, where we can pretend we've left the city behind us. I stroll down the paths until I've lost all sense of time, my mind has slipped the track of frustration, rejection, and loneliness, and I simply *am*.

I stop for lunch on an old stone bridge, leaning over the edge, mesmerized by the still water below reflecting a hazy sky, crisscrossing tree trunks, and the tops of buildings so elegant I doubt they'd even let me through the front door. After wandering awhile longer, I finally head home, skirting around the natural history museum, trying to reconnect with West 80th. A clapboard sign is propped in the center of the path, announcing: *Free and open to the public today: The Hayden Planetarium.*

I stop suddenly, my torso lurching forward at the abrupt change of direction.

The Hayden Planetarium. I know that name. I reach out a hand to steady myself as memory eclipses the world around me, replacing it with an early October evening nearly two years ago—one of my first Friday-night dinners at the Schmidt house. We all bundled up and went out behind the barn to where Jesse had his homemade telescope trained on the stars. The Soviets had just launched *Sputnik* into orbit, and he was determined to see the thing with his own eyes. He'd already rigged up a shortwave radio to listen to its *beep-beep-beep-beep* signal. The whole country was whipped up into a frenzy over that blasted satellite, but this sort of thing was nothing new for Jesse—he'd been watching the night sky for years.

Joy smirked. "Remember when Jesse sent a letter to the Hayden Planetarium when he was all of ten years old, begging the chairman to reserve a spot for him in the first interplanetary tour?"

"Yeah." Lois chuckled. "He was only supposed to pick one planet to visit, but he checked every single one, and the moon, too, for good measure."

A sheepish smile curved over Jesse's lips, probably because I was there to witness the ribbing. But nothing—not their teasing nor the good-hearted laughter that followed—could pry his eyes off the sky. That is, not until it was time to drive me home, when he drew me into the barn's shadow, making some excuse about needing to check that he'd capped the lenses or something. Really, he only wanted a minute alone with me.

It might have taken Jesse another six months to kiss me if I hadn't backed him up against the barn that night and made my intentions clear. I was rattling like a leaf, I was so nervous. But then, so was he. Things between us were just beginning then, bright and hopeful as newborn stars.

I close my eyes as the memory fades, trying to hang on to that feeling for a moment longer. I dart a look around me, then step onto the grass, through a line of young trees, and toward an enormous sphere like a concrete moon rising above the museum's stolid red brick exterior. I hesitate in the entryway. It doesn't seem right going in there without him—coming here would be a sort of religious pilgrimage for Jesse. But then, it doesn't seem right not to, either. So I wander through the planetarium, past the Zeiss projector, the Viking rocket, and the Copernican exhibit with our solar system in orbit on the ceiling.

Jesse should be here. Yes, of course, because the two of us belong together. But also . . . he deserves better than a life working the earth when all he wants is to be among the stars.

-31-

MONDAY MORNING I try to give myself a pep talk along the lines of *Every morning is a fresh start!* or *New day, new opportunity!* but desperation is a demon that I can't seem to get off my back. Either I book a show by Friday or I book a train ticket home. For luck, I borrow a pair of patent leather heels from Sue Ellen down the hall and spend an extra thirty minutes smoothing the frizz out of my curls. I force down a bowl of oatmeal and a cup of strong coffee, no matter that my nerves seem to want to bring it all back up again.

The whole way across town, I run my lines, my lips moving in a silent recital of the new monologue I've been working on. It's from *Seven Brides for Seven Brothers*, which is sort of repulsive when you actually think about it: a handful of petulant man-children kidnapping a bunch of women because they don't know how to talk to one unless she's *literally* a captive audience. Not my favorite musical, but it's popular, and apparently mass appeal more than substance is what casting directors are after.

I've got the lipstick in my purse and a kerchief for blotting this time. I've powdered my freckles into submission. I'm wearing

Marsha's red sheath dress, and every time I start feeling uneasy at the way it hugs my hips, I remind myself that I'm not Mazie today. I'm Marilyn or Ingrid or Liz. I belong in a dress like this. And I deserve the spotlight.

The line is long, and maybe it's only that I've been to so many of these now, but all the girls waiting to audition seem a little tight around the eyes and pinched at the mouth, like we're already beat. When they call my name, I turn on that *thing* every actress worth her socks has got and sail onto the stage like a grand madam at a party she's spent months planning down to the very last detail.

"Mazie Butterfield," I say. "Pleased to meet you." Then I launch into my monologue.

It's not always good when I sink deep into a character. Sometimes I can let it slip a little, veer into the overdramatic. Other times it falls flat, and I can't put into words why, or what goes wrong. Not this time, though. It's good. Real good. I can feel it. I'm not just pretending to be Milly. I *am* Milly. And I'm giving that husband of mine an earful.

But still, halfway through, the director flops a hand in the air. "Thank you. That's all."

I just stand there, stunned. I should hustle off the stage with what dignity I have left, but I can't seem to move off my mark. I nailed the scene the best I know how, and if *that*—lucky shoes, lipstick, and all—isn't good enough, maybe I *should* head home to Nebraska. The casting director leans in to confer with the others, and I can't help but catch a few choice phrases. *Hefty. Plain. Midwestern.* They seep right through the fog in my head, and I scurry for the wings like a kicked dog. I'm almost out of sight when the director stands.

"You there, uh—Mazie. Hold on."

I whirl back around, but the bravado I called up on the way in has left me. It's cold in the theatre now. I wish I'd worn a sweater.

"You're not right for my show."

The casting director jabs her elbow into the director's ribs, rolling her eyes to the track lights above. "What he means to say is, we might have something else for you."

The director clears his throat. "My friend Harbuckle was nearly done and dusted—halfway through rehearsals—when his talent went scurrying for the hills. The Rodgers and Hammerstein hills, if you take my meaning. Don't know what the big deal is about a bunch of nuns and Nazis, but *eeeeverybody's* clamoring to be a part of their new show."

I glide toward the front of the stage, barely breathing. Is he saying what I think he's saying?

"Harbuckle needs to find replacements, and fast. It isn't an open call—they've already gone through all that. They need somebody *now*, and you're the right kind of . . ." The director gestures vaguely at me, his mouth turning down in a grimace.

Hefty? Plain? Midwestern? Yeah. Got it.

"Here." The casting director scribbles on a sheet of paper, tears it from the pad, and leans out over the row of chairs to hand it to me. "This is the address and the hour when they'll be seeing a few alternates. Good luck to you."

I don't remember walking off that stage or collecting my

things. And I have no idea how I'm able to find my way home. When I cross the threshold into Mrs. Cooper's boardinghouse, I pull my hand out of my pocket and blink a few times just to be sure. It's really there, really real. My knuckles are bone white, gripping that paper so tight I don't think the devil himself could pry it away from me.

-32-

IN THE MORNING, I tuck my purse into the crook of my arm and step out of the bedroom, closing the door quietly behind me. I cross to the mirror at the end of the hall and twist to check my reflection. I smooth the front of my dress. No matter what everybody else seems to think, all that oatmeal (and maybe all that walking across town and back again) has done a number on my waistline. My clothes fit differently now—it's not only the home cooking sloughing off, it's also the dancer's muscles I spent so long building up going soft. The city is whittling away chunks of me, one nervous audition at a time.

I wish I could afford lessons—I miss how strong it makes me feel to work my body harder than I ever would without Mme Durant's critical eye. All those casting directors seem to think "thick" or "hefty" is a bad thing. But where I'm from, strong is a good thing. It's beautiful.

I make my way slowly downstairs, trying to clear my head of that oh-so-predictable rush of doubts. Seems to me that every artist—painter, writer, actor—has a tiny voice inside her head that's always heckling: *Who do you think you are? How dare you reach for those stars? They're so far beyond the likes of you, you'll never touch so much as stardust.*

I know I'm green. I know there are folks who've got ten times the experience I do. I mean, I've only ever been in one professional production, and even that was all thanks to Nana. It was last fall; she'd clipped an announcement out of the *Lincoln Journal Star* and cornered me after supper to show me the casting call for a regional theatre production of *Anything Goes*.

"But—I can't do this!" I exclaimed. "Rehearsals in Lincoln every evening? Daddy and Otis need the truck here at the farm. Besides, paying for the gasoline would wipe my savings clean, and then what would be the point?"

Nana gave me one of her signature looks. "With that attitude, you'll never land this part, much less one on Broadway."

Coming from anyone else, it would have been a slap across the face. But Nana believed in me—sometimes even more than I did.

"You're right."

"Course I am. Now, listen up. I rang the casting director, and as it turns out, they need a few youngsters in their company. See, here: *Girl, soloist.* The underage actors are only called to rehearsal every other Saturday."

"No," I breathed.

"Last time that farm boy of yours came calling, I mentioned the transportation predicament, and wouldn't you know it—he said he'd be pleased to drive you, seeing as how the run would be over before planting begins. As for auditions, well, your nana can only arrange for so much . . ."

I squealed with glee, leaping around the room. And Nana

heard nothing for the next few weeks except *What should I sing?* and *What should I wear?* over and over again.

Wouldn't you know it—I got the part, and Jesse drove me to every single rehearsal and the performances, too. To make it up to him, I read out loud the whole way there and back out of this *dry as unbuttered toast* book about the launches of *Sputnik 1* and *2* and the eminence of the Soviet Union in space.

Half of me is terrified I'll never land a part outside Nebraska, and the other half knows that if I do, I won't have Jesse along to make me laugh at myself when I flub my lines or trip over my own feet getting offstage, or to swing me around and then, when he sets me back down to earth, kiss me until it's all gone—the jitters and the nerves and the whole wide world.

And suddenly, I miss him every bit as bad as the minute I left. It's not that I didn't expect the city to be lonely. I knew being away from him would knock the wind out of me. I guess I just thought it would hit hard and then I'd put it behind me. I thought that because I always knew how we'd end, maybe it wouldn't hurt so much when we did.

I take a breath and try to clear my head. Then I blow a kiss to each of the framed playbills lining the entryway and head out. This audition has to be a good one. It *has* to be.

I get to the suite of offices thirty minutes early. That's long enough to warm up my body and my voice, but not so long that my nerves can knock me off my game. When I step up to the receptionist's table, I'm the only girl in the waiting room.

She peers at me over a pair of wire-rimmed glasses. "Can I help you?"

"Yes, thank you. My name is Mazie Butterfield, here to see"—I glance down at the paper—"a Mr. Harbuckle?"

"This is a closed audition. We just showed the last girl in, and your name isn't on my list."

She wouldn't send me away without being seen, would she? I hold the paper out. "Yes, but I was sent here special, by a friend of the producer's. He said I was just what Mr. Harbuckle's looking for, that I should come to this address at this exact time." Can she hear the desperation in my voice?

She sighs. "One moment, please."

She rises from behind the desk and disappears into the adjoining room. I roll my ankles and my neck while I wait for her to reappear. When the heavy office door finally reopens, it isn't the receptionist who answers, but a male voice with a thick Boston accent. "Well, hurry on in here!"

The receptionist gives me a look, so I suppose that means me. The girl who just finished her audition scurries back into the waiting room, while I hustle through that door before they can change their minds.

"This is Mr. Harbuckle." The receptionist nods at the portly man behind a wide metal desk. He's leaning forward on his elbows, the fabric of his suit jacket straining over his shoulders. He's got an unlit cigar clamped between his teeth, but that doesn't stop him from talking around it, and plenty loud, too.

"I'm producing the show, and this here"—he jerks a thumb at a smaller man seated in a wooden chair beside him—"is the director, Gerard Pierce." He flings a hand at me, by which I gather that I'm supposed to begin.

"Pleased to meet you both! I'm Mazie Butterfield, and I'll begin with a song."

I launch into "People Will Say We're in Love." For an office, the acoustics aren't half-bad, and since I don't have to worry about filling a whole theatre, I can really play with the tone, starting soft and building until my voice fills the whole room, rich and full of emotion. I get so caught up, I forget this is an audition and I just sing.

Mr. Harbuckle leans back in his seat with a grin. He holds up a hand after I finish the long high note and keeps it there while he leans conspiratorially toward the director. "She's better than the others we saw today."

This guy's only got one volume, apparently: loud.

The director crosses his arms over his chest. "True."

"I think she'll do fine!"

Is this real? My fingers start to tingle. After all I've been through, and how close I am to packing it in and heading home—

"Miss—what did you say your name was? Butterbun?"

Lord.

"Butterfield. Mazie Butterfield."

Maybe Peggy was right about the name—maybe I need to change that, too. After all, it worked for Rita Hayworth and Marilyn Monroe.

Harbuckle chews on the end of his cigar. "How much did they tell you about this production, Miss Butterfield?"

"Not a word. But they seemed to think I'd be right for the part."

"Indeed. We've got a bang-up show written by Kelley and Sotts and headlined by Clive Booker and Gloria Jamison."

I gasp, my hand flying up to cover my mouth. Pierce's eyes narrow at that, a slow smile dawning.

Harbuckle leans forward. "It's an industrial sponsored by the Von Steer tractor company, and let me assure you, they aren't sparing any expense in rolling out their new model to showrooms all across the Corn Belt."

Wait. What? "The Corn Belt?" My voice is small. My breath hitches. *This isn't a Broadway show?*

"On Monday, we head out on tour. The production has a small cast but a big production value. We'll be putting on a total of ten shows, and don't you worry, the union has negotiated a pretty penny for you actors."

I'm just starting to feel my toes again. *The Corn Belt?*

"This whole thing is nuts." Pierce rakes a hand through his thinning black hair. "We don't have time to teach her the songs, much less the reel of square dances—that number alone took the cast an entire day to get right."

Corn Belt or not, there is no way on God's green earth I am going to let this chance slip away. I flip my hair back and smile for all I'm worth. "Are you doing the Chicken Plucker? Or are you going with an old standby like the Salty Dog Breakdown? Pocket Full of Dreams? Pistol Packin' Mama? 'Cause I know them all. My uncle Lem called more square dances than anybody in Jefferson County, and who do you think filled in when an odd number of people showed up?"

Pierce tilts his head to the side, his pale blue eyes scanning the length of me. I hold that smile through gritted teeth.

"You don't want this job," he says at last. "We started out with two understudies, and they both left for a better gig. We've restructured every single role, and the girl we're hiring today will cover all four female parts."

Pierce waits a minute for that to sink in.

"That's what we're offering, and trust me, you don't want it. The rest of the cast gets to have a few days off at each stop, and you would, too, per the contract, but understudies in a quick run like this one can't afford to do anything with that day off but study. You'll have new direction to absorb, line changes to learn, dance numbers to memorize from every single angle—and you might do all that work but still never get onstage, not even once." He interlaces his fingers behind his head and leans back in his chair, balancing on the back legs. "You don't want this job. Trust me."

His face is open—friendly, even. But something in his tone and the mocking tilt of his eyes tells me otherwise. I *need* this job. He knows it, and he thinks he's cornered me into begging for it.

Gerard Pierce may be a big name in this business, but he doesn't know me, and he doesn't know the first thing about what I want. I summon a *devil may care* chuckle and clamp a hand on my hip. "You're right. I don't want to go on a tour of the Corn Belt. I want to be here, in New York City, a part of a company that has a ten-year run on Broadway. I want to start out on the chorus line and work my way up as high as I can get.

"But as it turns out, Broadway isn't ready for me. You people can't see past where I come from, or the way I talk. So it seems like Broadway may need a little convincing. And if I'm honest, I might need to work at this a little more.

"You see, that's how I *know* I'm the girl for you. Nebraska folk are hardworking, determined people. Farmers can't help but be humbled by the fickle weather and the demands of crop-weary soil. If it's extra work this role needs, I'm your gal. I promise you, right here and now, I'm the best person for this job."

Harbuckle and Pierce share a long look, then the producer shrugs. "It's your call."

The director turns his attention back to me, drawing his palm across his chin as he looks me up and down again. "I'll take her under my wing and make sure she gets up to speed."

"It's settled then!" Harbuckle slaps the table, levering himself up to standing. He thrusts out his hand, and I leap forward to shake it.

-33-

I'M SO KEYED up, I can't sleep a wink. I flop this way, then that, sure Marsha's going to chuck a pillow at me if I don't settle down soon. I lift my wristwatch up to the light coming in the window—it isn't even ten o'clock. Back in Nebraska, the sun hasn't started going down yet. I bet Daddy's just pouring himself a tumbler of whiskey, and Momma's settling into her chair across the hearth from him.

I sit up and peel back the covers. I have a job now—I can afford a quick call. I wrap my housecoat around my waist and tiptoe into the hall and downstairs. I drop two quarters in the jar, dial the long-distance operator, and, quiet as I can, ask her to put me through.

"Hello?" Momma sounds a little confused. We don't get many telephone calls in the evening at the farmhouse.

"Hey, Momma," I whisper.

"Mazie?"

"It's good to hear your voice."

"Yours too, honey."

Something in her tone gives me pause. "Is everything okay?"

There's a long sigh on the line. "It'll be six weeks on Monday.

I suppose that means you're calling to let us know when to expect you at the station."

"Momma, I—"

"No, let me get this out. It was wrong to try and keep you here. I've always known you needed to leave—that you'd never be at ease with yourself unless you did. I've been thinking. Maybe when you come home, we can find some auditions around here. You know my second cousin Bertie in Omaha? I know she'd put you up in her spare room if you booked some regional theatre or concerts there. You'd make more money doing one eight-week run than you would in a whole year as a carhop."

"It's okay, Momma. I—"

"You could save up while you're working that show, then go back to New York, audition for a few more weeks, come home, and repeat the whole thing again if you need to."

I can hardly believe what she's saying.

"Mazie, honey, when you left, all I could think about was how to get you back home. But if this really is your dream, I want it to come true for you."

"Momma." It's barely above a whisper. I'm blinking hard and fast—a long-distance phone call is no time to choke up. I swallow, and my throat opens enough for me to try speaking again. "I can't tell you how much it means to hear you say that. But actually, I called to say I finally booked a show."

"You did? Oh, Mazie!"

I lick my lips. "I'm an understudy for a tour—I'll mail you a copy of the schedule when I get it. It's a summer gig, with an extra week in the contract if we end up needing it. We'll be traveling through Indiana, Illinois, Missouri, home to Nebraska, then north and east for a few stops, finishing in Cedar Rapids. The show is closed to the public, but maybe I can meet you and Daddy for dinner?"

"That'd be real nice, honey."

"They say I'll get my Equity card right up front. It all happened so fast—we leave next week, if you can believe it!"

I can hear the smile in her voice. "I'm so proud of you, honey."

And that's what wrecks me. "Thanks, Momma. I love you." Or at least that's what I try to say. I'm not sure she can make out anything more than blubbering before I hang up the phone.

-34-

THE NEXT MORNING, Mr. Harbuckle walks me through a quick introduction to the creative team, the crew, and the rest of the cast, then a contract signing and a tour of the place—all in the first hour of my first day of studio rehearsals.

I can't believe I'll be understudying Gloria Jamison! She's been on Broadway since she was a kid—and it shows. Even when she's only running lines her comedic timing is a master class, the way she delivers a line or angles her body toward the audience for the beats she knows will get a laugh. She's a pro, through and through.

Marsha says the big stars take these industrials for the money, but the calendar doesn't hurt, either. They can finish a summer tour in time to make rehearsals for another, bigger show opening in the winter and getting ready to round the corner into awards season. There's a strategy to it, but all that's light-years beyond me at this point.

Harbuckle starts up the stairs. "This is not the way things are supposed to go—replacements stepping in at the eleventh hour. Pierce is normally a pretty levelheaded guy, but so far everything that can go wrong casting this show has gone wrong. A director can't direct when the actors keep playing musical chairs."

He's huffing and puffing, getting ready to drop me at wardrobe, when Pierce grips my elbow and draws me over to a table at the end of a busy hallway. "I'll take it from here."

Pierce sits me in a folding chair, drags another one over, and leans across the table, his cheek hovering a little too close to my own. He slides a stack of pictures across the top of the table. Why is the director even sitting down with me one on one? Isn't there an assistant or second assistant who could be doing this?

"The cast is made up of four men and four women, with two understudies. The story goes that Ned is smitten with an upscale gal named Sally. Ned knows he'll never catch Sally's eye with the rusty tractor and ramshackle farm he inherited. He's determined to win her over, so he gets a loan and buys the newfangled tractor in the Von Steer showroom."

Pierce scoots even closer to peer at the script over my shoulder. I flinch back on instinct, then try to hide my reaction by digging in my purse for something to write with.

"You'll be covering all four female parts. First, Gloria's principal role as Sally, the object of Ned's affection. Next, Fiona plays the receptionist at the Von Steer showroom as well as Sally's best friend, Gemma. She married a nice guy but a poor one, and she's suffering for that choice now." Pierce points to each actor's picture as he ticks down the line of characters. "Next you'll cover Darlene. She plays no less than six characters, from Ned's mother to Sally's dim friend, Ethel, then a boy at the barn raising, the glamour girl in the Von Steer showroom reclining across the tractor's bucket,

Ned's schoolmarm in flashback, and Ned's high school rival's svelte wife."

Pierce drapes an arm over the back of my chair, stretching across me to point out the last picture. "Finally, there's Wanda. She's mostly filler—an extra body, be it man or woman, boy or girl, in nearabout every scene. Hers will be the most challenging to cover, because of the backstage choreography of each quick change."

I feel myself shrinking inward the longer he talks. He was right yesterday when he said I'd be nuts to take this job. Every one of those actors sings and dances and has at least a smattering of lines. I have absolutely no idea how I'm going to learn everything in three days and keep it all straight.

Pierce's arm slips a little lower down the back of my chair. "Don't be alarmed—I said I'd take you under my wing, and I will."

I sit up, ramrod straight, inching forward, away from his hand on the small of my back. I'm pretty darn sure that under his wing is nowhere I want to be.

When Pierce is finally summoned to approve a staging decision, he strolls away, calling over his shoulder, "Just remember, if everything goes right, you'll never even step onstage."

I don't know whether that's supposed to make me feel better or worse. I slump over the table. What I do know is that nobody'd better call out in the first couple of weeks—it's going to take some time before I'm ready to cover even one of those parts.

Before anybody else tries to take me under their wing, I set off for the rehearsal room. Poring over scripts will only get me so far—I need to see the scenes in action. The actresses are huddled in a corner, whispering. I screw up my courage and go to stand near them, thinking their close circle might open for me when I arrive, but it doesn't. I'm stuck standing near them, but not with them, until the only thing that would make the moment more awkward is if I left again for no apparent reason, so I just keep standing there, mortified.

The group finally disbands when one assistant or another claps his hands, calling the actors to the stage. Only then do the girls meet my eyes. Wanda and Darlene had their backs to me, so maybe they didn't see me before—their faces are friendly enough. Gloria seems to be in her own world. But Fiona is another story.

"Well. You're mighty friendly with the director, aren't you?"

I open my mouth to protest, but she sweeps past me before I can set the record straight. I trail after them and find an open seat beside the stage manager, who looks to be about Lois's age, and every bit as gruff. She's got a clipboard clamped across her chest and a penlight between her teeth. She's wearing dark slacks and work shoes like the rest of the crew, and her hair is cropped short, stuffed under a herringbone flat cap.

"Hello," I whisper.

"Hold this," she says in return, dropping a thick three-ring binder into my lap and shooting to her feet. "Just the one ladder—we'll have the set pieces in place tomorrow."

I scan the pages. Today they're blocking the end of the first scene, when Sally and Ned are singing a duet in counterpoint: poor, lovesick Ned is in the hayloft pining for Sally like a bull with a stomachache, while her eyes are on the horizon, wishing for more than the life she was born into. I lean forward in my chair, softly so it doesn't squeak and spoil the moment, and return the binder when the stage manager gets back to her seat.

"Name's Gwyn." She reaches over to shake my hand. "The number one rule of understudying is: learn those traffic patterns quick so you don't kill anyone."

"Sure," I say as nonchalantly as I can. *Kill anyone? Seriously?*

Clive cheats his chiseled cheekbones and strong jaw up to catch the lights, like he knows every angle that'll make the ladies swoon and the men puff up their chests, imagining themselves a manly specimen like him. I'm sure they've rehearsed the scene a dozen times already, but even so, all eyes are riveted on the pair of them. Clive and Gloria seem to have every single person in the room head over heels in love with one—or both—of them.

I am *so* out of my league.

All over again, I'm longing for those leisurely drives to rehearsal from Fairbury to Lincoln with Jesse. I could jabber away for fifteen minutes straight about every last thing I was worried about, and somehow he'd have me laughing at myself and my overactive imagination before we arrived. Then I'd waltz into a rehearsal room full of professional actors feeling like I could go toe to toe with any one of them.

I could really use that shot of confidence right about now.

-35-

I GRAB A hamburger on the way back to Mrs. Cooper's since I missed dinner, then I stop in the pharmacy on the corner to buy some Epsom salts to soak my sore feet—I won't get a bath until the morning, and they are killing me! I take it slow all the way home, trying to shake the memory of being with Jesse, that easy feeling of being together.

When I get inside, I drop my bags in the entryway and make for the telephone on the sideboard. I give the long-distance operator the code to the Schmidt farmhouse, wait through a pause and a few clicks, and then:

Brrrrring.

Calling to tell Jesse I landed a part seemed like such a good idea when I was walking home from rehearsal. But now that the line is live, I'm not so sure. What if Mama Schmidt answers, and she's upset with me? The whole family is probably furious about how things ended.

Brrrrring.

Or what if Jesse picks up, but he's angry I never answered his letter? What if he hangs up? I *did* write back, a dozen times. I just never mailed any of those responses. It's no good rationalizing it to myself. I should forget all about this, hang up the—

"Schmidt residence."

Oh, criminy. "Hey there, Lois, it's Mazie. I was hoping to speak with Jesse. If you don't mind—"

"Are you in trouble?"

"Pardon?"

"Are you in some kind of danger you need saving from?"

"Of course not. Why would you say that?"

"Are you coming home, to stay?"

"No. I only wanted to tell Jesse that—"

"Then I do mind. As a matter of fact, I mind you stirring things up very much."

"Just put your brother on the phone, Lois. Please."

"I will not. And if you had half a heart, you wouldn't want me to. There's nothing you could say that'll make things any easier for him. Be honest—who you're really interested in soothing is yourself."

I don't have anything to say to that. If I could only talk to him . . .

At length, Lois sighs. "Look, Mazie, I don't mean to come down so hard on you. Just—let him go. Jesse's having a tough enough time settling into farming full time as it is. If you aren't going to be here beside him, step for step, then let him go. Don't call the house again."

There's a click on the other end of the line. My hand drops to my chest, pushing back against the pressure building beneath my ribs. I set the receiver down on the cradle. Jesse's struggling? I knew he would, but still—hearing that he's hurting when I'm not there for him, that he lost me and then he lost his freedom.

Lois is right. Calling the farmhouse wasn't just selfish. It was cruel.

I'm up before the sun the next morning. I could hardly sleep, what with Lois's scolding ringing in my ears. I choke down three cups of coffee trying to ward off the buzzing between my temples.

Most of the morning is spent at the rehearsal studio, where the first act is in tech—we've only got two more days of rehearsal before we hit the road. In the afternoon, we work through the last bits of choreography for the second act. I wasn't bluffing about the square dances—I know every one back to front, and I can dance the men's part just as well as the women's for most of them. It's a good thing, too, because when Wanda gets called away for a costume fitting, they slot me into her spot.

Before I know it, I'm holding hands with Dixon and listening for Gwyn's cue. I've barely exchanged two words with Dixon up to this point—he must be ten years older than me! But his smile is generous. He's tall and slender, with curly brown hair and the beginnings of a full beard bristling across his cheeks. The fiddler steps onto a box where the orchestra pit should be and starts playing "Turkey in the Straw."

"Everybody balance and everybody swing, take your partner and promenade the ring."

We trot around the studio, arm in arm, in time to the fiddler's tapping foot. It's the same as filling in for Uncle Lem back home, except this time the point of nearly every move is to get Ned and Sally heading downstage, in the spotlight, where the audience can witness romance budding before their eyes.

"First couple swing in the center . . ."

Of course that's Ned and Sally, him acting every bit the gentleman, and her holding herself ever so slightly back from his embrace.

"Four gents a left-hand star . . ."

Us girls swish our skirts while the boys show off a bit.

"Right to your partner where you are . . ."

I know this dance like the back of my hand, so I focus on learning from Dixon and the rest how to *act* like I'm square dancing, always cheating your face toward the audience, dipping a shoulder or swinging a hip far beyond what the dance requires to make the scene a riot of movement for the audience. I keep my mouth shut, but the fact is, they're not even doing the dance right the whole way through. Whatever fancy consultant they paid to choreograph this number was padding his résumé, that's for darn sure.

When the dance ends and Gwyn claps her hands, sending us back to our places for the beginning of the number, Wanda slides into her spot. I go back to my chair in the corner, where I can see all the pieces to this puzzle in motion. Much as I loved being up there with the rest of the actors, I've got a job to do. For now, this is exactly where I need to be.

-36-

I BEGGED OFF a copy of the sheet music to bring home with me yesterday—thank heaven Mrs. Muth insisted I learn to sight-read. Last night I parked it at the piano, switching between vocal parts and trying to marry each character to the tone and texture of my voice. Mrs. Cooper joined me, singing along in her rich alto, turning the pages, and even offering a few suggestions. I've only ever played one part in any given show before, and now, learning all these different roles—infusing backstory, dialect, and heart into each character—I feel like I'm drawing close to the heart of the show in a way I never knew was possible. It's all so much *more* than I ever imagined. It's damn hard, but I love it!

Rehearsals are moving so fast I feel like I've been sprinting for days. It's a thrill being part of a production just getting on its feet, it's just . . . the rest of the actors don't seem to know I exist. Except Fiona, that is. It's pretty clear she dislikes me already.

It seems like I was just packing my things to make my way to the city and now here I am in Mrs. Cooper's entryway, my suitcase and hatbox in hand, ready to leave again. I fiddle with the buttons down my coat. Summer came to the city practically overnight, and already it's stifling in the narrow entryway. If I had the space, I'd shove the coat into my suitcase, but the poor old thing is packed tight as a jar of pickles.

I leave a letter for Mrs. Cooper, thanking her for taking me in and for looking out for us all, in her way. Marsha is out at an audition—heck, the whole third floor is empty. I wish Peggy were still around to see me off with a hug and one of her pep talks. I'd even settle for Evie at this point—any familiar face to mark whether I stay or go. I put my shoulders back and heft my luggage, resigned to setting out alone, when Mrs. Cooper steps into the entryway.

She presses a slim book into my hands.

"Oh. I didn't expect . . ." I shift my weight onto one foot while I try to find the right words. I settle for a sheepish smile. "Thank you. What's it for, exactly?"

Mrs. Cooper rolls her eyes, hard. "Girl, it's a good thing you can sing."

I shrug and try another smile.

"You're the understudy for how many people—four?"

I nod.

"Anytime the stage manager opens her mouth, you'll want to take notes—in pencil, with a good eraser handy. Every time the choreographer changes his mind about a combination, or whenever the director shifts the blocking, moving where the characters stand onstage, you'll need to remember it exactly. Don't think they'll tell you twice just because you're new. You've got to be ready to step onstage for any one of those parts at a moment's notice."

"*Oh.* Right. Thank you, Mrs. Cooper." And because I know by now she's not half as tough as she makes out, I dart in to give her a quick hug. I'm sure she can't afford to get attached to all the dreamers who flit in and out of her doors, but even if it is one-sided, I'm going to miss her when I'm gone.

I yank open the door, blinking hard. I didn't think my dream come to life would look like a tour of the Midwest or singing songs about tractors or watching the production from offstage. But it's close. And close enough is good enough for me. For now, anyway.

By the time I get to the parking lot where the tour bus waits, idling, nearly every seat is taken, the entire cast and crew settled in for the first leg. I hand my suitcase to a member of the crew, hoping nobody else notices how shabby it is. Inside, Harbuckle and Pierce are in the first two seats, conferring across the aisle over some last-minute changes for opening night. Harbuckle is coming to see the first show, and then he'll check in on the tour again in Omaha, while Pierce is along for the duration since the show got off to such a rocky start.

I keep moving—I don't want to sit anywhere near Pierce.

The next row of seats holds the stage manager, lighting technician, and technical director. The stage crew is clear at the back, with the musicians in front of them, and the wardrobe department next. In between, it's all laid out like the playbill will be, I suppose, with the principals toward the front and the rest filling in the seats behind them.

I spy an empty seat halfway back, opposite Charles, the male understudy, and sidle down the aisle. I smile at everyone as I pass, trying not to appear *too* eager to make eye contact, though no one even seems to notice me. Halfway there, I trip over a strap looped across the aisle and pitch forward with a shriek.

Oof! I land on my stomach, my ribs high-centered on my hatbox, my face hovering inches above the floor. I flail like an upturned bug trying to get my breath back. There's no way to hoist myself back to standing with a single shred of dignity intact.

A set of large hands cinches around my waist and yanks, and the next thing I know, I'm upright again. And I can breathe, thank heaven. I blow a puff of air over my forehead to flop my hair back where it belongs. Well, didn't I want everybody to notice me? *Sheesh.*

The hands on my waist let go. "I was hoping we'd meet."

I twist around, and there's that million-dollar smile. Clive extends a hand, and I'm reasonably sure I remember how to shake his in return.

Say something. Quick. Something witty.

I make a show of dusting off my knees. "Is that how you pick up all the girls?"

The bus goes silent except for a snicker coming from somewhere behind me.

Clive's smile collapses. "Uh . . . no?"

"Oh—I mean. I didn't mean—" I cut my losses and scurry to my seat.

"*Christ,* tell me she didn't sprain an ankle," the dance captain gripes as I plop down in the empty seat. "If I have to train one more person only for them to up and leave, I quit. You hear me, Pierce? I'll quit."

I duck down in my seat as far as I can. Nobody's even trying to hide their laughter now. The thing about Fairbury is I could do the stupidest thing—I could blow my solo or drop a whole tray of milkshakes—and folks would just shrug it off. In fact, the other carhops would be there in a flash to mop up the spilled cream and sweep up the broken glass so I could have a minute in the back to compose myself. Then Momma and Daddy would've made me recount the whole thing at least once so they could have a good chuckle at my expense, and Jesse would have had me laughing at myself so hard there wouldn't be any room left for the embarrassment currently burning a hole in my belly.

But all those weeks when money was shrinking and I kept hearing *no, no,* and *thank you, miss, but no,* I pictured the day I'd have to leave the city more times than I can count. I thought I'd be mortified, heading home because I ran out of money before I caught a break. Well, I *am* mortified, but only because I made a fool of myself.

Heck, if it's this or heading home, I'll take it, bruised ego, skinned knees, and all.

The engine coughs and sputters, and the bus sways onto the city streets. From my angle, scrunched down in my seat, I've got a prime view of the tops of the buildings outlining the sky as we roll by. They look like backlit sets, dim rectangles and triangles jutting up into the late-morning glow.

Yeah, I'll take it all—the rejection, the loneliness, the embarrassment; I'm still here, aren't I? I landed a contract, and I'm headed out on tour with actors I'm honored to share a stage with. I'm going to learn a heck of a lot from this show. And booking this one might open doors for my next one. The New York skyline flies past, and the smile on my face spills over into laughter. I'll happily take it all.

-37-

AFTER A FEW hours, Gwyn shoves in next to me, a pencil clamped between her teeth and her show binder in her hands. "You get carsick?"

"Oh, hi! Not usually. Why?"

"We've got work to do. Let me see your notes."

I pull the scattering of loose pages from my purse and my copies of the script and score from under the seat. She adds a tour schedule to the pile.

"Might I recommend one of these?" Gwyn wiggles her binder and her eyebrows, too, so there's no chance I miss her meaning. "I'll even let you borrow my hole punch."

"Uh, thanks?"

Gwyn drags a finger down the list of performances. "Von Steer planned this tour to swing through the Corn Belt, aiming with each stop for that sweet spot between the heart of farm country, proximity to a Von Steer showroom, and a theatre grand enough for this production. They foot the bill, so they call the shots. The whole reason to stage this show is to entertain and educate the salesmen, motivate them to beat their quotas, and have them humming catchy show tunes all the while. When push comes to shove, though, we'll play anywhere that can accommodate our sets—and the tractor, of course, the real star of the show—through the back door."

I nod. "Good to know where the rest of us rate."

"Exactly. But it also means there's no hustle to sell tickets. We'll play to packed houses the entire tour. Of course, the audience is mostly men—why do you think Gloria has cucumber coins perched on her eyelids during breaks?" Gwyn elbows me in the ribs, whispering, "And that crate of Pond's cold cream the stagehands haul everywhere we go? It's written into her contract."

"You're joking."

"I wouldn't!" She feigns innocence, then laughs. "Whether the noble salesman remembers the dimensions of the new tractor model and all its shiny features, he *will* recall her dewy skin and that brilliant smile all for him."

She flips to the front of her notebook, walking me through stage directions for each page of the script while I check her comments against my notes. I doubt very much that Gwyn's the sentimental sort—she may have only come to sit with me because there was work to do. But maybe, just maybe, someone besides me wants to see me succeed.

The following morning, when the bus clips a curb turning into the motel parking lot in Lafayette, Indiana, our first stop, I'm nearly thrown onto the floor again. I sit up, groggy, hanging on to my seat-back for all I'm worth. There's a crick in my neck and a rubbery taste in my mouth. The sun is low in the sky, and my stomach is demanding breakfast.

It's a rest day for the actors while the crew puts the sets in place and tests the curtains and stage lights. We've got a three-piece orchestra plus a piano player, and they'll need some time to tune the instruments and let them adjust to the humidity, or lack of it, in the theatre.

My motel room has two twin beds covered in beaded cotton spreads and gold lamé throw pillows. The scruffy carpet is the same avocado green as the curtains, and the wallpaper is a dizzying constellation of golden starbursts. I drop my suitcase on one of the beds and undo the straps; with a click, it falls open like a shucked clam.

I sag against the window frame and peek through the curtains as voices float by outside. Wanda and Darlene are headed out shopping, purses tucked under their arms. I suppose I shouldn't feel left out—they hardly know me. I've only been with the company for a few days. I let the curtain fall shut. Even if they had invited me, I can't spare the time. Pierce was right about one thing: I've got my hands full memorizing this show.

I change into something fresh, tuck my copy of the script under my arm, and cross the street to a café. The moon is a pale sliver above. The minute I step inside, the smell of bacon sizzling and eggs frying has me missing home so bad my eyes sting. I order the biggest breakfast I've had in months and take my time eating, reading as I go and downing cup after cup of strong coffee.

Gwyn and I decided I should start with Sally, then learn

the other parts as I'm able. On the page, Sally's a Grace Kelly, all smooth sophistication. She thinks she's miles too good for every other human in her orbit, and it seems like there's not too much going on between her ears besides visions of sparkling jewelry and shimmering chiffon.

When I've finished, I leave an extra nickel for the waitress and head back across the street to the motel. The sunrise shift is the pits when half your customers aren't even eating, just huddling someplace warm until the day starts in earnest. Lord knows, I could be slinging burgers and pouring milkshakes again all too quickly. Now that I've tasted this life, I wouldn't be able to even pretend the other was good enough for me.

"Mazie!" Pierce calls as I cross the motel parking lot, standing half-in, half-out of his motel room a few doors down from mine. "Come here a minute."

I tuck my key back in my purse and hug the script over my chest. As I draw near, he steps out onto the sidewalk and waves me inside. I dart a look behind me. Just me and him, alone? He's the boss, though. I have to do what he says, don't I?

I grip the pages even tighter and turn to the side, making myself as slim as possible to slip through the door without brushing against him. I scan the room, my pulse hammering in my ears. There are two beds and one tiny table between them, but no chairs in sight. No way am I sitting on one of those beds. I perch on the windowsill, the metal frame digging into my rear as Pierce shuts the door behind him.

"You've been running Sally's lines?"

I nod. Maybe I should suggest we go back to the café?

"Good, good. Let's pick up right after the square dance finishes." He leans one hand against the doorframe, the other propped on his hip. "Well, come on over here."

I glance at the slice of daylight visible between the curtains. I wish I'd pretended not to hear him call my name. I wish I'd never left my room. I open the script to the second act and flip to the barn dance scene.

"You don't need that. Come on, it's best to get the scene in your body from the beginning. I'll feed you your lines."

I raise a fist to my lips and, though Mrs. Muth would scold, clear my throat to buy myself a second to think. "What I really need is help double-checking my notes on traffic patterns on- and offstage. I'll get to the scene-by-scene work later. Maybe I'll just ask Gwyn—"

"I know what you need." His voice is smooth, practically purring. "I said I'd help you, and I'm not about to go back on my word."

I freeze, halfway to standing, still gripping the pages across my chest. I had no problem at the Frosty Top dumping milkshakes over a patron's head if he got too friendly. But I had nothing to lose—if I got canned, I could always go work for Uncle Cal.

Here, I have a whole heck of a lot to lose. And this guy knows it.

"Relax," Pierce says, running his hands up and down my arms.

I jump back, knocking the lampshade over, leaving the bulb bare, exposed and flickering. Pierce takes another step toward me, his hand snaking around my waist. "I'm only helping you, like I said I would."

I dart around him and fumble with the door handle. "I never asked for this sort of help." I yank open the door. The outside air rushes over me, and I gulp it in, grateful.

"Whatever do you mean?"

Momma taught me to be polite. Daddy insisted I respect my elders. But they also taught me to speak the truth. I back onto the sidewalk. "I expect you to keep your hands to yourself, sir."

Pierce's eyes harden, his dark brows snapping together. "Who do you think you are? You don't get to talk like that to me. Not if you want to go *anywhere* in this business."

There's nothing to say to that. For all I know, he's right. I've seen my share of young women bitten when they know full well there's a snake in the grass; they can see its flickering tongue and hear its rattle. But somebody says, *No, no—that's not a snake,* and rather than be contrary, they squeeze their eyes shut while the fangs sink in.

I hurry back to my own room.

Pierce steps out onto the sidewalk after me, his voice pitched just loud enough so I hear every word, and as calm as if he's ordering soup. "You'll be finished. Do you hear me? I'll see to it you never work in show business again."

I shut the door to my motel room. My hands are shaking so bad it takes three tries until the little brass peg will drop into the slot so I can slide the chain across. I push a chair against the door for good measure and crouch on the edge of the bed, half expecting Pierce to break through the door at any minute. I try to get my racing pulse to listen to what my brain's saying—he's not the kind to bust down a door. He's one of them that prefers to tell so many sweet-sounding lies a person starts to question the truth they know in their own minds. But still, I can't stop shaking.

The day crawls by, then the sun sinks, turning the thick curtains orange, then mauve, then a sullen gray. Eventually the cast trickles back from town. They parade between their rooms all evening, hollering and jeering like this tour is one big party while I sit alone, adrenaline rattling out of me, leaving me hollow as an empty silo.

-38-

THE NEXT MORNING, I do my best to focus on the work and put what happened with Pierce behind me. He didn't mean those threats, surely? He wouldn't take this show away from me? Or my chance at ever booking another one. Could he really do that?

Our first performance is at the Mars Theatre east of the Wabash River. From the street, the sturdy old building might be anything—a hotel, a department store, or even a bunch of apartments. But once you get inside, she doesn't hide her charm—dripping chandeliers and gold trim everywhere you look.

I get to the theatre early. The last thing I want is to end up in a room alone with Pierce again, so I trail after Gwyn the whole afternoon, making some excuse about how it would help to see the production through her eyes and promising to stay out of the way.

Later, when the half-hour call sounds, I peek through the curtain to watch the audience mill around and find their seats. It's a packed house, more than a thousand people all told. I'm not even performing tonight, but still, the sight of such an enormous audience is terrifying! Everywhere you look, it's salesmen in suits, with the exception of the regional managers' wives. The women stroll in, pearls sweeping across their bare necks and fur coats draped over their shoulders like this is the biggest society event of the season. Except the public isn't even invited—it's an exclusive performance for the sales team. Nobody else is allowed through the door. Heck, the rest of town probably doesn't even know we're here.

The house lights dim, the overture begins, and my skin ripples with goose bumps. The curtain rises on Ned lit by a single spot. The makeup artists have smeared grease over Clive's forehead and across the oiled muscle of his upper arm. He puts his whole bodyweight into the wrench in his hands, working on the rusty old tractor he inherited with the family farm.

The orchestra dies down, and he hurls the wrench onto the oilcloth. He kicks the tire and turns to face the audience. Cold, without a hint of a lead-in, he belts the first note, frustration and shattered hopes resonating through his warm baritone.

> *Tell me there's a trick to getting ahead.*
> *Even a fella like me, down as down can be.*
> *Tell me I'm not out, not yet,*
> *not for good.*

He's like a gorilla beating its chest. If the audience wasn't ready to be wooed before, they are now. But Clive makes it look natural, like he's having a conversation with the audience, man to man.

> *Maybe I got a hamstrung start,*
> *but there's gotta be a way to make my way.*

Tell me I'm not out, not yet,
not for good.

He ends the song barely above a whisper. The audience is silent, breathing with him: inhale, exhale. Everyone out there is on Ned's side now. Clive's brilliant; there's no denying it.

The light shifts, illuminating the backdrop. It's a cornfield in silhouette, the tassels jiggling in the wind. Farmhands drift onstage, sagging after a long day's work, rubbing their backs and grumbling. They gather downstage to give Ned a good ribbing about that dang machine, jostling our hero around the stage until the conversation tumbles into another song. They chuck their farm implements to the side and chant in a rolling bass:

> *You gotta get low, low, low*
> *to dig that hoe, hoe, hoe.*
> *You get a mighty ache-ahhhhh*
> *a-workin' that-a rake.*

They scuff and slide across the stage, until Ned finally throws up his hands and stamps off stage left. I know the traffic patterns well enough by now to stay out of the way as Louis and Dixon dart into the wings inches from where I'm standing (though I have to duck out of the way of a flying rake). The curtains swish closed, and a lone spot drops on Gloria now, standing alone on the apron of the stage, perfect to the last stray hair. A few whistles float out from that big black monster of an audience, but you'd never know it to look at her. Gloria is one hundred percent in character, and Sally wouldn't spare a single thought for the fools out there who, emboldened by the darkness all around, think their no-good catcalling is a way to impress any woman. She homes in on that darkness and croons her longing for a life better than the one she was handed.

Me? I'm spellbound. By all these people I get to work with, or if not exactly *with*, then near. I may not be Gloria's caliber— heck, I'm not even close. But if I get to watch her each night and learn from her, then I'm one step closer to where I hope to be. I may not be going on for a single scene tonight, but I'm *here*. And so far I've managed to be wherever Pierce is not. I'm counting that as a win.

It isn't like me to hide from a problem, scuttling like a prairie dog between burrows, dodging a hungry coyote. But I've never been in a situation like this before, where the thing I've dreamed of having my whole life is being threatened by the one person who has the power to take it all away from me.

Before Sally's final verse, a second spot drops opposite where she stands. It's Ned in that hayloft, downtrodden as he's ever been, still covered in engine grease. He knows how very far out of his league Sally is, but that doesn't stop him from loving her from afar. He sings to her while she finishes her song, and their mournful harmonies twine together.

The lights cut, and I sit back while the audience roars their approval. The show is on its feet, and boy, does it have legs. When Peggy insisted industrials were good shows, I only half believed her. But I should have. Heck, you'd hardly know the whole point of this thing is to sell tractors.

The next scene begins with the boys bragging about their tractors' features. Sure, there are a lot of specifics shoehorned into the lyrics that the salesmen will want to remember, but it's a hilarious number, full of innuendo, and the audience is busting a gut. I close my eyes and picture the stage in my mind, the actors shifting like chess pieces as the song progresses.

"It's working!" Darlene whispers, grabbing my arm as she scurries past. By the time the next song starts, I'm all alone backstage, ready to block out the dance steps for "I Don't Need a Man." In the coming scene, Sally and her friends are baking pies for the barn raising that weekend. Not unlike the last number, the girls are all going on about their man's features, making no small point of the fact that Sally hasn't got one.

I work through the jazzy steps, determined to get each move right. It's one thing to copy what you see in the movies and another to be in line next to professional dancers. I follow the cast rushing back downstairs to the dressing rooms, where Charles is bent over in the hallway, one elbow propped on a knee, the other arm pumping a barbell so he stays in "show shape," as he likes to remind me every time I walk in on him in the middle of a sweaty push-up/jump rope/chin-up circuit. I slide past him, trying not to be too obvious about holding my breath, and duck into the women's dressing room.

Darlene's face is flushed with excitement. "There is *nothing* like getting real-time feedback from an audience. Nothing."

Wanda nods. "It's a drug, I swear."

I scoot into the back corner to avoid the dressers buzzing around the actors, swapping out wigs, helping them strip down to their undergarments and into a new costume. It's thrilling to be this close to it all.

The makeup artist hovers over Fiona, laying on the rouge so her character always looks like she just finished wringing scalding water out of the wash basin.

"Did you hear them burst out laughing at the tractors' features bit?"

"Of course they liked *that* part," Wanda scoffs. "It's a theatre full of men—they probably hold their own pissing contests once a week."

"That's not all they're measuring," Fiona adds with a wink.

Even Gloria laughs at that. The makeup artist hops back over to Gloria to spend an extra moment powdering the shadows beneath her eyes. Is she not sleeping well in the motel?

Wanda spins around in her chair. "Did you see the way they jeered at the bank clerk?"

"Who knew, right?" Fiona says.

Darlene shrugs. "I guess it makes sense that the salesman who only wants to close the deal and the loan officer standing in his way wouldn't be the best of friends."

"Oh yeah—back home, nobody likes bankers," I say. "Why, just last fall, they . . ." A chime sounds overhead, and I back against the wall, out of the way, as the girls scurry for the stairs and to their places for the second act.

My excitement drains away. I make my way back upstairs and out of sight. I'm not a part of this company, not really. But I don't know how much more I could sacrifice to this dream. I already left my home and family. I gave up Jesse, leaving my heart back in Nebraska—how could that not be enough?

The second act starts off with a bang—the barn raising where all the boys' muscles have been oiled so they glisten in the lights while they heave and thrust. Next is the scene in the beauty parlor when the girls are all having their curls put up. They're trying to make Sally forget how she swore off being poor, to think about how good Ned looks in his overalls instead. It's tight choreography with a little slapstick thrown in, so the timing has to be spot-on.

Next comes the barn dance when it's all Sally can do to hold herself back from Ned. And finally, the big reveal: the new tractor with all its attachments and newfangled technology that will ensure the farm is a success. Sally and Ned kiss, and the crowd goes wild.

But the thrill of it all falls flat for me.

After the show, Gloria makes her excuses and heads back to her room while the rest of the cast mingles with the salesmen, signing autographs and record jackets. Then, before I know it, the girls take off to go dancing and the boys head out to the bar around the corner. I hustle back to my motel room, trying to convince myself they only forgot to ask me along, that they didn't exclude me on purpose. I avoided Pierce the entire day, and I am not about to risk ruining that now.

So I sit in the dark, the yellow glare of the streetlights seeping through the perforations in the limp curtains. I never thought I'd see my dreams come true, or a version of them anyway, only to find myself unhappier than I've ever been. I should take this opportunity to transfer my notes into the little book Mrs. Cooper gave me.

I know if she were here, she'd let me have it for throwing myself a pity party, but I can't bring myself to care, not tonight. I turn on the clock radio on the bedside table and twist the knob until it lands on static, the steady hiss and scratch scrubbing away the world outside, and the racket in my head.

-39-

AFTER ALL THE turnover in the casting process, the costume mistress, a petite woman with a snorting laugh named Kathleen, is finally finished with alterations for the main players and ready to turn her attention to me. The crew couldn't care less whether it was me or Laurette Taylor going on; their day doesn't change so long as whoever it is knows her traffic patterns, onstage and off, and collects and deposits her props where and when she's supposed to.

But every time there's a casting change, Kathleen has to redo work she's already done. To refit the understudy costumes for me, she has to pick apart her seams and let out every single one. And that's no small order since the understudy before me was tall enough but skinny as a beanpole. It isn't that I've got a lot of extra around my midsection, but my rib cage is broad and the muscles in my stomach and back are ropy from doing chores from sunup to sundown pretty much since I could walk.

While Kathleen measures and scribbles down notes, I stand with my arms outstretched, marveling at the array of watercolor sketches she's got pinned to the wall. There must be a dozen of them, one for each costume, and she's infused each painting with some essential part of that character.

"These are gorgeous."

"Thanks," Kathleen says through a mouthful of pins while she cinches a corset over my rib cage.

Just then, Pierce peeks into the room. I clamp my arms over my bust—I'm only half-dressed! He looks me up and down with a proprietary smirk, then laughs and backs slowly out of the room.

"Better lay off the butter, Butterfield."

The joy drops out of the moment, and I cower, half-dressed, reaching for a spare length of fabric to cover myself.

"Ignore him," Kathleen mutters when he's gone.

She seems so dainty with those big doe eyes framed by blocky glasses, but there's nothing timid about Kathleen. My gaze skitters between her and the empty doorframe. Gerard Pierce is a big name in this business, whereas I only just got this job. How am I supposed to ignore him?

"I mean it," Kathleen says, more forcefully this time. "Don't give him a second thought."

I offer her a weak smile. "I just wish he'd leave me alone, you know?"

"I do. But remember—just because he's dishing it out, that doesn't mean you have to take it. He may be the boss of this show, but he doesn't own any of us."

I want to believe her. But Pierce's threats are like a dust storm at a summer picnic, showering grit over everything; whether you can see it or not, you'll be chewing sand all day, no matter how many times you try to swish your mouth clean.

If this were Fairbury, I'd call his bluff, and I'd have backup: Momma and Daddy, Jesse, and, hell, every one of the Schmidts. No way would I let some smooth talker get the better of me. But I'm too far from Nebraska right now, too far from everyone who loves me.

As much as Pierce gives me the creeps, he is right about one thing: I *don't* know how this business works. Maybe all he has to do is whisper the word *difficult* in connection to me a time or two and whatever slim chance I had at booking that next gig dries up like a highway after a July thunderstorm. Since I don't want to risk the trouble that confronting him might bring, I figure the next best thing is to put my head down and make myself indispensable to the show. So I throw myself into preparing for my understudy roles and make a plan to focus on somebody new each night, checking my notes against their performance to see what's changed and what I've gotten wrong. At this pace, I should be ready to get onstage halfway through the tour, which—nobody should get hurt or violently ill before then, right?

At our second performance at the Virginia Theatre in Champaign, Illinois, I decide that since I already watched Gloria in the last show, I'll move on to the most fragmented part: Wanda's. If I didn't know her round face beneath the wigs and all that stage makeup, I'd hardly be able to follow her through all those costume changes.

The first act isn't half as tight as it was on opening night. The boys mess up their traffic patterns in the first scene and have to play off the collisions as intentional—luckily no one is stabbed with a pitchfork in the process. And the harmony is off in the pie-baking scene, too—we'll just have to hope half the audience is tone-deaf.

During intermission, I patter down the narrow stairs to the dressing room after Wanda. "You're *amazing* out there—I don't know how you do it!"

Wanda's just tossing a smile over her shoulder when she gasps, her eyes flying open. A shriek and a tumble sound behind me. I whip around to see Darlene, palms pressing against the walls on either side, her left ankle caught beneath her at an ugly angle.

Wanda and I rush to lift her down to the dressing room and get her settled in a chair. I run to borrow a pillow from the stagehands so she can prop the rapidly swelling foot up on the makeup counter. By the time I get back, Darlene is flanked by Harbuckle and Pierce, with Gwyn peering over their shoulders, clutching her clipboard as if she could beat back disaster with it.

Wanda and I exchange a look of terror. Darlene is not going back on tonight, that much is clear. My breath catches in my throat and I choke on it, coughing into my hand, my eyes bulging as Wanda takes me by the shoulders and shoves me into a chair, spinning it to face the mirror.

"Okay, Nebraska. I guess that means you're on." She rips the bow out of my hair and starts putting up pin curls.

As if on cue, the wig mistress scurries in next, an assortment of feathered and big-bowed hairpieces clipped on top of her head, the wig for Darlene's next character splayed between her fingers. She jams it down on my head, pulling the back down over my flyaway strands and cursing the whole time.

Ow. I think she drew blood.

The PA system crackles, Gwyn's assistant on the microphone. "Ms. Butterfield to stage right. Ms. Butterfield, please, to stage right."

"But I'm not ready!"

"Yes you are." Wanda does a hasty job with a tin of blush and a tube of lipstick and shoves me out of the chair. "You can do this!"

Gwyn follows me up the narrow stairs, herding me like a sheepdog. "Whatever you do, *walk* down the stairs for your costume changes and hold on to the handrail, for chrissake!"

I scurry toward the wings, where Kathleen is waiting with my costume. The intermission always seems so leisurely when you're waiting backstage. But tonight? I swear I blinked once and it's over. I have never, not even once, rehearsed this part. Sure, I watched from the house during tech. And I've taken a million notes. But none of that prepares you for actually stepping onto the stage.

When it's my cue, I saunter on beside Fiona, mouthing a silent conversation while the main story is playing out downstage. The heat from the lights hits me like a wave—I have to remember not to look directly into them. My brain is scrambling to transmit the stage directions from my notebook to my hands and feet. I'm thinking so hard about what steps to take and where, what part I'm supposed to be singing, I completely forget about the audience until halfway through the first number. I can't explain it—when you're standing in an empty theatre with the house lights off, the place feels like any empty building. But when you're up onstage and there are living, breathing people in all those seats, even if you can't see them, and even if every single one of them is holding their breath, you can sense them out there, watching, listening, *feeling* right along with you.

I freeze, forget to breathe, my body suddenly thick as a block of ice. I couldn't move if my life depended on it. The biggest stage I ever performed on back home was for an audience of a few hundred people, give or take. And I know for a fact that there are no fewer than *fourteen* hundred people out there tonight.

Maybe only ten seconds have passed, but every single one of them feels like a lifetime. The next thing I know, Gloria loops her arm through mine and sashays downstage, towing me right along with her. She deposits me in Dixon's arms, and he twirls me back upstage and out of the spotlight. As soon as his back is to the audience, he makes a face, scrunching up his eyes and sticking his tongue out at me.

I bite back a laugh. "You're going to be great!" Dixon whispers, squeezing my hand before spinning me back toward where I'm supposed to be standing.

And from that moment forward, I have the time of my life. I don't hit all my marks—not even close. If I'm not sure of the harmony, I drop in a half beat after everybody else to make sure I don't knock the whole arrangement off. When it's time for the finale and the big tractor reveal with all its newfangled attachments, I'm weak with frazzled nerves and arcing joy.

The second the curtain drops, I sink to the ground, hugging my shins. I did it! I held my own out there with the pros, and with next to no rehearsal time. That could have been a complete disaster, but somehow I was able to step into that three-dimensional moving puzzle without scattering the pieces too badly. I drop my head onto my knees while the adrenaline courses out of me.

I remember myself after a few breathless moments and rush over to Gloria's side. "You saved me out there! Thank you."

Her face is pale under all that makeup. Dark smudges stain

the skin beneath her eyes. She offers a weak smile. "We help each other. It's what we do." Fiona takes Gloria's arm and steers her past me with a pointed glare.

Kathleen's waiting for me backstage, a pincushion strapped to her wrist.

"What's her problem?"

"Fiona?" Kathleen lifts my arms up over my head and works at a split seam down my rib cage. "Well, you did forget to bring the shovel onstage during the barn dance, so Clive had it on hand for the finale; since you forgot, Fiona had to find a way to get backstage and on again with the shovel without missing a beat."

"Oh." The lights above the stage flick off one by one, and the rest of the cast trails downstairs. "Should I go apologize?"

"Nah—that sort of thing happens all the time when an understudy is thrown in without enough rehearsal time. Don't mind her."

Kathleen ducks under my arm to snip a few loose threads. "Fiona has been at this for a long time. She does tours every summer, and single-performance industrials at yearly sales meetings for everything from cars to washing machines. She's worked for everything she's got, but she's not young anymore. The longer you do this, the harder it gets on your body. She's nearing the end of her career and that big break still hasn't come."

"Oh." I scuff my toe against a piece of tape on the floor, the edge curling away from the rest.

When Kathleen steps away to confer with the wig mistress, Pierce sidles up behind me. "I can see you're struggling with the barn raising scene. Why don't you let me arrange a put-in? I know it'll settle your nerves."

I *wish* he meant a put-in rehearsal with the rest of the cast. I grit my teeth and force a wan smile. But Pierce doesn't even notice—he's already walking away. He doesn't really want to get me up to speed; he just wants to get me alone again. Heat washes over me and settles low in my belly. I should have said something. I should have stood up for myself.

Back in the dressing room, I change out of the ill-fitting costume and back into my own clothes. I wipe the stage makeup off my face, wishing I could just as easily wipe away Pierce's not-so-subtle come-ons. Kathleen and I make a plan to finish altering the understudy costumes together. She'll help me run lines while I sew hems and a few simple darts even a child couldn't mess up.

Darlene scoots her chair up to my spot at the mirror. "You saved the show tonight, you know?"

I suppose I did. I should be on cloud nine right now—but I can't shake what happened with Pierce, how I just stood there when, if it were anyone else on the planet, I would have put him in his place.

I get one slap on the back from Gwyn, which I guess is her way of showing wholehearted approval. I'm exhausted. My nerves are completely shot. I did my job. And for how little preparation I've had, I did great! Pierce doesn't get to take that away from me.

-40-

I GET CALLED up again at the very next stop in Jacksonville, Illinois. But it isn't a supporting role I'm asked to step in for this time. It's Sally. I start shaking so bad when I hear, I can't even take a sip of water without spilling it down my dress. Gwyn's talking, but all I hear is a roaring inside my head: the voices of all those people who said I was too green, too hick, or too hefty for a job as a chorus girl, never mind the star of the show.

The only person more terrified than me is Kathleen—my costumes for the principal role aren't even close to ready. So an hour before curtain, Kathleen is ripping apart seams and pinning me into the dress. If I take even one wrong step, they're going to split, and the entire audience will be laughing at me.

"Ms. Butterfield, this is your lift call. Ms. Butterfield to the stage, please."

I swear, every drop of blood drains out of me. I start walking, Kathleen bent over and scurrying along, trying to stretch the material over my hips.

She lets go when I take my place backstage, where Clive is pacing, waiting for me. He takes one look at the nervous crowd trailing behind me and shoos everyone away. Gwyn sputters, but he claps her on the shoulders and, with a smile and a disarming little spin, sends her back to the wings. When he turns to face me, he's all business. Clive holds my hands in his, the easy charm gone. It's maybe the first time I'm seeing him and not the leading man.

"You've never rehearsed this role?"

I jiggle my head, still too rattled to come up with anything resembling a coherent response.

"I didn't think so." He swears under his breath. "All right. We're going to modify things a little, and then you and me are going to practice, for real, once we get to Missouri."

We sing through the duet at the end of the first scene, and that, at least, goes well enough. Then he takes me through the courting scene, when Ned is leaping all over a bunch of haybales, sweet-talking Sally into giving in.

"*Christ!* Are those pins?" Clive yanks his hand back, shaking it out and then sticking his knuckle in his mouth. "Don't answer that. Listen, you just go out there and do the best you can. We'll run through the tricky parts of act two during intermission." He grabs my hands again and lifts them up, tight to his chest. "Do you trust me?"

I nod. I barely know him, but if I can't trust my scene partner, I'm sunk.

The PA system crackles to life again, only this time it's broadcasting through the entire building. "For this evening's performance, the part of Sally will be played by Mazie Butterfield." An audible groan from the audience floats through the thick stage curtains.

My cheeks are on fire. I can't do this. The show hasn't even started, and already they hate me.

Clive squeezes my hands to get my attention. "Don't let that get to you, you hear? Gloria is a household name—of course they're disappointed not to see her. What they don't know is what a revelation you're going to be."

My vision goes all fuzzy at the edges, and he gives me a little shake again. "Say it. You're going to be amazing."

"You're going to be amazing," I mumble.

"No, dummy. *You're* going to be amazing."

Right. I put my shoulders back. "I'm going to be amazing."

"That's it." He crosses his arms over his chest and takes a step back. "We're all with you out there. If you're unsure of your spot, we'll do a little shove-with-love. And if you can't remember the line, one of us will feed it to you. We'll get you through this. Okay?"

"Okay."

He glances behind him. "We've got about three minutes. What can I get you? Water? Aspirin? What do you need?"

I cast around myself. It's dark and cold behind the curtain. If I could only ground myself a little on the stage, feel my body in these costumes.

"I could use a wooden chair."

"You got it."

I close my eyes, turning my hips out and lifting my chin as if Mme Durant herself were watching the point in my toes and the slope of my spine. I open my arms into second position and the chair back is there, beneath my palm. I rest my fingers on the wood and begin to move through a warm-up. By the time the call for places comes, my breath is back, my mind is clear, and my entire being is humming with excitement.

It's showtime.

-41-

BEING ONSTAGE IS like an out-of-body experience—the part of my brain that worries and panics and doubts that I really can do this shuts down completely and I just *feel* out there. I know my timing's off in a few places, and Fiona picks up a few lines I drop. But I've been singing Sally's songs in the shower ever since I landed the understudy role, and my voice smooths over the rough spots in the rest of my performance.

The scenes with Clive are the easiest. I become Sally and he becomes Ned and we just *are*. Every time I make my exit, Gwyn is right there with my notebook in her hands, propped open to my next scene for a quick refresh of the script. While Gloria's dresser flits around me, swapping out costumes and then backing away so Kathleen can pin me into them, Gwyn holds the page up at eye level so I can go over my notes for the coming scene—those notes I copied into my notebook night after night, alone in my motel room while the rest of the cast was out on the town. And then I close my eyes and picture Gloria onstage: confident, composed, regal, even. I don't have to own this role; I just have to channel Gloria for one night.

I'm waiting in the wings for the finale when the orchestra swells, the signal to drive the new Von Steer tractor out onstage. The engine chortles to life behind me, and I breathe deep, ready to make my last entrance. But the tractor belches a black cloud directly in my face, and instead of gliding onstage, I double over, hacking and spitting. Clive grabs my hand and drags me with him. I can't stop coughing, and I'd be willing to bet there's soot all over my face.

Clive does his best to hide my coughing by turning me upstage every other second, but he's shaking with laughter and finally, *finally*, I relax, following his lead as if we're in a dance hall and no one is watching us. The tractor rolls onstage to wild applause. The engine cuts with another puff of black smoke. I flinch and Clive guffaws, unable to hide it this time. He runs his hand along the bright red hood that's been buffed to a mirror shine.

"She's a beaut, isn't she?" he manages to say through his laughter. With a wink and a knowing nod for the audience, he spins me out so my skirt shirrs around my hips. With a flick of the wrist, he draws me against him and dips me, one hand spanning the small of my back and the other circling under my hips.

He leans in for a kiss, and everything roars up around me: the whooping crowd, the heat of the lights, and the electricity sizzling through me. I wrap my arms around Clive's neck and kiss him back. I give up hanging on and melt, the adrenaline and relief and maybe a little leftover tractor exhaust coursing through me.

I don't know how long it takes my brain to connect that the hall has gone quiet again and Clive's not so much trying to pull me into him as pry himself away from me—it can't have been more than a few seconds. Can it? I mean, there are *rules* about how long and how deep you can kiss somebody onstage.

When I do finally stagger out of that dip, he darts away with a nervous grin. Why, *oh why* doesn't this stage have a trapdoor? Gwyn could give the sign, and the stage crew could drop me out of sight.

Somehow my feet get me moving through the reprise of the square dance number that serves as our curtain call, the cast stamping and clapping in time as each of the four couples takes their bows and finishes surrounding the shiny tractor, which, of course, gets the biggest applause of all.

Despite my embarrassment, all that love (even if it is directed at the tractor) rolls over me and gets me smiling so big my face hurts. I can't *wait* to do this again.

-42-

WHEN THE LAST curtain drops, I hightail it for the dressing room, slam the door, and launch myself face-first onto the couch. It's musty as hell, but it's the only way I can think to smother my flaming cheeks. Maybe everyone will think I'm asleep. Or just plain dead. Either one would be fine, really.

There's a knock at the door. "Mazie?"

I groan, shoving my face deeper into the cushions. Clive is the last person I want to talk to right now.

"Go away!"

"Not a chance." The door squeaks open and closes softly again. "Oh good, you're still decent."

I am never pulling my face out of these couch cushions. *Not ever.*

He lets out a nervous laugh. "You were amazing out there tonight—I had a great time working opposite you."

"You did?"

"I did. You're the real deal, even if you are new at this."

I'm more than ready to get my nose out of these cushions now that I've had a moment to consider how little I know about the couch's previous occupants.

"You and me—that kiss—listen, I think we could be a real team, but . . ." He looks up, his face written over with worry. "I'm not interested in women, if you take my meaning."

"Oh." I start to sit up. He's looking at me sidelong, sort of flinching, like he's waiting to see if I'll lash out. *"Oh."*

"They're not my type, you see."

I do.

He begins pacing the narrow room. "This life wears on a person, you know? I wouldn't trade it for anything, but always playing a part, coming off as the man's man (and not in a good way)—it's exhausting. I can't play a part in real life, too, or I'll lose my goddamn mind."

"Believe me, I understand."

"Don't get me wrong, I love show business," he continues. "But traveling all the time, hopping from show to show—it doesn't leave much room for a personal life."

I sniff away the last of my mortification and pat the cushion beside me. "Let me guess—you're hopelessly in love with a guy who lives on the other side of the country?"

"No." He slumps against the cushions. "Nothing that tragic. Truth is, I haven't found anybody to feel that way about—not yet."

"I'd say that's tragic enough."

He's quiet for a minute. "Yeah, it is."

We sit in silence on that disgusting couch for I don't know how long. Every once in a while, someone ambles by the door, giggling and stage whispering about my all-too-public mortification. Finally, Clive slaps my knee and stands, offering a hand. "Come on now. Let's get out there and show them there's nothing to be ashamed of."

I let him pull me through the door. When we emerge, a cheer erupts, and Wanda, Darlene, and Dixon surround me. Fiona makes for the wings with a plastic smile, but hey, I'll take it. A fake smile is better than nothing, right? Clive hefts me up onto his shoulder.

"The pins! The pins—" But my protests dissolve into laughter as he spins me in a dizzy circle.

When my feet finally touch the ground, Pierce is right there, arms crossed over his chest, a sneer pulling at his lip. "You sure flubbed your way through the courting scene, and don't pretend we didn't all see how you embarrassed yourself during the finale."

My fingertips begin to tingle, my ears ringing. I feel myself shrinking again, recoiling from his words. So this is how it's going to be? I don't give in to his sleazy come-ons, so he grinds me beneath his heel like a cigarette butt? In public, no less?

Clive cinches a hand around my waist and jabs a finger at our director. "What *you* are is lucky that Miss Butterfield here is quick on her toes and even quicker to cover *your* ass. She needs put-in rehearsals for each part she covers if you expect us to do any better than avoiding disaster the next time somebody calls in."

Pierce opens his mouth to protest, but Clive has already steered me out of range. "Let him stew on that," he mutters. "And you—get out of those pins. It's a miracle you haven't punctured a lung already. We've got some celebrating to do!"

-43-

THE NEXT MORNING comes too early, and I stumble onto the bus half-awake. The minute my head comes into view, Clive jams his fingertips between his teeth for an ear-splitting whistle. Wanda and Darlene are beaming, and Charles is on his feet, cheering me on, though he looks a tad jealous, too.

I cut my eyes toward Gloria. She's staring out the window, her lips drawn in a tight line. I want to say something about what an honor it was, just that once, to step into the role she originated, but she doesn't look up. I scoot back to my seat—and manage to get there without falling on my face this time. I'll find a more private moment and try to talk to her again later.

I tug Momma's crocheted hat down clear to my nose, determined to sleep the whole way to Missouri. But every time I close my eyes, I see cheering audiences and feel the cast and crew pulling together—maybe even pulling for me. Except for Pierce, that is. Then I circle back to worrying whether his public criticism is going to get worse, and whether Clive calling him out will only make things harder for me.

After a half hour on the road, the bus jerks to a stop on the side of the highway. There's a commotion up front, and the door squeaks open. Gloria stumbles down the steps, a hand clapped over her mouth.

The bus fills with whispers. I slide toward the front and kneel beside Clive. "What's going on?"

He glances at me, then turns back to the window. Gloria is kneeling in the middle of a cornfield, one palm pressed tight against her mouth, her other arm curled over her stomach.

"Gwyn said she caught a stomach bug last night. But Gloria's been sick for weeks, though she's hid it well enough until now." He dips his head down, continuing in a low voice. "I've got three older sisters. I know what morning sickness looks like."

"You think she's *pregnant*?"

Fiona practically vaults over her seat and into my face. "Look— you're just a child. You don't have any idea how hard it is to have a family and a career. Gloria's got three kids at home. She thought this show was her way back onstage. She didn't want another baby, but what is a married woman supposed to do?" Fiona flops back onto her seat and mutters the rest under her breath. "It's bad luck, that's what it is."

I slink down beside Clive. I left home thinking I was ready for anything. But there's so much I don't understand—and not only about theatre. I peek out the window. Gloria is standing again, her fingers pressed against her lips. Her eyes are pinched closed, her spine hunched as if she took a fist to the gut. She's not even trying to hide it from the rest of us now.

All I can think is I don't ever want that to be me.

-44-

AFTER BREAKFAST THE following morning, a rap sounds on my motel room door. I'm in the middle of my makeshift barre— my hair's a wispy mess and I'm only wearing my leotard. I peek through the curtains to make sure it isn't Pierce, and Gwyn knocks again, more forcefully this time. She hustles in as I open the door, all business.

"Gloria has left the company." She slaps a stack of papers on the little round table by the window, dropping a pen on top. "Your contract has been adjusted; all we need is your signature."

I see her mouth moving. I hear the words, but they make no sense.

"*Yoo-hoo!*" Gwyn snaps her fingers beneath my nose. "Wake up! Should I have brought a pot of coffee with me?"

Gloria's gone? But I never got to say thank you—I learned so much by watching her.

Wait. "What contract?"

"The principal role, dummy. For the remaining seven shows, you're our Sally."

"*No.*"

Gwyn nods, her eyebrows wiggling like caterpillars.

"Are you serious?"

"*Mm-hmm.*"

"But . . . what about Fiona? She has way more experience than me."

"You're right about that. Fiona was Pierce's choice, but she doesn't know the part. You do—well, more than anyone else, that is."

I lean my hip against the vanity. I forgot about Pierce for half a second—what price will he assign to my promotion? "There's no way he is okay with me taking the lead."

That gets a smirk out of Gwyn. "Pierce doesn't have much of a choice now, does he?"

He doesn't? I drop onto the edge of the bed, letting that sink in for a moment. Is it possible he doesn't have the sway over my career he keeps insisting he does? That thought is like a sheet of river ice breaking up after a long winter and tumbling downstream, leaving nothing but cool, clean water behind.

"Besides, it isn't him who has to rearrange everything now that we don't have an understudy if any of you ladies call in. Charles is going to have to lay off the weights and start practicing dancing in skirts and heels."

Gwyn's snorting at her own joke, but I can only muster a half smile.

"So if I agree, I'd be taking the role away from Fiona?"

"Yes and no. I can tear this contract up and start getting her up to speed if that's what you'd like." Gwyn pauses, then snaps her fingers under my nose a second time. "Haven't you heard of a little thing called show *business*? Every time you land a role, it could have gone to someone else. That's the game."

It's one thing to earn something outright; it's another to take advantage of Gloria's condition and a lucky break that puts me a toe in front of the person who deserves it. I know how folks back home would see it. I know what Daddy would say.

Gwyn ticks her head to the side. "Look, I fought for you in there. I know you can do this. But if you don't want the role . . ."

"No—I do. I want it."

Gwyn shakes her head, brow furrowed, watching me sidelong like I've lost my mind. "Obviously."

"I want it," I repeat, to convince myself as much as anything.

I barely know how to do the job I signed on for, much less a principal role. But like a well-timed voice-over, something Peggy said weeks ago pops into my head: *See if people don't treat you differently when you act like the spotlight's where you belong.* And I remember what she said about my name, too.

I swivel back to the mirror and snap the bronze cap off the tube of lipstick Peggy lent me for my very first audition. I lean forward, smearing cherry red across my lips, then press them together and blot, like she showed me. "I'll do it. But I've got one condition."

Gwyn quirks an eyebrow, like she didn't think I had it in me.

"I want my name above the title, right next to Clive's, like Gloria's was."

"We can do that."

"And I'll be using a stage name for the duration." I turn to face Gwyn, and since I can't quite locate my own confidence, I give it my best Peggy. "Mazie Malone is how I want it to read."

As the words cross my lips, my stomach heaves like it might bring my breakfast right back up again. How many times did I plead with Momma to understand that acting wasn't the same as lying? That I wasn't going to turn into somebody else just because I made playing a part my life's work? But I'm having a hard time convincing myself that changing everything about who I am, at least on the outside, is anything other than a lie.

And Jesse would never understand, not after all his family has been through on account of their German surname. They would never change it, even so. They'd never dream of doing something so opposite of what's true and real and honest.

Gwyn makes a few notes in the margin. "All right."

I lean over the pages to sign, never mind that my hands won't quit shaking.

"Miss Malone." Gwyn sees herself out with a smirk and a wry little bow.

-45-

IT'S ONE THING to prepare to cover a role at the last minute and another to own the part, to step into the role like you're stepping into your own skin. While I like that nervy feeling before a show, going onstage for a part that isn't in my body yet is beyond nerves—it's more like playing chicken with a freight train.

It's going to take a lot more rehearsal time to get ready—not that I'm complaining. I'd rather work in the days between shows anyhow. Maybe the better I am, the harder it will be for Pierce to make good on his threats.

I yank my hair out of its usual ponytail. Gloria always wore hers up in a twist, making her neck seem long as an antelope's. It takes about three dozen pins, but I finally arrive at something close. I darken my eyelids like she did, too, and sit back, blinking at my reflection. It's not like I've never put on eye pencil—I've worn all kinds of costumes and stage makeup. But that was for a role.

This is different—the idea of walking around all day looking a good deal more glamorous than I ever did back home feels downright strange. But Peggy was always going on about how you had to play the part of a star until even you believed it.

I suppose if I'm really going for it . . . I dust a layer of conceal-
ing powder over my freckles and turn away from the mirror before
I can change my mind. Fiona passes by on the sidewalk as I step
outside and turn the key in my motel room door. Guilt billows up
like a cloud of steam all around me. She glances at my dress and
rolls her eyes skyward. "You sure have taken the whole 'girl from
the sticks' character work to heart."

"Pardon?"

"I get it—a little method acting never did anybody any harm."
She spins away with a wan smile.

The words sound innocent enough. Her tone, however, is anything but. Is she poking fun at my clothes? Heat rises in my cheeks
as I watch her saunter off. She must know the lead would have
been hers if it weren't for me. And it's just like Fiona to be spiteful
about it.

Never mind her. I was right to jump at Gwyn's offer, wasn't I?

I head across the street to the diner and straight to the counter
to place a takeaway order. The waitresses flit between customers—
they look tired already, early as it is. I don't want to be in their
shoes again, not ever. I don't miss fry grease in my hair, not one bit.
But before I left home, I was comfortable in my own skin. I didn't
constantly feel like I needed to change how I looked or talked or
who I was to do my job. That's the thing about growing up in a
small town—everybody knows you, and has since you were born.
Momma would say you are who you are; it's no use putting on
airs. Then Daddy would say something about the long line of
Butterfields while Nana made a face behind his back and I had to
do my best not to bust up laughing and give her away.

But it's more than not being able to escape who you are and where you're from—I was proud of who I was back then, inside and out. And now? I'm not so sure. I collect my order, shake off my misgivings, and head back to the motel. I swing by Clive's room on my way to the theatre, a tray with a half dozen cups of coffee and a deli sandwich for lunch balanced in one hand, my notebook and script tucked under the other. He isn't under any obligation to run scenes with me, but he did promise to help. I think he and Gwyn are the only ones who believe I can pull off this whole leading-lady thing.

"Mornin'!" I can't keep the overeager smile off my face.

Clive grabs one of the coffee cups and slurps in response.

"Kathleen laid out the costumes so I can do the scenes in full dress. I'm thinking we start with the vocals in the opening number, then run through the courting scene one more time—I practiced the dance steps last night in my room, subbing the haybales for the second bed in my room." A nervous laugh titters out of me, but Clive only grunts and takes another swig.

"Then the barn raising, barn dance, and the finale? Gwyn is meeting me later to run through the other scenes."

"She cleared the stage for us this morning?"

"Yep. And she asked the stagehands to have the props on hand when we need them."

"Is that who the other coffees are for?"

I flash a smile. "A little bribery never hurt anybody."

He chuckles and lifts my books out from under my arm.

"Ah, so you *are* a gentleman."

On a dime, Clive pivots, batting Ned's lovesick eyes at me. I nearly drop the tray on the sidewalk, and we're both still laughing when he bows me through the stage door. All that pressure cramming into my brain fades away, and by the time we step onstage together, I feel like I belong there. Like a professional. Like I'm earning my place in that spotlight, inch by inch.

We sing through our duet twice. I get so caught up in it, I have to remind myself of the notes I took when I was watching Gloria—how she played the scene—and I do my best to mimic her performance. We run through the dialogue a few times so it feels less like a bunch of words on the page and more like a conversation between almost-lovers. Clive helps me hit my marks, pausing to shift me into place when I get it wrong. Finally we run through the dance, working the lifts until he's dripping with sweat and I feel like I can trust the muscle memory. Then, with a peck on the cheek and one final spin, Clive slides offstage.

"My turn?" Gwyn twirls on in a parody of his graceful exit, her binder splayed between her hands.

"I'm all yours."

"Excellent. Let's bake some pies then, shall we?" She drops her binder on the butcher block, and I roll out an imaginary lump of dough with a wooden rolling pin while we run lines. Gwyn has to stop me every so often when I drop my head like I would if I were really in Momma's kitchen, putting all my weight into my work. She grabs my shoulders, yanking them back and tilting my face up to the lights.

"You're going to have to match Gloria's blocking, from your toes clear to your head."

We move on to the song next. Gwyn's got a wretched singing voice, so she doesn't bother adding off-key harmonies. In the call-and-response section, she speaks the lines at tempo at least, so I can get a sense of the timing. Sally's vocal parts are nearly always melody, so they're easier than smaller parts that might not demand so much of my voice but would require me to listen closely and really think in order to hit every note.

When we break for lunch, Gwyn makes for the wings and I sit alone on the apron, dangling my feet over the edge of the stage. I drape a sheet over the costume while I tuck into my pastrami sandwich, saving the pickle for last. The theatre is empty except for the stage crew running through a lighting check. By the time I finish my lunch, even they are gone.

I move to the center of the stage. I'm tired from the morning's rehearsal, but I'm not going to pass up a chance to hear myself fill the theatre with nothing but my voice. I start with a warm-up, humming scales at first, then voicing them stronger and stronger, focusing farther and farther away until I'm projecting to the back of the house.

And then I forget about everything and anyone else who might wander into the theatre. I just sing. The sound resonates, swelling to fill the cavernous space. My tone brightens as a smile stretches out the words—I can't help it. I'm swoony, dreamy, helplessly in love with this.

-46-

MISSOURI IS SO close to home I swear I can feel Nebraska calling me. I've missed the wide-open spaces, the slow and steady pace of things, and the people. I'd be missing Nana no matter where I hung my hat on this earth, but being so long without Momma and Daddy doesn't seem natural, especially with how Daddy and I left things. And Jesse—well, being close enough that a hard drive through the night could get me there with enough time to scale the lattice leading up to his window, slip under the covers, and curl around him—it makes it tough to do something as simple as drawing breath. It makes me wish I were back in New York, far enough away that I didn't daydream about hijacking the tour bus just to have five minutes alone with him.

The playbill has been redone with my name at the top. The marquee, too. Well, my stage name, anyhow. Tonight we're playing in a gorgeous opera house built in the thirties that has hosted the touring companies of *South Pacific*, *The King and I*, and *My Fair Lady*. It makes me tingle all over just thinking about the actors who've stood in that very spot, all the hearts laid bare on that stage.

I've got my entrances and exits down. I don't only have

scribbled notes about where to be when, I've stood there and I've sung from there and I've danced my way through every single step, in rehearsal, at least. I *think* I'm doing Sally justice. At least, I hope so. Kathleen worked through the night to finish my costumes, and after an early-morning fitting to be sure, she grabs my hand and whisks me outside.

"Time to celebrate. Lord knows we both need it!"

I follow her to the curb in front of the motel. She lifts one arm to hail a taxi and glances back over her shoulder, looking me up and down. "I heard what Fiona said about your clothes the other day. It was spiteful, plain and simple." Kathleen offers an apologetic grin. "But she isn't wrong."

"Really?" I trace my eyebrow with my pointer finger, dipping my head slightly to take a second look at my dress. It isn't store-bought, but it's well-made. It can't be *that* bad, surely?

"Come on." Kathleen draws me into the taxi. "This will be fun."

"Okay." Though we got a paycheck on Saturday, I'm not going to spend my salary on fancy clothes. But I'm also not going to turn down a chance to get out of that motel room.

We zip through town to a quiet street lined with boutiques. Kathleen chatters away about the show she worked on before this one and about the Hollywood costume shops she hopes to send samples to as soon as the tour's finished. She asks about home, and I find myself rambling about the farm, and losing Nana, and how I worry about Momma and Daddy all alone in that big old farmhouse. And, because I can't help myself, I tell her about Jesse.

When we sweep into the first shop, she dismisses the

saleswoman with a disarming smile. Kathleen knows my measurements better than I do after all those costumes, so I trail behind while she scours the racks, tapping a delicate finger along her lips as she considers each item.

She selects a half dozen outfits, then steers me toward the dressing room. "Try these. It isn't so much how they look on you—you're an actress, you can wear anything. It's about how the clothes make you feel. Start with the cigarette pants."

I step inside the tiny dressing room, wincing a little at the mirrors on all sides. I slip out of my homemade dress and hang it on a hook beside the outfits Kathleen chose. *Oh.* We did our best to keep it clean, but beside these new clothes, my old dress looks *so* shabby and out of date. My hands fly up to cover my cheeks, no matter that I'm alone in the dressing room with no one to see me blush.

Okay, so maybe I do need to make a little room in the budget for clothes.

I step into the pants first. I have no idea what to call the fabric, but it's sleek black with small polka dots. The waist is high, tailored at an angular V and secured with a thin leather belt. The legs fit snug, ending above the ankle.

I pull the peasant top over my head, shake out my hair, and have a look. My midriff is exposed, a pale triangle of flesh just below my ribs. Before I have the chance to even twist to see what it looks like from the back, Kathleen whisks the curtain aside. She leans back, considering.

"Well, you look amazing. But how do you feel?"

I consider my reflection. It isn't anything like the dresses that make it seem as though I'm trying to wedge myself into the shape of someone half my size and twice as delicate. But it isn't *me*, either. I can't explain it, and I've certainly never imagined wearing something so . . . dramatic.

"You don't have to say a word." Kathleen yanks the curtain shut again. "Take that off and try the hostess gown."

"The what?"

"The coat-looking thing with the opening at the waist and the capri pant beneath."

Ah. It's a midnight-blue fitted top with a flaring almost-skirt over striped pants. As I draw it over my shoulders, I can tell before I fasten a single button that it's light-years more *me* than the last one. I slide the pants on, then button the high neck down to my waist. I catch myself smiling without even meaning to. I didn't know I could look like this.

When I open the curtain, Kathleen's face mirrors my own.

"Wow. You look incredible! That would be perfect for an opening night, don't you think?"

"It really would." I feel *amazing.* I never knew that what a person wears on the outside could have such a profound effect on how they feel on the inside. I reach for the tag—*yikes!*

Kathleen peeks at the price. "Oh. Tell you what—I'll make you a better one custom when you land your next job."

"You'd do that for me?"

"Of course! Now, what we need is something versatile that can work just as well for one of Harbuckle's after-parties as a long afternoon on the bus."

She ducks out of the dressing room, and I take one last look at myself in the hostess gown. I run my fingers along the sharp tailoring at the collar and down the slit before I begin unbuttoning again. Someday.

I try on a trapeze dress next, which is a definite no. And the chemise—it makes me look like a potato sack that's grown limbs. We move on to the next shop, where it's more of the same. Too suave, too matronly, too frilly. I've almost given up when we step inside the last boutique. It isn't like the others—there aren't racks and racks of clothes to choose from. There are only a half dozen dress forms, and behind each one, a towering shelf with stacks of each design in an array of sizes and colors.

Kathleen takes one step inside, gasps, and clasps her hands in front of her. "Oh *yes*."

She twirls in a circle at the center of the mannequins and, rather than shooing the salesperson away, says, "We'd like to try the battle jacket in slate and navy and the pantsuit in every color you've got."

She was right—I have no idea how, but when I shrug into the arms and tug the pantsuit up over my shoulders, it's like stepping into a second skin. The neck is high, like a simple T-shirt, and the cuffs go clear to my wrists. There's a knot at the waist, and the pants flare just the right amount at the hips, narrowing to hug my calves. When I step outside, Kathleen raises her eyebrows and claps as if I just sang an aria.

"It's perfect," I breathe.

She chuckles. "It's a Givenchy knockoff is what it is, but that makes it just right for our budget." She tosses the battle jacket over my shoulders—it looks like the one Daddy wore during the war. The elastic hugs my waist, and the thick lapels add a splash of color.

"It looks smashing on you, but what we're really after is *that*." She points at the grin I can't tamp down. "This business is fifty percent talent and fifty percent confidence. You're selling yourself short if you don't start dressing like where you are is where you belong."

I cringe and flip the tags over. Kathleen was right! These are definitely knockoff prices, though they're certainly not cheap. I could probably get two sets—the black and maybe the emerald— and one jacket. But I've never even dreamed of spending so much on clothes before.

"You've earned this, Mazie." There's a warning note to Kathleen's voice.

A tight breath sighs out of me. "It's just, my nana sent me to New York with all the money she'd saved over her whole life. I have to make the most of every dime. I can't afford to waste anything— not time, not money, not even something Pierce might be able to teach me—at arm's-length, mind. I owe it to her."

Kathleen comes to stand beside me, peering over my shoulder at our reflection. "I didn't know your nana, but if I had to guess? That money was less about pinching pennies and more about giving you wings."

I drop my head, shaking it slowly side to side. It's exactly the sort of thing Nana would say if she were here. And it eases up on the ache a little to think that she's still here with me, in a way.

I roll up two pantsuits and a jacket and plunk down my money. I don't have it all figured out, not even close. But I'm getting there, Nana, I promise.

-47-

OUR NEXT PERFORMANCE is tight as a drum, the quick changes timed to the last second and the dance numbers sharp. When I sing, I can feel the audience tip forward in their seats, wishing right along with me. We get to the last scene before intermission, and I can feel the crowd holding their breath, seeing Sally and Ned together for the first time.

"Come on, gimme a chance." Clive pulls off Ned's desperation perfectly—he's got one foot on the ground and the other one propped on the haybale where I'm seated.

"Oh, Ned." My legs are crossed at the ankles, my face tilted toward the audience and down, eyelashes fluttering, just like Gloria used to. "It isn't you—"

"That's what all the girls say," he spins out with a hapless shrug, "when they're turning a fella away."

I swing my head dramatically back around and begin at a whisper: "If only you were . . .

a tailor or a grocer or a door-to-door salesman,
a plumber or a teacher or a radio repairman,

a carpenter, or a lumberjack, or an elevator operator,
a janitor, or a traffic cop, or a milkman, or a haberdasher . . ."

I stand and take a step toward him. "I would let myself—"
One more step. "I wouldn't be able to stop myself—" Then I lean in,
like it's against my will. I lick my lips and lead with my chin, my
eyelids dropping dangerously low.

"So what—you're too good for a farmer?" He turns his back to
me, and the crowd grumbles, right on cue.

"It's not like that." Now it's my chance to swing away. "You
wouldn't understand."

He comes up behind me and lays a hand on my shoulder. "But
I want to."

In the orchestra pit, a lone banjo sends out a spray of notes in
a mournful minor key.

> *"Daddy worked long hours.*
> *Momma toiled even longer.*
> *Day in, day out, sun up, sun down,*
> *gotta get the hay baled,*
> *gotta call the vet out,*
> *gotta get the roof patched,*
> *gotta bring the crops in.*
>
> *All they could give was never enough.*
> *Cold coming, storm brewing, bills rolling in . . ."*

The arrangement scatters, slowing as the story comes to a close.

"Plow horse came up lame,
 crop died on the vine,
 the bank took the farm,
 took everything from them."

He spins me slowly to face him and folds his arms around me. I keep my hands tucked against my chest but drop my head onto his shoulder.

"All they had was never enough." I push him away, then stand tall and speak into the darkness. "I swore that would never be me."

"Sally, I'm awful sorry for your folks—I am. And while I can't make promises about the weather, if you stick with me, you won't have to worry—my new Von Steer will take care of us, and your folks, too."

"You can't know that—it's only a tractor."

He gasps, the entire cast and crew joining in backstage for effect. The audience of Von Steer salesmen is heckling and jeering now, and Ned saunters toward them, arms outstretched. "Let me tell you a little about this tractor. It can plow a field in an hour that would take a team of horses all week. Why, you've never seen anything like the new S model."

The music kicks up, and he strikes a pose in the middle of the stage.

"It's got a two-stroke air-cooled big diesel engine,
 a fifty-two HP; eight-speed transmission,
 power steering, power brakes, live PTO,

and when you really need it most,
POWER IMPLEMENT RAISING!"

That gets a chorus of whistles from the audience, and Clive takes the opportunity to draw in a quick breath.

"For threshing, hauling, excavating,
spraying, shelling, cultivating . . ."

I join him center stage, tapping my foot along with the clapping audience as he rattles off another dozen newfangled features. "You don't say? Well, how about:

binding, disking, middlebusting,
hulling, seeding, pulverizing?"

"Don't get me started! This tractor can:

cut corn, rake hay, saw wood, dry grain,
pull stumps, crush rock, grind feed, shell peas—"

I grab his arm, laughing, trying to drag him offstage. "All right, all right!"

While I'm tugging his arm, he keeps shouting all that the various attachments can do to a field of corn, gamely stumbling toward the wings with me. The audience is laughing, egging him on as he rattles off another spurt of handy features. Finally, when we're almost offstage, he turns, serious, and takes my hand in both of his. The music fades, and he proclaims, "I'm telling you, Sally: You can depend on me. And *we* can depend on Von Steer."

Clive and I hold that pose, staring into each other's eyes while the audience leaps to their feet. And that feeling—joy bubbling up from my toes clear to the tippy-top of my head—I wouldn't trade it for anything.

-48-

WHEN THE SHOW'S over, I'm the first one out of the theatre. The sky is black, the stars hidden, low clouds lit from beneath by the streetlights. I need some time to myself to sort out my emotions— tomorrow the crew will pack up the show, and the next day we'll be barreling down the highway till we're within spitting distance of Nebraska. Before I get more than half a block away, Kathleen busts through the door after me, my coat slung over her arm.

"Mazie! What's the big hurry?"

I cross my arms and duck my head. The air is warm, but the rain is coming down in buckets, bouncing off the pavement and pooling in the street. Apparently April showers like to hang around through July in Missouri.

"You wouldn't understand."

She throws the coat over my shoulders and links arms with me. "Try me."

We hurry across the street to a diner not unlike the one where I used to work, with vinyl booths and stools pulled up to a chrome bar framing soda and milkshake machines. We perch on a pair of bright red stools and order malted milkshakes. When they arrive, we clink glasses like they're filled with champagne. Then Kathleen takes her straw between her teeth and peers sideways at me. "I don't get it—you were a hit tonight! What's there to be so glum about?"

I swipe the strands of wet hair away from my face. "We're playing St. Joseph in a couple of nights. It's only a few hours from home."

"So you're feeling homesick?" She shakes her head. "I forget sometimes how young you are."

"Of course I miss home. But that's no different whether I'm in Manhattan or Omaha." I take a sip, stalling. I hadn't expected anyone to follow me out into the rain. I'd planned to do my sulking alone. "The whole reason I left home was to become a big Broadway star, and I wasn't quiet about saying so. I mean—this production is amazing, and I know any work in this business is good work. Besides, I'm learning, and maybe this gig will make booking that next one even easier, it's just—"

"You're singing about tractors."

I slump onto the counter. "I'm singing about tractors! I mean, of course I'm proud of this show. But it isn't exactly the triumphant homecoming I imagined."

Kathleen dips her straw into the glass, poking out any air holes hiding below. "I suppose a lot of the folks back home are farmers?"

"*Mm-hmm.*"

"And I bet you know a few Von Steer salesmen, too."

"I do."

"You're afraid word will get out."

I nod, trying not to feel miserable about how ridiculous it is that I'm miserable about this. "To them, our show probably seems no different from community theatre on the high school stage."

"Well, that's understandable—outside New York, who really gets what this business is like on the inside?"

"Exactly. And what if Jesse hears folks talk like that and comes to believe I left for no good reason? What if he thinks I don't . . ." I trail off. I can't finish that sentence. The pendulum lights above our heads flicker, and suddenly everything in the diner seems overly bright.

"So tell him."

I tamp my straw against the sludgy bottom of my milkshake glass. I want to. The only problem is, if I do that, if I tell him that I still love him, then I'm admitting, against all logic, that I'm holding out hope. And that isn't fair to either one of us.

No. I can't say a word.

-49-

CLIVE IS A walking encyclopedia when it comes to historic theatres. Before every performance, when the cast gathers behind the curtain, holding hands while the orchestra begins the overture, he regales us with stories about the building we're about to perform in. Here in St. Joseph, the Missouri Theater has a sculptural, vibrant interior to match the towering façade out front. It was built in the twenties to house silent films, then talkies, and now packed houses of popcorn-eating, soda-sipping audiences for hit movies like *Gidget* and *Sleeping Beauty*. Clive's stories always make a performance seem like it's about something bigger than tractors, salesmen, and profit margins. He gets us all believing our show is a part of a greater legacy, sharing this all-American art form we've given our lives to.

But tonight I don't really hear any of it; I can't quit thinking about Jesse.

At the end of the show, when the final curtain comes down, we all scramble for the dressing rooms beneath the stage. My feet are killing me—I ran that beauty parlor number two dozen times this afternoon with Gwyn because I wasn't hitting my marks cleanly enough. It's a complex scene. The sets fold in on themselves, turned by a giant winch offstage to pivot the scenery from inside the shop to outside in a matter of seconds. The timing is tricky, but all that practice paid off, and for the first time, I was able to relax and enjoy myself during that scene tonight.

I slide out of the costume and into my new black pantsuit. I wipe off all the stage makeup except the lipstick and sit back with a sigh. I blink a few times at my reflection. Even though it's only been three months, the girl who left Nebraska and this one staring back at me are lifetimes apart. My cheeks are thinner and the rest of me is, too. My eyes look, well, not wiser, but maybe a touch less innocent. I've learned how to sweep my hair up into a twist to highlight my jaw and cheekbones. Even my posture is different somehow. All I know is, if the old me passed the new me on the sidewalk, she'd probably think I was some smart city broad who had everything figured out.

But I don't. The work is exhilarating, and I love the challenge every single day to stretch and grow. But I'm lonely. I'm starting to loathe motel rooms. And if I'm honest, I haven't been truly happy since I left home.

The rest of the actors are going out, but all I can think about is how much I want to soak my poor feet in a tub of Epsom salts. I climb the stairs slowly, leaning on the handrail so it groans under me. Backstage, the crew is finishing up for the night—they'll strike the sets tomorrow and pack everything into the truck for our next show in Omaha.

Now that the audience is gone, the curtains are flung wide to reveal the empty house, save a lone usher strolling through the aisles to collect stray playbills and commemorative records. I cross to the apron one more time and close my eyes to see if I can call up the feeling of the audience out there in the blackness—I'd swear every single one of their hearts was beating in time while I sang tonight.

Behind me there's only silence, so when someone's chin touches down at the nape of my neck, a hand grazing my hip, I leap away like a startled jackrabbit.

"What on earth?!" I exclaim as I whip around.

It's Pierce. I bite down so hard it draws blood.

He says something in a low voice, but I don't catch it over the roaring in my ears. He gives me that bemused smile—the one that proclaims him innocent and me crazy to think there's anything threatening beneath his polished veneer.

"I said you looked great out there tonight." He isn't looking at my face. "I'm going to ask Kathleen to take your costumes in a little at the ribs. We want those salesmen to get a good look at what you've got to offer." He reaches out to demonstrate, chuckling when I sidle out of the way.

Pierce walks offstage, and I'm left all alone out there, trembling. The sound of his laughter is hushed by the thick curtains edging the proscenium, and swallowed by the stairwell as he trots downstairs. Why can't he just leave me alone? I hug my arms around my midsection, trying to get ahold of the shudders rippling through me.

"Mazie?"

That voice—I spin around, my mouth going dry as a ball of cotton. "Jesse?" It's barely a whisper.

He's standing in the wings beside Gwyn's station, holding a cluster of flowers in one hand and a folded playbill in the other. A frown creases his forehead as he looks between me and the stairwell.

I come to my senses, cross the stage, and throw my arms around his neck until every inch of me presses against him. Too late, I remember I'm not supposed to do that kind of thing anymore. I slide back a step, trying to read his face.

I can't figure out what to do with my hands. Unbidden, they find the front of his shirt and grip the collar, pulling us close again. He smells like straw and dark soil. His cheek is scratchy against mine, his eyelashes brushing the tip of my nose.

"You're burning up." I can't believe he's here.

"Yeah." Jesse licks his lips. He's nervous. I've known this boy since we were both in diapers, and I've never seen him so nervous. "I was waiting outside the stage door for the longest time—it's sweltering out there. But then this gal with a pincushion strapped to her wrist spotted me and brought me here."

I draw away, just far enough so I can look at him. "Kathleen? You met my friend Kathleen?"

He smiles. "She seems real nice."

And that's almost worse than the nervous. He's being polite now, to *me*. My arms drop to my sides, and I back up a step. "I'm sorry. If I had known you were coming . . ."

"Nelly heard you were in this show, and I cut a deal with Eddie down at Von Steer for his ticket." He grips the hair at the back of his head, the ends curling around his fingers. "I thought I'd surprise you. But I guess that was all wrong—"

I've got to say something, and quick. "No. I'm so glad you came." There. The truth. "It's good to see you."

His eyes dart around, anywhere but at my face, landing once again on the stairwell. "Who was that guy?"

My face flares with heat. Jesse saw that? "He's the director. He's not . . . I didn't want him to—"

"Yeah, that was clear as day. I kept thinking you'd give him an earful, but you didn't. I can't figure out why not." He looks genuinely confused, and also sad. "Do you want me to go find him and tell him to leave you alone?"

"No!" I don't mean to snap. I shake my head and reach for Jesse's hand, but his stays clamped onto those flowers, and after a beat, my arm falls back to my side. "It's complicated."

He looks up, meeting my eyes sidelong. "You know, if I hadn't watched you up on that stage and checked the program nearabout a hundred times, I'd hardly recognize you, Mazie."

The pause stretches too long. I want to pull him close and kiss the confused off his face. But it doesn't seem fair—I'm not coming home, not if I can help it. My plans haven't changed. I suppose I can say that much.

"Nothing has changed." It comes out almost pleading.

"No? I've never, not once, seen you let someone walk all over you. *That's* changed. That and your name." His voice is flat, his eyes empty.

"This isn't Nebraska, Jesse. What you see isn't always what you get. The rest of the world doesn't play by those rules. Either you bend or they break you."

Jesse sets the flowers, already bruised and wilting around the edges, down on Gwyn's stool and backs away. He can't leave like this; it's going to kill me.

He pauses, a dozen different emotions floating over his face. "I get that this is a big dream you're chasing. I understand why you needed to go. But what I can't wrap my head around is why you decided that the Mazie Butterfield I knew and loved wasn't good enough."

He slips away into the shadows.

Loved? Past tense? It drops me to my knees.

I want a do-over. I want to run after him and beg him to understand, but I can't seem to move. Long after Jesse's gone, I huddle alone on the stage, hugging my midsection as if my arms are the only things still holding me together.

-50-

THE NEXT MORNING, our bus pulls into Omaha under a hazy summer sky. At least the weather is being considerate of my foul mood. I mean, let's not get carried away with any green clouds or funnels touching down, but a sunny blue sky full of chirping birds at this moment in time would be downright obnoxious.

At least I'm back in Nebraska. I wish I were home, where I could curl up on the sofa next to Momma and let her solid, steady presence chip away at the block of ice in my chest. I wish I could sit in the tall grass by Nana's grave and let it all spill out of me—the confusion, the worry, and the disappointment.

Harbuckle is waiting outside the bus to greet us all. He'll be watching the show with the regional sales manager, and as long as he likes what he sees, we won't see him again until the tour is over. I stumble down the bus steps like one of those actresses with a pill problem, hiding bloodshot eyes behind a pair of dark sunglasses. But of course, pills aren't what's killing me on the inside. A busted-up heart is.

It was one thing to be away from Jesse after we'd broken up, when I could still believe that he was right there if I ever came home. But now that he apparently despises who I've become—now that he doesn't even love me anymore—I can't bear it.

If it were up to me, I'd head to my motel room, draw the curtains, and stay there until showtime tomorrow. But somebody leaked to the whole cast that today is my birthday. So no matter how much I want to sink into a puddle, they aren't going to let me.

They're taking me to the dive bar on the corner, and I'm not about to remind them that I'm only turning eighteen. Besides, it's not like I've never had a drink of liquor. Momma always ladled a teacup of her mulled wine for each of us on Christmas Eve. And after those really hard days in the fields, Daddy would sip a little whiskey straight from the bottle before leaving the barn. When I worked beside him the whole day through, I got some, too. I don't need anyone trotting me out to the nearest watering hole and showing me the ropes. But after being so lonesome the first half of the tour, I'm grateful for friends who want to do something nice for me.

So when Kathleen raps on my door, I put on a smile and fake happy the best I know how. Gwyn and Clive are already bellied up to the bar. I order a French 75 just like Madeleine LeBeau in *Casablanca*. The glass is frosted halfway to the rim, my fingertips leaving wobbly ovals behind. The sugar-soaked gin slides down my throat like a sip of ice-cold stream water. Fire hits my belly and warms my cheeks, and I welcome the heat, ordering a second before I'm even halfway through the first.

When I wake the next morning with an ache splitting my

head like an axe through firewood, I remember ordering a third drink. I do not recall a fourth. I've got a vague recollection of a dance-off on the sawdust floor. But the one thing I'm sure of is how the night ended: me slumped on the bar, crying over Jesse and making everyone else just as miserable as me.

-51-

I DON'T HAVE any intention of leaving my motel room until show-time. I turn the television on and twist the volume dial down. I don't want to see anyone—I just can't bear to be alone with my thoughts right now. The bubble screen flickers between *I Love Lucy* reruns and footage of the *Explorer 6* launch, plus about a million diagrams of the satellite's elliptical orbit.

Of course, the stupid launch only makes me think of Jesse and everything that went so wrong so fast. I keep running over and over what I should have said, how I should have run after him and held on until I could make him see *me* behind all the changes on the outside. I drag the extra pillow over my head and groan, punching the mattress a few times for good measure.

The worst part is that he's right—who I am and where I come from is nothing to be ashamed of. I didn't go all the way to New York City to lose myself. It's one thing to work hard to be the very best at this job that I can. And it's another to twist myself into something I'm not to do so. There's got to be a way to meet my dreams on my own terms.

When I can't hide any longer, I leave my sunglasses in the

room and chuck the lipstick, face powder, and eye pencil in the trash on the way out. I'm keeping the pantsuit, though. That feels more like me than circle skirts ever did, like a cross between the overalls I wore around the farm and the simple leotard and tights I've danced in since I was four years old.

After a few minutes' walk, I reach the Orpheum Theater. I used to beg Momma and Daddy to take me there when I was a little girl, but we weren't the kind of people who could afford something like that just for the fun of it. So I take it all in now. The moment I step onstage, I feel the old place wrap itself around me. I breathe in the history soaked into the heavy curtains in the wings and the tapestries mounted to the walls to dampen the sound.

I read an interview once from a movie star who crisscrossed the country, then the continent, selling war bonds and singing for the troops. She talked about how it's easy to play the part on a good day, when your personal life is in order and luck is with you, but that a real actor's mettle is tested when times turn hard and you still have to give it all for the troops every night.

Seeing as how I can barely keep my mind out of the wallows, tonight's performance is going to be tough. It'll be easy enough to summon the melancholy for Sally's first number, I suppose. But the rest? It'll take every bit of talent I've got to sell happy and in love.

I close the door to my dressing room and prep for the show quietly, taking my time through a ballet warm-up, using the makeup counter as my barre. Next comes a vocal warm-up, while I step into the undergarments and pin curl my hair flat against my scalp. I crack the door, not so much that I'm inviting conversation, but enough to let the wig mistress in when she's ready for me. I begin patting the thick stage makeup onto my cheeks and forehead, my arpeggios becoming stronger and more ambitious.

And it works: the ballet centers me, and the quiet is calming. I get to thinking—Gloria had the whole audience hanging on her every gesture before she ever opened her mouth. I can't compete with that. So as of this moment, I'm done trying.

I may not have half Sally's class, but I know how she feels, born into a certain kind of life and wishing for more. I know the weight of family legacy in a place, and pride in that work. It's no good trying to imitate Gloria's performance, to live up to her presence onstage. I'll never be more than a carbon copy, not if I'm trying to be someone else.

But maybe what I bring to the character is just as powerful.

After the curtain goes down on the first number, I step onto the apron and the spot drops on me, hot and so bright I have to remind myself not to squint. For the first time ever, I let go of what I think the role is supposed to be. I focus on the balcony filigree and feel my way into the character. When Clive's harmony drops in halfway through, I barely notice.

I make it through the first act without giving in to the sadness that's dug in beneath my skin. Instead of heading downstairs with the rest of the cast during intermission, I push through the stage door for a breath of fresh Nebraska air. I close my eyes and lean back against the brick, tilting my face up to the night sky. A moth flings itself at the outdoor light above my head, searing its paltry wings on the bare bulb popping and fizzling in its cracked plastic casing.

The stage door swings open, and I dart out of the way. It's Pierce. My eyes narrow. Of course it is. The moth drops to the sidewalk, its wings singed to dust.

"Your delivery is all wrong." Pierce reaches out to tug at a loose thread on my shoulder. "That hick accent of yours is sullying Sally's polish. Can't you at least fake classy?"

I yank my arm free and slide around him. Jesse's right. Whatever I may have talked myself into believing, no job is worth this. I'm done letting Pierce threaten me.

"Listen, I know more about Sally than you ever could. I've worked my ass off for this role, and I'm doing a fantastic job. You want to fire me? Go ahead, tell Harbuckle you're going to cut loose his only Sally. Go on."

I throw open the stage door.

"But don't you ever touch me again."

The beauty parlor scene is my favorite, maybe because I've had to work at it so hard. The number is zippy and peppy, and the choreography is tricky as hell. We get to the part where all four of us stroll outside, our hair as glossy as candy apples. The cue for the sets to split in half comes from me: mid-stride, I place my palm on the door and push through, that one motion peeling back both walls of the set. At least that's what it's supposed to look like.

In reality, I could never push those sets myself, not even if I used both hands and gave it every bit of my strength. Backstage, the stagehand at the winch times the moving set to my approaching footsteps. But tonight, when I toss that last laugh over my shoulder at the girls and flip up my hand to press it against the "door," I can tell right away something's not right.

The set doesn't budge. I can feel it sort of rumble, like a car that's revving to go but the driver hasn't popped the clutch yet. The girls are fanned out like a flock of birds behind me with nowhere to go but straight into the set walls. Sweat breaks out on my upper lip. I watched the cast practice this moment in tech for an entire afternoon when I first joined the company, and we've performed this number a half dozen times since. The sets have never stuck once.

The missed beat stretches out, and the audience begins to stir. I've got one shot at salvaging this, and it has to be quick. Since the door won't open for me, and the windows of the beauty parlor are nothing but cutouts anyway, I say my line with a shrug and vault out the window like a teenager sneaking out of the house. I stroll downstage, singing and giving the choreography a little something extra until I feel the girls fill in the space around me. We nail the last eight-count in unison and hold that last, long chord, our arms outstretched as the horns trill in the orchestra pit beneath us. I slap my hands against my thighs as the note cuts off.

Behind me, there's a sound like a grenade going off, and we all hit the deck. The audience gasps. I may not be able to see more than the first few rows, but that tells me all I need to know. Their hands are all raised, frozen in that moment before they burst into applause. It's almost comical—every single mouth dropped open in an astonished O.

Fiona begins to cough, and no wonder—a cloud of dust billows up all around us. And then the house curtain closes right in front of my nose. Clinging to one another, Wanda, Fiona, Darlene, and I scramble to our feet and spin around. The sets are mangled, splintered wood and toppled furniture scattered all over the stage.

I shove my hands into the folds of Sally's circle skirt to try and hide how bad I'm shaking. If I hadn't leaped out that window, I'd be crushed somewhere in that mess of lumber. We all would have been.

"Is everybody okay?"

Gwyn scurries around trying to get everybody up and moving so the crew can do something about the busted sets while Harbuckle shoves the Von Steer regional manager through the curtain.

"Just talk about the new model," he hisses. "Stall any way you can!"

The crew clears enough space for the tractor's entrance, then lowers a painted drop to hide the wreckage. We limp through the barn dance and finale, and when the show is finally over, the whole cast and half the crew ends up huddled inside a single dressing room. Folks are sitting on dressing tables and along the wall; no fewer than six people are squeezed onto the couch in the corner. Nobody is talking, but we're all thinking the same thing: *Is the tour over? Can we recover from this?*

There's always an element of danger in putting on a flashy show. Dancers leap down raked stages and through set pieces. Hell, Mary Martin flew above the stage on wires eight performances a week in *Peter Pan*. You hear of mishaps in shows, but they're usually something people laugh off afterward.

Nobody's laughing now.

The dressing room door squeaks open, and in walks Pierce,

scratching his head and looking like he'd rather be anywhere else. Harbuckle is a step behind him, his hands jammed into his suit pockets.

"The technical director thinks it'll take a week to repair everything," he says. "Gwyn is rescheduling the last four stops on the tour. I won't be returning to New York as planned. I'll be right here with you all to see that this thing is done right. I'm afraid we'll have to invoke the week extension clause in your contracts. But we *will* finish this run."

Harbuckle says that last bit like he's rallying the troops or something, but it lands flat as a pancake. He removes his hat and twists the poor thing in his hands. "Taking all that into account, there's no need for you all to be here while repairs are being made. So that means you've all got the week off."

Whispers fill in the space all around me, and Harbuckle grins. "Rest up. Take some time to get your heads right and put this behind you so we're all ready to finish strong."

Pierce is still glowering by the door. At me. "What were you thinking, going through that window? If you hadn't put the stress of your bodyweight on the sets, they would have moved as intended."

"Me?" It comes out feeble, like a child's voice. "The winch was stuck. We could all hear it. If I didn't do something, and quick, we would have been—"

He cuts me off. "You can't cowgirl something like this. Do you have any idea how much those sets cost? How much it will set this company back to rebuild them?"

"But I didn't . . ."

Fiona shoves her way in front of me. "That girl saved my life tonight, or at the very least, my legs. And hers and hers and his, too." She jabs her finger into Pierce's chest, pushing him backward one jab at a time until he stumbles out of the dressing room. "The only words you should have for her right now are *Thank you kindly for saving my scrawny ass.*"

Fiona slams the door and whirls around to face the rest of us. "I don't know about you all, but I am *never* signing on for a show with that son of a bitch again."

Folks say theatre people are like family, and I never really got that from anything I'd experienced before. I always thought it was because I had a sterling family already and didn't need any surrogates to step in where the Butterfields had already laid claim.

But now I get it, completely. With one last lewd gesture toward the door, Fiona comes for me. She wraps her arms around my neck, and the next thing I know, I've got every single person in that room holding on to me, or the closest they can get, anyway.

It chips away at the miserable, the scared, and the bits of bravado I'd called up to get me through the day. It warms me to my core. And when they finally step back, all that's left is a single, solitary thought.

I'm going home.

-52-

THE FOLLOWING MORNING, I pour three coffees from the carafe in the motel's front office. I've had plenty of practice balancing teetering trays of brimming cups, but I'm so excited, it's a miracle I don't drop them all. I'm really going home!

All I want is to sleep in my own bed. I want to sit on the porch swing, counting fireflies. I want to work side by side with Daddy in the barn. I want to watch Momma kneading bread, that familiar *slap, slap, slap* ringing through the kitchen. If what I need is to be reminded who I am, they're the ones to do it.

And I want to make things right with Jesse. I have to.

I rap on Kathleen's door first.

"Aren't you a dear!" She pushes her eye mask higher up on her forehead and takes the cup with both hands, lifting it to her lips like it's filled with liquid gold.

"You're staying here?"

"Yep."

"I can't convince you to come home with me? Momma says there's plenty of room, and you're more than welcome."

"Not a chance."

"And you won't tell me about the samples you're working on?"

"I'll do better than that." She levels a finger in my direction as she backs away. "I'll show you. Next week."

I stop at Clive's door next. He opens the door, leaning through the gap and squinting at the overly bright sun.

I hand him a coffee and lift mine for a quick sip. "I'm going home to Fairbury for the break. Wanna come?"

"Tempting," he says through a yawn. "But I'm headed back to Lincoln. I've got a buddy there who runs a local theatre group. Frank and I did a tour together years ago, and he's been on me to visit for years."

"Suit yourself. I'm going to stuff myself on Momma's home cooking, alternate between my pajamas and an old pair of overalls, and never bring a hot iron anywhere near my hair."

"Sounds glamorous."

"Ha! Not at all glamorous. But it's going to be glorious, all the same. I'll see you in a week."

I check out with Gwyn, heft my patched-up, strapped-together suitcase, blow a flurry of kisses to my friends, and cross the street to board the Greyhound bus.

Otis comes to get me at the station, and I'm practically bouncing up and down in my seat by the time we pull down our long dirt drive. When I bust through the front door, Momma pokes her head out of the kitchen, drying her hands on the towel stitched to the side of her apron. She slaps her thighs and flings her arms open, and I dive into them. She's laughing through her tears, and now I'm crying, too.

She finally pulls back to give me one of her looks. "Your daddy's waiting for you in the barn."

I leave my things in the hallway and head outside. The dirt beneath my feet is hard as rocks, a sure sign of a hot, dry summer. I hope the crops are faring okay. When I get to the barn, Daddy's not even pretending to work. He's sitting on a haybale, wringing a washrag between his hands. He looks up as my shadow reaches the toes of his boots, his eyes searching mine. Then his face softens, and he blows out a long breath.

"You're home."

I bite my lip to keep from rushing in.

Daddy drops his head and scrubs a hand through what hair he has left. "I should have written, I know, but I saw your leaving as you rejecting us—this place, this family, me. I didn't think you'd ever come back."

I swallow, hard. "I'd never do that. There's no denying I needed to go. But I should have stuck around until the grief wasn't quite so raw for any of us."

He levers himself upright. For the first time, I can see the toll the years of hard work have taken, the way his shoulders bend forward, how he squints a little in the dim light of the barn. Why didn't I notice that before? I close the space between us and wrap my arms around his middle.

"Even if I never live here again, this is always home."

Suddenly a week on the farm seems like nowhere near long enough.

-53-

I CARRY THE luggage up to my room, but instead of going inside, I wander into Nana's. Whatever traces hung around right after she died—a hint of her Turkish perfume, her warmth, her sass—they're gone. All over again, losing her sinks me. If there was ever a time I needed the lash of her sharp tongue, it's now.

I make my way downstairs to lunch. Momma can't stop beaming, while Daddy hardly eats, taking in what's left of our family gathered around the old walnut table with a bemused smile.

"We thought we wouldn't see you for weeks yet."

"That was the plan, but like I told Momma on the phone, our sets busted and we can't perform until they've been repaired. The tour will start up again next week and we'll need to finish our run." I spear a trio of green beans with my fork. "I ought to have another show opening after this one is over, but I don't."

"You'll go back to the city even so?" It's clear Momma's trying to keep the disappointment from her voice.

"Yeah—I've saved some money from this tour, and I'm hoping it'll float me long enough to book another show. But most of the other actors already have something lined up."

"You're still getting on your feet. It takes time to learn something new." Daddy reaches out and squeezes my hand. "Be patient with yourself."

Talk spins away from me, to Momma's favorite chicken who's quit laying in this heat, the new roof everybody's chipping in for to fix the leak at the parsonage, and the Wilkins' new soybean crop. My gaze travels around the room while they talk, to the lace curtains over the window, the worn wood floor, the pale yellow wallpaper all around—everything just as I left it. A lazy smile spreads across my face; being home is like lying down in a ray of sunlight. I lean back in my chair, soaking it all in.

There's only one thing that still needs setting right. "Daddy, can I borrow the truck tomorrow?"

My parents exchange a look before Momma answers. "Jesse's not home, if that's what you're after."

"What? Where is he?"

"Mr. Schmidt had business out of town, and Jesse went in his stead, to take the trouble of traveling all the way there and back off his papa's shoulders."

I sit back in my chair. "Well, that's some timing."

Momma stirs the soup in her bowl and sets down the spoon without eating a drop. "Honey, he knew you were coming. We went to the movies last night, and, you see, Nelly was there. She asked after you, like she always does, and when we told her you were coming, well, she seemed to think he'd make himself scarce."

He left *because* he knew I was coming home?

Momma wrings the napkin in her lap. "Did you two have another disagreement?"

My face crumples, and I bite my lip, hard. I stare at my plate, the glare of the overhead light glancing off the china.

Daddy reaches across the table and takes my hand in his. "The truck is yours if you want it."

"Thanks." I manage a weak smile, though I know it's nowhere near convincing.

After supper, I watch the sun set from the porch swing, Nana's cherry tree quilt wrapped around me for comfort even though it's still sweltering out. I watch the fireflies dance through the dusk. And I watch the moon rise, tugging the first star of the evening halfway across the sky.

-54-

JESSE ISN'T HOME, so there's no point in going to the Schmidt farm. It's just, if I don't go over there and see for myself, I'll always wonder if there was more I could have done to patch things up between us. And I am not willing to spend the rest of my life wondering how things might have turned out if I were only braver.

I cut the engine when I pull into the drive and hop out of the truck. I glance toward the house, then the barn, and back again. I can't stop by and *not* visit with the family, but if Mama Schmidt is angry with me, or even half as disappointed as I think she might be, it's gonna hurt.

So I pick the barn for starters. It's two stories of weathered wood with horse stalls along one wall and a hayloft above. The center is an open area big enough to drive the tractor in out of the weather or to drop one attachment and pick up another. I spot Papa Schmidt on horseback in the fields. Lois is with him, of course, testing the soil and rubbing the leaves between her fingers.

I cross to the middle of the hay-strewn floor and turn in a slow circle. Jesse isn't here. There's no reason for me to stick around, no reason to torture myself with this place drenched in memories of the two of us. The last thing I want to do is go into that farmhouse and face his mother. But I was raised better than to run away, so I head back to the truck, lean in the open window, and grab the basket of raspberry muffins Momma sent over. My boots feel like lead beneath my feet, and I shove my extra hand deep into the pocket of my overalls. They're hopelessly baggy on me now, but my new clothes don't fit on the farm, either.

I rap my knuckles against the wooden doorframe, feeling like a kid caught leaving the grocery store with a fistful of candy. When Mama Schmidt's solid frame darkens the screen, confusion, then joy, and finally pity settles onto her round face.

"Mazie, *schatzie*, what a surprise! Come in, child." She props the door open with one arm and folds me into an embrace with the other.

"From your *mutti*, yes?" She takes the basket from my hand and ushers me through to the kitchen. "Delicious."

Mama Schmidt sets the muffins aside and slides a bucket of apple peels over to the table with her toe. She hands me an apron and sets out two paring knives and a wide bowl between us. Then she fishes a dozen apples from the sink and sets them out on the table. The peels and cores will go to the hogs, and early as these apples are, they'll be for sauce more than likely.

She sets in, doing enough talking for both of us, chatting about the farm and the family, the movie Nelly treated them all to for Joy's birthday, Rose's blue ribbon at the science fair, and on and on until it begins to feel like I never left. She's quicker with the paring knife than I am—I'm sure my contribution to the slices piling up in the bowl is hardly worth the trouble. But the simple work in my hands is welcome, and the familiar cadence of her thickly accented speech puts me at ease.

I barely notice when she's stopped talking altogether, but I feel the weight of her gaze on me. I glance up and there it is, that pitying look again. "My son walks around this place with that same gloom about him. Heartsick, the both of you."

It's the first time she's mentioned Jesse. "Yes."

I can't bear to offer anything less than the truth, not to her, but I can't bring myself to burden her with any more of it, either. She sighs and stops her work long enough to gather my hands between hers. Mama Schmidt isn't one to offer pleasantries simply to have something to say. I thank her for the conversation and slip away before Lois and Papa Schmidt come in from the fields.

As the truck tires crunch over the gravel drive, I watch the old farmhouse grow smaller and smaller in the rearview mirror. I take a breath, and it doesn't hitch in my chest quite as painfully as it did on the way in. Maybe I can't make things right with Jesse. He doesn't love me anymore—he said as much to my face. And he clearly doesn't want to see me.

Maybe what we really needed was something awful between us, to drive us far enough apart so we really could move on. But at least I know now that I don't have to live in a world where Mama Schmidt thinks ill of me. Maybe that's all I can ask for.

-55-

THE FOLLOWING MORNING, I'm up before the sun. I change into my leotard and tights and pin my hair up in a bun. I make my way downstairs and help myself to a cup of coffee. Momma kisses me on the cheek without breaking off the hymn she's humming. She's making sausage and biscuits for breakfast and can hardly believe it when I beg off with only one egg.

"I'm going to ballet class, Momma. Save me some for when I get back?"

"Will do."

I set my cup in the sink and back slowly out of the kitchen. I want to remember this—the smells and the sizzle, the way the early sunlight falls on her cheek, and how good this old house feels when she's at the heart of it.

It's a quick drive into town, and the nerves build in my stomach the whole way there. It seemed like such a fun idea—surprising Mme Durant in her advanced class. But I've been gone for months. Maybe she changed the time? Or the class might be full. I haven't had a ballet teacher since I left Fairbury—my form is sure to be horrid. I should turn around, change into my overalls, and start hauling pig slop and scattering chicken feed.

But one thing this tour has taught me? That voice—the one that tries to make me feel small and silly—is not my friend. I want to see my teacher. I want her to be proud of me. I want to work up a good sweat and see if who I'm becoming and who I was have the important things in common.

I slip into the ballet studio while Mme Durant is changing the record. Her back is to the class, so I find my way to an empty spot at the barre and roll out my ankles, point and flex my toes, ready for her first command.

The room is quiet except for the sound of ballet slippers gliding across the hardwood floor. Then the first bars of Debussy's Arabesque no. 1 fill the room, and class begins. We're moving through the familiar patterns when she spots me at last. Mme Durant's eyebrows shoot up, and her laugh is like a sigh. The rest of the students continue while she glides over to me. She lays her palms against my cheeks for a second, then steps briskly away.

"You're back?"

"Only for a few days, Madame. I'm in a touring production."

She nods, and a small smile tugs at her lips, though she's quick to erase it with a sniff. "Well, clearly your posture has suffered with all that time on the road. Shoulders back. Chin up. Tuck that abdomen. Extend through your fingertips. There, that's better."

Satisfied, she strolls down the line, calling each change of position, adjusting turnout here and lift there, while I sink into the familiar sequence, and deeper into myself.

-56-

AFTER TWO MORE days without leaving the farm, I am rested as I'm ever going to get. So when Clive calls after lunch on Friday inviting me to Lincoln for a dinner party, I jump at the chance.

For the first time all week, I brush my hair till it's sleek as a bolt of silk and slick the waves back like Grace Kelly. I pull out one of my old button-down shirts and tuck the tails into a pair of cigarette pants Kathleen tailored for me. At the last minute, I knot a scarf around my neck, slip into my loafers, and have a look at the result in the hall mirror. I'm still figuring out who I am, not to mention how I want the rest of the world to see me. For tonight, anyway, this feels right.

Daddy lets me take the truck again, but not before he checks the oil and the tire pressure and at least a dozen other things that we both know are perfectly in order. He's so happy to have me home, I think he'd agree if I asked to drive the tractor all the way to Lincoln.

It's a gorgeous August night, and the sun seems in no hurry to set. I crank up the radio, roll the window down, and lean out, sticking my face into the warm summer wind blowing by. To hell with my hair—it never really looked that much like Grace Kelly's in the first place. Before I know it, I'm singing at the top of my lungs. Not about tractors or Ned's assets or baking peach pie but "Whole Lotta Lovin'" by Fats Domino and "Dream Lover" by Bobby Darin and "Donna" by Ritchie Valens.

I know my way to Lincoln well enough, but when it comes time to pull off the highway, I have to unfold the Rand McNally in the passenger seat, tracing each turn on the map until I arrive at a bungalow a few blocks away from the capitol. I feel provincial as could be toting another basket of Momma's raspberry muffins, but it's better than showing up empty-handed, I suppose.

When I press the buzzer, Clive whips open the door and yanks me inside, then dips in to drop a kiss on my cheek. "Mazie, meet my friend Frank. Frank, Mazie."

"Home cooking?" Frank says with a little bow as he takes the basket out of my hands. "Bless you."

Clive shows me into the next room, where a pair of young men stand in the kitchen, one stirring a pot of something heavenly and the other dangling a wine goblet from his fingertips and whispering in (or maybe nibbling on?) the other's ear. I couldn't name the spices simmering away on the stove if I tried. I hurry to follow Clive into the living room, staring like the hillbilly I am at the abstract paintings on the walls, when I hear another voice, one I'd know anywhere.

"What the hell is she doing here?"

It's like walking face-first into a spiderweb. I spin around and there's Lois, propped against a chaise longue. She's got a highball glass perched on one knee, and her other arm is draped across the torso of a petite brunette woman curled between her legs. Lois is wearing a pair of men's slacks, rolled and pressed, with a collared shirt not unlike the one I've got on.

I've . . . never seen her in anything but overalls. And she never lets anybody touch her. My face is on fire. I snap my mouth shut, scrambling to figure out where my courage has gone to.

"Hello, Lois."

Clive and Frank, hell, everybody in that room is looking between the two of us like they don't know whether to expect a fistfight or a punch line at the end of whatever this is.

Lois doesn't answer, not directly. Instead she glares at me, all the while speaking to the woman she's with. "That's the one I told you about. The girl who wrecked my baby brother."

Clive gasps like he's onstage. "You're Jesse's sister?"

Lois turns that glare on him next, her eyes hard, like she's not sure yet whose side Clive is on.

I swipe the glass out of his hand and knock the bourbon back with a gulp and a grimace. "Yep."

The house has gone silent except for the Brazilian jazz on the record player. I'm sure Clive regrets inviting me. And right about now, I'd rather be anywhere else in the whole universe.

-57-

IF NOT FOR Lois, dinner would have been lovely. Frank serves curried chicken and rice, and I try to pretend like my ears aren't about to steam clear off—I've never tasted anything that spicy. All throughout dinner, there is somebody leaning across the table, offering to fill my glass. I don't have another sip, though, not after that first shot. If I'm barreling toward a standoff with Lois, I need to be steady on my own two feet. After a dessert of pecan pie, everybody makes their way onto the screened-in porch to welcome a scattering of stars blinking in the night sky.

I scurry to intercept Lois's girlfriend and stick out my hand. I may not have the first clue how to talk to Lois without arguing, but I can get off on the right foot with Vivi. "It really is lovely to meet you. I'm only sorry this is the first time I've had the pleasure."

Lois rolls her eyes, hard, but Vivi takes my hand in both of hers and gives me a thousand-watt smile. "Just think"—she reaches back and grabs Lois's hand, slapping it into mine until we're shaking hands, whether we want to or not—"in a parallel universe, you and I could have been sisters."

Her smile is so infectious, by the time she leaves us to join the others outside, I'm grinning, too. Lois drops my hand, thrusting both of hers deep into her pockets.

"I like her," I hurry to say before the goodwill Vivi tried to force on us vanishes completely. "A lot. How did you two meet?"

Lois doesn't answer for a long moment. Instead, she studies my face, like she's trying to decide if I get to know anything about this other side of her she's clearly kept hidden for a reason. Finally, she sighs and leans against the glass, watching the crowd outside while she selects her words.

"It was a different world when I was your age. There was none of this chasing dreams you kids are always going on about. That wasn't an option. This country was in the middle of a war that could have stretched on for decades, a war it felt like we might lose at any moment. Everybody gave everything they had—their crops, their free time, their sons, husbands, and brothers.

"I dropped out of school when I was sixteen. Papa was on the continent—he still won't tell us what, exactly, he was doing. So I was up at dawn every day to work the farm, then I rode the bus after lunch to the army airfield on the outskirts of Lincoln to work as a mechanic. Mama was called in for translating work all the time—not that she'll talk about that, either—so it was up to me to earn an income and up to Joy to raise Jesse and our sisters. The two of us were burning the candle at both ends just to keep the family going."

That rocks me back a bit. I never really understood why Lois held so much sway with Jesse, why he never would cross her. Or why she cared so much how I handled things with him.

"It was mostly young women at the airfield, except for a few old fellas and some young men left behind for one medical reason or another. It changes your perspective after a while, doing a job like that—doing a damn good job, in fact, and earning a wage for it. You get to thinking your contribution has value. You get to thinking maybe there's a way of living that doesn't include needing a man to provide for you.

"And once you don't *need* a man, well, some of us got to wondering if we even wanted one." She looks me dead in the eye. "I don't. Never have. But I sure was sweet on Vivi, since the first moment I laid eyes on her."

I've known Lois for every one of my eighteen years, and I've never heard her talk like this. I wonder how much she's even told Jesse. "You've been together all this time?"

Lois nods. "Fifteen years, come spring. That is, she lives here and I live on the farm, but we spend our weekends together. We belong to each other."

I don't want to say the wrong thing. I don't want to do anything to stop her, to make her remember this is *me* she's talking to. "Are you scared?"

"Of being found out?" She sucks in a tight breath and puts her shoulders back. "It's less dangerous in the cities, that's for sure. We could run away together, go where nobody knows us, and live sort of free. But I've given my whole life to that farm. I know that soil and every inch of that house. To leave it now—"

"Wait. You actually *want* to run the farm?"

"Why do you think I'm busting my ass every day if not to show Papa that I can?" That scowl is back. "I don't have a lot of options, Mazie. When the war was over and the soldiers came home, the airfield closed. All that opportunity was gone in a blink. Nobody would hire a woman mechanic. It wasn't just a *no*, either. It was a *How dare you try to take a job away from one of our boys coming home?*

"But all those things I learned at the airfield, turns out they're mighty useful, considering all the machinery we've got nowadays. I'd be proud to take over the family farm. It's just . . . not the way these things are done. The best I can hope for is that when Jesse does take over, he'll split it with me, fifty-fifty."

"But . . . that's not right. Why should he be the one to take over just 'cause he's a boy? It isn't fair, not to either one of you. He doesn't even want the farm."

"Shit, Mazie, I know you're not dumb. I just can't figure out how you and I live on the same planet and you're *still* so damn naïve."

She's trying to get a rise out of me. But it's not going to work, not this time. I'd be willing to bet half the reason she's so tough on the outside is that she's been bracing, all these years, for a fight. Well, I'm not going to give it to her.

"If you love Jesse half as much as you claim to, you'll come home and make a life here. I'll share the running of the farm with him. None of us will get everything we want, but we'll each get a piece of it. Believe me, that's more than just about everybody else I know."

"You really think that's what's best for Jesse? Chained to a farm he doesn't want and married to someone he can't make happy? We'd be together, but he'd be miserable watching the sky every night and pining after the career he might have had. And me? Knowing I had a chance to make a life for myself on the stage, but I turned my back on it? How long before I resent him for that? And how long until he stops looking at the sky altogether?"

"Then let him go."

I should have expected it, but still, her words are a kick in the teeth. My head rears back as if she actually struck me.

"Really, Lois? You can't understand that it's impossible for me to forget about him? Could *you*? Could you just let Vivi go?" She recoils like I slapped her across the face. Any minute we might really start swinging. "This is who I am. Sure, I've got big dreams. But so does your brother."

Before she can say anything more, Clive slips back inside. *"Heyyyy.* Everything okay in here?" He glances between us with a worried little frown. And then he stage-whispers, "We can all hear you outside."

I wrap my arms around Clive's waist and squeeze as if I could wring all my pent-up frustration out of him. "Sorry. No more yelling." I let go and swat him back toward the porch. "I'll behave. Promise."

Then, looking anywhere but at Lois, I say, "I think Vivi's divine." I flick my gaze up to her face before following Clive outdoors. It's like looking straight at the sun. "Even if things are over for good between me and Jesse, you're still family. I can't speak for the rest of folks in town, but you can let your guard down with me."

-58-

THE LAST DAY at the farm before I'm due back in Omaha, Momma, Daddy, and I head down to the Little Blue for a swim. We cram into the cab of the truck with a picnic basket full of sandwiches, dilly beans, and cherry tarts propped on my knees.

The current is swift, the water clear all the way down to the gravelly riverbed lined with gray and green, almost blue, and the occasional red stones. Elm and cottonwood trees line the banks, offering shade to cut the heat and fluttering their broad leaves in the breeze.

Momma somersaults in the water like a kid, giggling and sweeping her hair away from her face each time she surfaces. I'm about to join her, but Daddy stops me, patting the rocks beside him.

"I've been meaning to say something ever since you came home."

I sit next to him, hooking my knees with my elbows and pulling them into my chest. "What is it?"

"I was real hard on you when you left. I couldn't understand."

"It's okay—"

"No, let me get this said. It's important. I see now that there's a difference between running from something and running *toward* something."

"Yeah." I swallow, hard.

"It took guts to leave here. I said before that a Butterfield wouldn't run like you did, but that's only true 'cause none of us have ever left. Seems to me, seeing something worth fighting for and going after it with your whole heart is exactly the kind of thing that would do the Butterfield name proud."

I drop my head onto Daddy's shoulder. Peggy was right. You never do outgrow wanting your parents to be proud of you. I close my eyes and let his words seep in through every pore. I want to be proud of me, too.

When we get back to the house, Momma leads me by the hand to Nana's room. I sit on the bed while she reaches above the armoire.

"We haven't wanted to disturb her things. Not yet, anyhow. But I was in here cleaning a few weeks ago, and when it came time to dust up here"—she pulls down a leather suitcase and sets it on the ground, then levers up onto her tiptoes again—"I saw these."

She pulls down a smaller suitcase, then a hatbox and a soft-sided leather overnight bag, all in matching cream with brass latches and locks at the joining. Four matching pieces, lined up in a row. They've been stacked on top of her armoire for as long as I can remember—it's funny how a thing can be such a fixture in your everyday life, you don't even see it anymore.

"Your grandmother bought these when she was young—she had some big voyage planned that she never was able to take. These old things may not be the peak of style at the moment, but she kept them in mint condition. I think she always hoped they'd take her somewhere before the end."

Momma comes to sit beside me on the bed. She holds one of my hands in both of hers, and we sit there for a moment, both of us overcome. At length, she sniffs a few times, dabs a handkerchief beneath her nose, and says, "I know for a fact your nana would want you to have them."

It's felt so good to be home, surrounded by these people who are so easy to love, and being in a place where I'm free to be myself. I wish to God I could hold on to this happy. My life would be so much easier if I could only be content to stay. I may not be itching to get back to Gerard Pierce and those songs about tractors, but the restless tugs at me even with my heart this full.

Nana understood that. She, of all people, knew what it felt like to be trapped by the place you call home. I can't help feeling like this homecoming is only to show me that home isn't here anymore, not in the same way. I need a bigger stage than this—there's no escaping it. Even with that big blue sky and the wide-open spaces all around us, life out here is too small for me.

I'm just going to have to find a way to hold on to a little bit of home when I go.

-59-

WHEN MORNING BREAKS, I climb the low hill behind the barn, my steps slow and my heart heavy. The branches from the old oak tree shade the ground like a lace parasol, scattering the sun's glare in dappled shadows. Three generations of Butterfields have been laid to rest here between the tree's knobby roots. The weather has scrubbed the names from all but the most recent of the simple wooden crosses marking the graves.

I sit in the dirt, leaning back against the old tree's gnarled trunk, blowing a long sigh through my lips. "I sure do miss you, Nana."

There's no answer, not even a rumble from the clouds or a gentle wind across my brow that I could talk myself into believing is her speaking to me from the beyond. The fields stretch as far as the eye can see, leaves hanging limp off the stalks. In the distance, the Little Blue cuts through the land, its path every bit as meandering as my own seems to be.

"I know if you were here, you'd have some choice words for me." I pluck a blade of grass and split it down the middle. "I don't know how everything became so complicated. I thought if I got myself to New York City and booked a show, that would be it—I'd be on my way, and that would be enough."

I squint up at the bright blue sky. It's gonna to be a scorcher today. There'll be no hiding from the sun on the open road.

"Jesse's right, you know. I think I lost myself somewhere along the way. I'm not even sure how, it happened so gradually. I came home to make things right with him, but I think that might have been wrong, too. Truth is, it'll probably be easier for all of us if he thinks I'm not someone he wants anymore."

The wind picks up, fluttering the tassels in the cornfield and clattering the leaves overhead. I close my eyes and let it roll over me.

"I don't *want* to let him go, even though I know I should."

If Nana were here, she'd give me a nudge in the right direction—hell, she'd give me a swift kick in the behind. I sit bolt upright. Maybe it's high time I learned how to deliver one of those kicks on my own.

I check the time. I've got thirty minutes before Daddy will come in from the barn to drive me to the bus depot. It isn't long, but it should be just enough to get out what I've got to say.

I drive like a bat out of hell to the Schmidt farm. When I get to the turnoff, I peek down the long driveway to make sure Jesse's truck is still gone—I'm not here to hurt him. I park in front of the barn and hurry inside before I can change my mind. It's dim in there, the tractor parked in the middle of the dusty floor, a pair of long legs sticking out the underside.

"Lois, get out here. I need to talk to you."

She slides out from under the tangle of machinery, eyebrows arched, her face quickly shifting from surprise to anger. "Mazie? What in the hell do you think you're—"

"No. It's my turn. Seeing as how you've got zero reservations about telling me exactly how I should and should *not* be living my life, I figured I'll give it a go and you can see how you like it."

Lois wipes the grease from her fingers onto a rag dangling from the hip pocket of her overalls and rests her elbows on her knees. "This isn't the place—"

"I don't care. You are going to hear me out." I swallow. It feels like there is a peach pit lodged there, the spines jabbing at my throat and blocking any words that want to come through. "Jesse should be in college, and you know it as well as I do. It would be a damn shame to waste all those brains on a bunch of corn."

She takes her time standing up. "You came here to tell me farmers are stupid?" Lois is not a small woman. All the Schmidts are tall, but she's solid, too, her arms built like a boxer's from all those years working on heavy machinery.

"Oh, come on, Lois. Quit putting words in my mouth." I feel like a bee buzzing around a steer's nose. "I'm saying this is not the life your brother wants. You know if he were free to choose, he sure as shit wouldn't stick around here."

"And just where does he belong—in New York, with you?"

I thrust my chin out. "He should get the chance to chase his dreams just like I'm chasing mine. And him and me? We should get the chance to try. If he's stuck here, we've got nothing, no shot. But, Lois, it doesn't have to be that way."

I grab her arm. "You told me yourself that you want this farm. So what if land is supposed to pass from father to son? When did anybody get anywhere by paying attention to *supposed to*?"

Lois jams her fists on her hips, her lips drawn in a thin line just like her mother's whenever Nelly tests the last scrap of her patience.

"You're a grown woman. What are you so afraid of—that your papa will tell you straight to your face that you can't do it? That he won't abide a woman running the family farm? At least then you'd know." I can't keep the pleading out of my voice. "But what if he says yes?"

"It's not that simple."

"Dammit, Lois. Just . . . just ask yourself if you're willing to spend your whole life wishing for something you can't have. Ask yourself how many more of us have to be made miserable before you decide to *do* something about it?"

The broad door at the back of the barn groans open, the wheels grating against the grit as it slides out of the way.

"Don't answer that." I swipe an arm across my eyes and scuttle around the tractor's shoulder-high wheel well. I don't want Papa Schmidt to see me like this. I sidle along the bug-covered grate and make a break for that rectangle of too-bright afternoon sunshine.

"Lois? What's going on?"

Jesse's voice hits me like an arrow between my shoulder blades, piercing my lungs and stopping me in my tracks.

"Mazie?"

I've never heard him say my name like that. Hard, and

hopeless. I can't help it—I turn back for one last look. He's standing half-in, half-out of the shadow, hay dust lazing in the air all around him. His work shirt is smeared in dirt, and he's got a streak of grease across his forehead and down one cheek. His big brown eyes blink and settle on me, and it's all I can take.

I can't make things right between him and me. The kindest thing I can do for both of us is to leave before I make things worse. I hurry out of there as fast as my legs will carry me.

A crash sounds from inside the barn. "What the hell, Lois?"

The sound of their arguing chases me all the way to the truck. I clamber inside, slamming the door and revving the engine to drown everything else out. Dammit. He wasn't supposed to be there. He wasn't supposed to ever know.

Dammit.

I thought I was done hurting him. Now I've gone and given him another reason to be glad he's rid of me. I throw the truck in gear and peel out of the driveway. I can't stop the ugly, choking sobs that heave out of me anymore. I'm swerving something awful, but I can't seem to hold the wheel straight. It's all I can do to hang on and keep myself upright long enough to make it down the driveway and out of sight.

-60-

IT'S HARDER SAYING goodbye to Momma and Daddy the second time around, now that I know how it feels to be so far away, and how lonely New York City can be. At the last minute, Momma presses two embroidered handkerchiefs into my palm, one for me and one for Mrs. Cooper. Truth is, Mrs. Cooper is far too good a businesswoman to also play mother to us all. But it puts Momma at ease thinking somebody is looking out for me in the big city, so I don't tell her any different. I promise I'll visit again as soon as I can, and I swear to myself that the minute I land a real show on Broadway, I'll spring for tickets and bring them both out to watch.

I find a seat by myself on the Greyhound bus. The windows are down despite the noise—even with the wind ripping past, the air is hot. I stare out the window, yanked between excitement at heading back to the production, sadness at leaving home, and desperation at the way things with Jesse and me have taken a sharp turn for the worse. When I'm dropped on the curb with my new set of luggage, Gwyn is waiting outside the tour bus, clipboard in hand, to welcome us all back. Pierce dodges my eyes when I climb aboard—good, it's his turn to slink out of my way.

Everybody's chatty on board the bus, and no wonder—they've just wrapped up a week of vacation in a part of the country they've never seen before. But this week wasn't a lark for me. It was real. And real life is complicated and messy, even the good times a little bittersweet. Nana tried to tell me as much months ago, only I didn't understand yet, not fully.

Kathleen beckons, and I slide in beside her. She's buzzing with excitement—her samples shipped yesterday. I can tell by the shadows under her eyes that she spent the whole week working. She tells me about each one as I thumb through the sketches, thrilled at this next possibility for her, all the while bracing myself to lose yet another new friend when Hollywood snatches her up.

The tapestry rolling by outside our window has barely changed since the first stop on tour. Green fields of corn flutter in the wind, with big blue skies stretching high above. I bet it'll be months before I dream at night about anything other than tall-growing, good old-fashioned Midwestern corn.

When we arrive in Sioux City, I set up my motel room like I always do, with my picture frames arranged on the bedside table and Jesse's ratty old shirt tucked under the pillow. I'm just deciding which I need first, dinner or a bath, when a knock sounds at my door. I peek through the shades and unbolt the lock. Harbuckle is standing on the walkway between the rooms and the row of parked cars, hands in his pockets, rocking back on his heels so his rather large belly strains against his suspender straps.

"Hello, Mr. Harbuckle," I say as I join him outside, closing the door to my room behind me. I lift a hand to shade my eyes. Seems like a heat wave hit overnight; I've already soaked through my shirt.

"Mazie," he begins. "Producer friend of mine came to see the show in St. Joseph—he's wrapping up a tour for Oldsmobile and has a Broadway show that begins rehearsals in September. He's got half the chorus already cast from his industrial that just wrapped and is looking for a few more actors."

Harbuckle is a decent man. He wouldn't be so cruel as to say all this without meaning *me*, would he? A whole river of sweat flows down my back.

"He picked out a few of you from the show that he'd like to see again. He's agreed to meet with you at our stop in South Dakota. Should I tell him you're in?"

"Yes!" I practically shout my answer at him.

Harbuckle chuckles. "I thought so."

Wanda darts into my room the minute he's out of sight, squealing, pulling Fiona with her.

"Can you believe it?"

I shake my head slowly. I can't—I've been terrified that this show was it for me. One and done, the closest to Broadway I'd ever get. Wanda flops backward onto the bed, kicking her heels and squealing some more.

Fiona takes the chair by the window. "I figured I'd be back to banging down agents' doors for months until I booked another show."

"Me too." I sink onto the padded vanity stool. My fingers and toes are tingling like they're coming back to life after a long sleep.

"But he only needs two of us." Fiona stiffens, like she's already preparing to distance herself from us.

I want the best for them both, I do. It's just—*I need this*. I need a sign that all this heartache hasn't been for nothing.

-61-

THE PERFORMANCE IN Sioux City goes off without a hitch, and the next one, too, in South Dakota. I shouldn't be able to focus at all, since Harbuckle set up the meeting for right after tonight's show, but there's something about playing Sally that takes me out of my own head. I don't know how to explain it except to say that I *feel* her. In a way, her struggles are a mirror of my own.

But once the curtain goes down, my whole body starts buzzing. It's what I've been hoping for—another production after this. A real one this time, on Broadway. Fiona, Wanda, and I find each other downstairs, and we hook our arms around one another's necks, shimmying into a tight circle of anticipation.

Fiona is the first to back away, closing herself off from us, the competition. "Break a leg."

I face the mirror and scrub the makeup from my cheeks, eyes, and lips until it's just me looking back. I pull my hair into a ponytail and step into my black pantsuit and a pair of red flats. I twist and turn, looking at my reflection in the mirror, the ends of my ponytail flicking against the back of my neck. I look like an actor. I look like somebody who believes in herself. I look like someone who's got a life's worth of stories to tell. Best of all, I look like *me*.

We climb the stairs from the dressing rooms and head back out onstage. The curtain is down, and Harbuckle is seated in a folding chair with a thin man in a crisp suit beside him. Harbuckle stands when he spots us.

"Ladies, this is Mr. Phelps; he'll see you one at a time. Why doesn't our leading lady go first?"

I feel like I stuck my finger in a socket—my whole body is zinging with electricity. Harbuckle ushers Wanda and Fiona into the lobby, their footsteps on the crushed carpet the only sound in the whole place. When the lobby door closes behind them, the house goes quiet. The stage is empty except for the two of us.

"Hello, Mazie."

"Pleased to meet you, Mr. Phelps."

"I've already heard you sing, and let me say, I am impressed."

"Thank you." I can't keep from smiling.

"And I've seen you onstage—you've got a solid presence up there. But I wanted to get a look up close."

My mouth twitches, and the smile begins to slide. "What do you mean?"

"Well, I'm sure I don't have to tell you, Broadway is hopping right now. There's a hit in every theatre and only so many theatregoers to win over. We've got to sell tickets if we're going to get this show on its feet, so we'll be doing things a little differently. I figure you industrial girls know a thing or two about selling by now?"

The smile is gone, and I think my heart has dropped clear out of my chest. *Selling what, exactly?*

"All of our actors will participate in an extensive publicity circuit. You must represent the show at all times. This look"—he twirls a slender finger, gesturing vaguely at my person—"may have been good enough for a tractor show, but my entire cast will be class personified. You'd need to drop ten pounds—*hmmm*, maybe twenty. And I think a few consultations with our linguist and makeup artist are in order." He keeps talking, but my ears may as well be plugged with cotton balls—all I hear is ringing.

Every spring back home when the snapping turtles wake from hibernation, they claw their way out of the mud and lumber toward the water, carrying on their backs the cubic foot of soil and greenery they hid beneath all winter long. Only when they reach those clear, cool lakes at last and sink underwater do all those extra layers slough away.

I *just* woke up. I just dragged myself out of the mud. I can't go back now—I can't.

I hold up a hand to stop him. "Mr. Phelps, I'd be pleased to be a part of your production. Being onstage is the greatest thrill I've ever known. I love laying a character over my own skin and creating something new. I love drawing gasps and tears and laughter from an audience. But *that's* playing a part." I extend my arms out to the side and let them slap back against my legs. "*This* is who I am."

He tilts his head and looks at me with a pitying expression. "Young lady, you clearly don't know how this business works."

"Maybe not." My voice breaks. I can't believe it's come to this. I can't believe that after everything, it isn't Broadway shutting me out; it's me walking away. "But this is who I am. I'm strong. I sound like the farm country I come from. I've got freckles across my nose and heft to my hips. I've got a voice that was made for the stage and a love for this work that will never dry up.

"And recently? I added to that list being the kind of young woman who knows who she is and what it is that really matters in this life. I'd give nearly anything to be on Broadway, to get to live my dreams eight performances a week. But I won't pretend to be something I'm not. I won't give up who I am, not for anything."

My smile's back—bittersweet, but it's there. I thank Mr. Phelps for his time, then I walk offstage and out of the theatre.

-62-

WANDA AND FIONA are beside themselves, thrilled to have booked Mr. Phelps's show. When I catch them shushing each other as I climb onto the bus the next morning, I plunk down on Fiona's seat, reaching a hand across the aisle for Wanda.

"Listen, you two. I'm happy for you. Sure, I'm disappointed that this show isn't for me, but that doesn't mean I can't be pleased as punch for you both."

Fiona digs in the bag at her feet. She hands me a copy of *Show Business* with a sheepish smile. "I had a friend send me this—I'm sorry I didn't pass it around sooner. I've already circled a few auditions for next week. Maybe you want to give them a look?"

I take the paper and step back into the aisle. I am determined not to spoil their party, but it's hard to be anything but devastated—this business is so much more complicated than I ever imagined. I manage a grin and head back to my seat.

We've only got two stops left on the tour: Rochester, Minnesota, and Cedar Rapids, Iowa. It's the end of summer, and lest we forget her power, the sun is drenching the middle of the country in a punishing heat wave. We soak through our costumes with each performance, and when the usual laundering isn't up to the task, Kathleen breaks out her spray bottle of diluted vodka, which does the trick.

Now that I'm done cowering from Pierce, I can enjoy the walk back to the motel from the theatre each night. I take my time, drinking in a sky full of stars while I still can. I'm going to miss this show when it's over. It's taught me so much about this work and the bigger picture behind the scenes. And I'm not afraid to say I'm doing a fabulous job. I can tell, and not just because of the way the audience roars to their feet at the curtain call. I'd know it anyhow. This is what it feels like to be sure of yourself, to be doing the thing you're meant to.

On the days when I'm performing, I practically wake up singing: humming warm-ups over my morning tea, sighing far above the highest high note I'll have to reach that night. And I've learned how to do a decent barre using the back of a wooden chair in a space no bigger than a closet.

I wear Nana's scarf swaddled over my neck and barely speak to anyone the whole day if I can help it. I get to the theatre before any of the other actors. Some slide in right before half hour, but I could never do that. I won't let myself forget that I was never supposed to be the lead, that nobody believed I could do it until I proved myself to them, one by one. So I work every day, finding something more I can draw from the character with each performance.

I didn't like Sally much when I first started playing her. Truth is, I thought she was stuck-up. What I came to realize stepping into her shoes night after night is that she keeps who she is close to the vest. She doesn't let just anybody in. And all that stuff I didn't like?

That's what the playwright thought of her; sad to say he didn't look much more than skin- and stereotype-deep. It's got nothing to do with who she really is.

In a way, getting to know Sally from the inside has helped me figure out how to be myself, to stand proud in who I am even when I'm different from what everybody else expects. Sally's quiet. She's a thinker, but that doesn't make her aloof. She has a high opinion of herself, but that doesn't make her a snob. Even if the newfangled tractor weren't enough to convince her to accept Ned's offer, that wouldn't make her cold. It would make her more like me, driven by something beyond the world she grew up in.

And I want to stay in this other world I've finally found my place in. I do. But I'd rather lose on my terms than win on anyone else's.

-63-

EVERYBODY'S WHISPERING IN dressing rooms and at bus stops—they've all got plans for what's next after this tour is over. Everyone but me. I guess it'll be a never-ending stream of auditions again—that's just part of this business. You work on a show until either you or it reaches the end of the run, and then you take all you've learned and any money you were able to save and you pray it'll hold you over until the next gig comes along.

In addition to the ones Fiona circled, I marked a few auditions for next week. I've managed to squirrel away a fair bit of money, more than what Nana gave me to get to New York in the first place. I don't trust that the next job will come when I need it—how can I? So I'll just have to work as hard as I can, for as long as it takes.

After the final curtain comes down on our last show, Harbuckle throws one hell of a party, more out of relief than anything else, I wager. Corporate suits from Von Steer fill the room, humming our tunes and raising glass after glass in the name of the almighty dollar they plan to rake in with their newly revved-up sales force.

Times like this, I've learned how to cross my arms in front of my chest and dangle my glass a good eight inches in front of me to keep the half-drunk salesmen as far away from my person as I can manage. But it always seems like the minute I shake one off, another ambles over.

It's been a grind getting through those last few performances, and I'm bone-tired. I can feel my eyes go glassy after the first saucer of bubbly. I just want to go back to my hotel room, pack my things, and sleep the whole way to New York.

I'm standing on aching feet, wishing I could leave the stupid party, when it hits me—I'm done here. I don't need to stay one moment longer. I set my glass down on a passing busboy's tray and hightail it outside. I'm nearly to my room when I hear footsteps closing in behind me. I grit my teeth, straighten my spine for a confrontation, and whirl around.

"Oh." It's Gwyn.

Her hands fly up. "Sorry—didn't mean to scare you. I wanted to chat, but I couldn't get a word in with all those fellas coming at you."

"It's okay. I'm going to pack a little, prep for an audition Monday morning, and then turn in early."

"Yeah—hey, that's what I wanted to talk to you about."

I quirk an eyebrow, and she gestures toward the door to my room. "After you."

I work the key in the lock, wave her in, and close the door behind us. I toss the key on the bed and shrug out of my jacket and the pumps that have been cutting into my heels all night. I turn my back so Gwyn can unzip my dress, then she sinks onto the side chair, swiveling away so I have a little privacy to strip down, slip into my pajamas, and wipe my face clean.

She pulls a can of beer out from the inside pocket of her jacket and flips the tab open, rushing to slurp the foam that spills over the top. I sink onto the vanity stool with a heavy sigh, brush out my hair, and smear a dollop of cold cream over my cheeks.

"I've got a part for you if you want it."

I spin around, banging my knee on the table leg. *"What?"*

Gwyn kicks her feet up on the bed and grins. Of course she waited until my face was covered in gunk to drop the news.

"Here's the deal: I have a friend who's been working on a show that'll start previews this fall in Boston, with the hopes to open off-Broadway soon. I was supposed to have a week of downtime, but now that this tour's gone long, I don't even get one day to rest—I'm hopping straight from this production into that one."

I grip the sides of my chair so hard the metal edges dig into the pads of my fingers.

"It's a revue, and they need to fill a few more spots in the singing ensemble. There's no square dancing, so I know you'll be bitterly disappointed."

I chuck my hairbrush at her, and she ducks, snorting with laughter.

"The whole show is a love letter to the continent—the Russian ballet, the Italian countryside, the romance of Paris, *blah, blah, blah.* Anyway, my friend needs people who can sing first and foremost, but who can fill in behind the ballerinas for a few numbers. I never would have thought of you if I weren't forced every single day to watch your little . . ." She makes a fiddly motion with her fingers.

"Barre?" I can barely choke the word out.

"Yeah, that. Anyway, my friend asked if I knew anyone who could step into rehearsals on day one. Had to be Equity. Had to be ready to understudy a couple of different parts, if need be. I mentioned you." Gwyn swings the chair around in a lazy circle, the pause stretching out unbearably long.

"And?"

She spins herself back around, a smile as big as the world stretched across her face. "She trusts me, and I trust you. So the part is yours."

"Really?" I whisper. "You wouldn't joke—not about this."

"I wouldn't."

I scream. A bloodcurdling, somebody-is-about-to-murder-me kind of scream.

Gwyn flies out of the chair. *"Jesus,* Mazie!"

I grab her cheeks, my face still smeared in cold cream I haven't had the chance to rub in, and plant a big old stage kiss right on her lips. She sputters away, wiping the stuff off her cheeks and grimacing.

"Honey, you're pretty, but you're not my type."

I'm laughing. I'm crying. I slide to the floor.

Gwyn chuckles, still wiping her mouth and pretending to spit as she sees herself out. "Actors."

-64-

THE BUS TRIP back to the city feels like a dreamy echo of the train ride that took me there in the first place. I'm too wound up to sleep, staring out the window at the sleepy towns and wide swaths of untouched land lining the highway, thinking about who I was then and who I am now, the bits I'm happy to shed and the parts of me I'm determined to never let go.

When we step off the tour bus for the last time, the cast exchanges addresses, some with promises to write and others with plans to meet up later in the week. It's hard to believe that after the flurry of rehearsals and bus rides, all those motels and ten dazzling performances, it's over.

The movie people love Kathleen, like I knew they would. Paramount Pictures is putting her on a plane to Hollywood in the morning. I wrap her in a big hug. "Thank you. For everything."

With a wink, she saunters off, and I wave until she disappears out of sight, a lump in my throat and a knot in my stomach. Nobody warned me that a casualty of life in the theatre was finding people who take you in like family, only to lose them again when a show wraps.

Clive makes me promise we'll have dinner next week at

Sardi's, and I'm so relieved at the thought of having a friend in the city, I nearly start blubbering right there in the parking lot.

Before I leave, I shake Mr. Harbuckle's hand. "Thank you for taking a chance on me. I'll always be grateful."

Pierce is standing right beside him, but I have nothing more to say to that man, so I simply turn on my heel, collect my suitcases, and walk away. I'm dying to get settled in at Mrs. Cooper's again, soak in a hot bath, and stretch out in a bed that's all mine and *not* barreling down the highway.

I hail a taxi and let it carry me straight to the boarding-house. Sure, I'll take the subway most days, but I've earned a little breathing room, at least. I watch the city stream by out the cloudy window. I haven't missed the brisk pace of this place. Or the noise. Or the smell, for that matter. But the energy is like nothing I've felt anywhere else, and by the time the taxi rolls to a stop, I'm on the edge of my seat, ready to get out there again.

I let myself into the boardinghouse and close the door softly behind me. Everything looks different. The old piano in the parlor, the framed playbills hanging in the hallway. The wallpaper that, if you don't look too close, could be mistaken for row after row of tall-growing Midwestern corn. On my way up to the third floor, I rap on Mrs. Cooper's door. I thought she might just nod and see me on my way, maybe even a little annoyed that I'd interrupted her solitary afternoon. But when she sees that it's me on the landing, she steps out and wraps me in a firm hug.

"Welcome home, Mazie. We're so glad you're back."

I'm so surprised I can barely summon a response. "Thank

you, ma'am." I press the handkerchief Momma embroidered into her hand and scurry upstairs.

I get my wish for peace and quiet soon enough. First I have to sit through the family dinner, though, where everybody wants to hear about the tour. The way those girls look at me, you'd think I was some big star like Kim Stanley or Katharine Hepburn. They have no idea what this business asks you to give, how easy it is to lose yourself in all the bright lights and big personalities. And I don't have the heart to break it to them, not tonight.

The next morning, I take a walk to reintroduce myself to the city. I stroll through the park, where men in suits and bowler hats pack together on the benches, hunched over deli sandwiches wrapped in wax paper and squinting at the sun, wishing they had better luck than working on a Saturday.

I spend the rest of the day haunting movie theaters, hopping from *It Started with a Kiss* to *North by Northwest* and finally *A Hole in the Head*. It's dark outside when I leave the theaters for good. The sidewalks are wet—the clouds must have finally let loose some of that hot summer rain.

Without really planning to, I make my way to Times Square. There's no point second-acting Broadway shows on the weekends, when the theatres are full, so I've never actually seen the weekend crowds lining up at the ticket booths. Every building is blazing with neon red, yellow, and electric pink lights drizzling onto the pavement and leaving wiggling trails along the wet streets. The theatres themselves are bathed in glistening white like beacons drawing the crowds to their doors.

Maybe, before too long, those crowds will be queuing to see me.

I'm still exhausted after a full night's sleep. I'd love to have a week off. But tired as I am, I'm even more excited for the first rehearsal.

Gwyn meets me outside the producer's office at noon and shows me into the room where we'll be doing the first table read. I take my seat in the outer circle. This is a much bigger company than the industrial, and the energy in the room is palpable. There's nothing that compares to opening a new show and making your mark on a brand-new character.

People trickle in, taking their places around the horseshoe of tables. They all seem to know one another—there's lots of backslapping hugs and hearty laughter, and nearly every actor has a scarf swaddling their throats. I'm tempted to reach into my bag and pull mine out, but I stop myself, shoving my hands beneath my thighs. It isn't like I'll be reading today, so there's no reason to keep my voice box warm. And I'm done contorting myself to be like everyone else. I may have to keep reminding myself of that fact every five minutes, but I am. I'm done.

Gwyn calls time, and everyone begins to applaud. Nobody's done anything yet, but as I look around the room, every single face is shining with uncontained joy for the work we're about to do, with love for the art and the craft of it. I join in, clapping so hard my palms sting. *This.* This feeling is exactly why I'm here. All of us working together to create something beautiful and real and true.

-65-

DAYS ROLL INTO weeks, the pace of rehearsals picking up like a freight train barreling down a straightaway. I'm not one of the principals, not this time. But that's okay—if you ask me, the ensemble is underrated. I mean, I'd understand being disappointed if a person never got to stand in the spotlight, to be the one to take a bow for a second and third ovation. But having your name in lights takes a toll, too. You can't hit a wrong note without the whole audience going sour on you. You can't let your smile slip, not once, not if you're sicker than a dog, not even if your heart is busted. And the way you're asked to not just play a character but become one, too? None of it is easy.

There's something to be said for taking a step back and letting yourself grow into a role. My name in the playbill is good old Butterfield, as it should be. And since I've been dancing up a storm in rehearsals these past weeks, the muscles in my legs are bulking up again. I'm getting stronger, finding my way back to myself.

The choreographer worked us hard today; when I leave the rehearsal studio to walk home, the air outside dries all that sweat in an instant. I hug my coat around my ribs, cinch Nana's scarf over my neck, and trot along, ducking in and around the moving stream of people. There's a nip of cold in the air I haven't felt since the spring.

But the city slows me down eventually. Truth be told, it stops me in my tracks. The leaves are going to turn any day—I swear I can hear the first whispers of that autumn rustle. Maybe I'll ask some of the girls from Mrs. Cooper's to head over to Central Park with me on my day off. We can get apple cider and roasted nuts and sit on a creaky bench, soaking up the city at its best.

It's crazy here. This business is even crazier. But I love it, every bit of it.

When I get back to the boardinghouse, there's a letter from Momma on the sideboard and a note on the message pad beside the telephone. Clive called, inviting me out to his favorite nightclub. I tuck the letter into my coat pocket, saving it for after my chores are done.

I need a bath, but I'll have to make it quick before my turn in the kitchen. I'm on bread-baking duty, which always reminds me of home, stepping through the front door to the smell of Momma's sourdough rising over the hearth.

Down in the kitchen, Mrs. Cooper works alongside me, prepping dumplings for the soup. She shucks every last bit of dough off her fingers, forming one final dumpling out of all those tiny shreds. They may come from different worlds, but there's a commonsense sameness between her and Momma that I find awfully comforting so far from home.

When I finally make it up to my room, a new girl is slumped on Peggy's bunk. She's got hair as orange as a pumpkin, and her clothes are wrinkled something awful. She's got her back to me, elbows deep in the trunk she brought with her. I remember my first, horrible trek across the city and thank the heavens I had the good sense not to travel with a trunk. I step back out into the hall and swipe the stack of newspapers off the sideboard, open the weekly to the second page, fold it down the middle, and slide back into our room.

The new girl has that greasy, sunken-eyed look from spending too long on a train to get here. I plunk onto the edge of her bed, and she jumps a little, her hand flying to cover the round O of her lips.

"I'm Mazie. And you are?"

"Ivy Pearl," she drawls.

"What's it going to be?" I slap the paper down on the bed and drag a finger down the row of casting calls. "Musical? One-act? Shakespeare?"

Ivy Pearl looks around her, like the excuses she's searching for are lying somewhere out of sight. "Oh, but I only just got here."

"Piece of advice?"

Ivy Pearl nods, her eyes blinking like busted stoplights.

"I'm guessing you've set aside every penny to your name to come here. And you've got enough for what—four weeks? Eight?" I don't wait for her to answer. "Well, let me tell you, those weeks are going to fly by, and before you know it, it'll be time to pack it in and head home.

"I promise you one thing: if you get to the end of your money and you have to leave, you are going to curse every single opportunity you let pass you by because you were too scared to reach out and take what you want. Now come on, pick something. I've got to be at rehearsal tomorrow by eleven, but that'll give us plenty of time to hit at least one of these on the way."

"You'd do that for me?"

"Course I would—don't believe everything you see in the movies. I'm also going to give up half my time in the bathroom, which starts in two minutes, so you'd better gather your things and get going. You look like you could use a soak even more than me."

Her hands fly up to her hair. "Is it that obvious?"

I waggle the show paper in her direction. "Take this with you. Oh, and Ivy Pearl? One more thing. You're going to hear from folks that you need to lose that drawl and dye your hair, or drop that southern second name of yours. Don't believe a one of 'em. The trick to making it in show biz is to be the best. Not the second-best Mary Martin or Julie Andrews or Gwen Verdon, but the very best Ivy Pearl there ever could be."

The poor girl hovers in the open doorway with the folded newspaper clutched to her chest, her eyebrows furrowed, her toiletry bag dangling from her wrist. "Should I . . ."

"Yeah. Get! I'll be banging down that bathroom door in exactly fifteen minutes. Don't you make me regret my generosity."

I chuckle as she scurries away, but the laughter dies in my throat when my gaze drops to the stack of papers scattered across the bed. The *Times* is front and center, and there, below the crease, a tiny column reads: *Last of Vanguards Is Fired Into Orbit*. My eyes slide to the window and the scrap of sky above the tops of the row houses across the street. I'd bet anything that tomorrow night Jesse will drive out to the middle of nowhere to see it, maybe all the way to the Sandhills. He'll be lying in the bed of his truck, staring at the stars and searching for satellites into the wee hours of the morning, trying to convince himself that that's close enough to the life he really wants.

-66-

TWO DAYS LATER, I'm elbow-deep in a bucket of potato peels when I hear the news on the radio. The Center for Radiophysics and Space Research in Ithaca is hosting a sky-watching party to spot that satellite. I've got the subway routes mostly memorized by now, at least the ones between here and Midtown, but I don't know the first thing about traveling upstate.

I hesitate, my hands dipping halfway back into the sack to grab another few spuds to scrub in the sink. This is nuts. It's not like going all the way up there will actually bring me any closer to Jesse. My chest tightens. I can't even rationalize it to myself, but I'm afraid that if I don't do this, if I don't make some effort to be close to him, even though there's still half the country between us, I'm giving up on us for good. I'm not ready to do that, no matter how hopeless it may be.

So I leave the potatoes where they are and dash upstairs. I check the bus schedule in the hallway and do some quick calculations. I have the next thirty-six hours off. I could rush up there and get back well before my next call. I set out across the hall to find somebody to wrangle into swapping shifts. Mine's more than halfway finished, so all I have to do is find one person who's got nowhere better to be and they'll take my offer for sure.

Ten minutes later I've swapped my kitchen scrubs for a pair of capris and a loose-fitting shirt. At the last minute, I grab my copy of the script and the notebook Mrs. Cooper gave me months ago and shove them into Nana's overnight bag. No reason I can't look over the blocking notes for my understudy roles one more time. I throw in a toothbrush and a change of clothes and call it good.

I grab enough cash for a few meals and a night at a motel. Six months ago I wouldn't have known the first thing about taking a quick trip like this. I'd probably have been too nervous to travel all that way on my own. But after a summer on the road, it's as natural as drawing breath.

I scurry down the stairs into the entryway and, as has become my habit, blow a kiss to each of Mrs. Cooper's framed playbills lining the walls. I bust out of the front door, pulling my sweater over my arms as I clatter down the front steps. I'm so in my own head that I barely notice somebody standing on the sidewalk at the bottom of the stairs. Halfway down, the hairs on my forearms lift away from my skin and my feet stutter to a stop. My breath stops, too.

There he is, a blanket draped over one arm and a grocery sack hanging from the crook of the other. I've dreamed of this moment, rehearsed a million times what I would do if Jesse ever showed up at my door. But my mind goes blank. If my heart weren't hammering against my chest like a bass drum, I'd assume it had given up along with my brain.

Jesse looks from my overnight bag to my face. He licks his lips. "Going somewhere?"

The blood rushes to my head, warming my cheeks and waking up my brain just in time. I drop down one more step. "You might not have heard—there was a satellite launch a couple of days ago."

A smile tugs at his lips. "I may have heard something along those lines."

I drop down one more step, my palm sliding along the stone railing. "I was going to take a bus somewhere far outside the city, away from all these lights, to see if I could watch it float across the sky."

"You're taking up a new hobby?"

A laugh catches in my throat, and I take one more step toward him. "There's a certain person I've been aching to feel close to. I thought if he and I were looking at the same sky at the same moment it wouldn't matter if there were a thousand miles separating us."

I come one step closer, and he shifts the blanket so his hand is free to reach for mine. I've always loved the way his face goes soft when he's looking at me.

"Would it ruin all your plans if I was just a little closer than that?" Jesse's hand is steady, holding mine.

I don't have the first clue what he's doing here—I don't know if anything has changed—but I'm not about to risk him misunderstanding this time. So I lean out over the steps between us, cinch my elbow behind his neck, and, well, pretty much crash on top of him. It's anything but graceful. His eyebrows jump up, and the grocery sack plops to the pavement, a plum and a wobbly pear making a break for it down the sidewalk.

Jesse wraps the hand still gripping mine around my back, and his other one, too, for good measure. It isn't a delicate kiss, one of those sweet reunion scenes you see onstage. It's desperation and hope and hurt crushing us against each other. It's everything we couldn't figure out how to say any other way.

When I finally pull back, we're both breathing hard. He leans over until my toes touch down. The city looks good on him. His sandy hair is all tousled; his skin soft and warm. I press my forehead against his and hold his face between my hands.

"How? How is this possible?"

Jesse smiles and kisses me again, quick this time, then bends to scoop up the fallen plum and pear. He shoulders the grocery sack and pulls me with him down the sidewalk. "I don't know what got into Lois, but she sat Mama and Papa down, laid out all the reasons why she should take over running the farm, and wouldn't quit until they came around to her way of thinking. Then she practically ran me off the farm." He pauses, tucks a stray hair behind my ear, then leans in for another kiss. This one's soft and lingering, ending in a slow smile. "I gather somebody gave her a swift kick in the ass."

I can't believe he's here. I can't quite keep myself from hoping it's for good. "Then you're free?"

"Free to enroll in classes in the physics department at NYU."

I grab his shirtfront. "You didn't!" At this rate, we'll never make it more than five steps away from Mrs. Cooper's front stoop.

Jesse chuckles. He covers my hands in his, and we stand there like idiots, grinning at each other in the middle of the sidewalk. "Freshman orientation begins tomorrow."

I thought I had to choose between my dreams and love—that life wouldn't let me have both. My chest is so tight I have to squeeze the air out of my lungs and force the words past my throat. "You're here to stay? In the city. With me?"

"Yeah."

And then I remember. "Oh—I leave for Boston next week."

"Boston?" His face falls.

Now I'm the one laughing. "It's an out-of-town tryout for my new show."

His eyebrows shoot up. "But you're coming back."

I reach up and draw a hand along his cheek, tan from a long summer in the fields. "I'll always come back—this city is where my dreams come alive, where *I* come alive."

Jesse smiles, those big brown eyes going soft. My hands find his again, and I hold on, as tight as I can. "Right here, this is where I belong."

A Note from the Author

IN THE YEARS after World War II, the United States was forging a new identity for itself, grappling with a boom in industry, a rapidly expanding economy, and a consumer-driven society. Among others, the auto industry was reaching new highs and searching for ways to bring drama and prestige to annual sales meetings. In a time before every home in America had a television, where better to look for star power and inspiration than Broadway?

After all, Broadway was experiencing a golden age of its own. Musicals such as *The King and I*, *Guys and Dolls*, *West Side Story*, and many more were enjoying yearslong runs on the Great White Way, some spurring national tours that extended the reach of this all-American art form across the country.

This unlikely marriage between art and commerce resulted in the quirky world of industrial musicals in which renowned Broadway directors, writers, composers, and choreographers created original productions put on by professional actors, dancers, and stage crews. The productions were impressive, but often secret—staged for an exclusive audience of salespeople.

The idea was a hit! The creatives loved the chance to flex their artistic muscles in a new arena and for a solid paycheck, too, while the target audience delighted in the experience. Industrial musicals waned as the decades passed, though thanks to a handful of intrepid collectors, their legacy will not be forgotten. Because of them, researching this book was an absolute delight!

I'd love to share a handful of my favorite resources for any readers interested in following my deep dive into this little-known era of musical theatre history.

I started out knowing next to nothing about musical theatre, so I began my education by watching the documentary film *Every Little Step* and listening intently to each episode of *The Ensemblist* podcast. To better understand Broadway in the 1950s and how it might have struck a young woman new to the scene, I turned to memoirs, notably Julie Andrews's *Home* and Florence Henderson's *Life Is Not a Stage*, as well as the compilation *Nothing Like a Dame: Conversations with the Great Women of Musical Theater* and the documentary film *Broadway, the Golden Age: By the Legends Who Were There*.

For an understanding of the complex life of swings, standbys, and understudies, I relied on *Broadway Swings: Covering the Ensemble in Musical Theatre* by J. Austin Eyer and Lyndy Franklin Smith, as well as the film *The Standbys*. And for a glimpse inside the gloriously wacky world of industrials, I turned to *Everything's Coming Up Profits* by Steve Young and Sport Murphy and the accompanying documentary *Bathtubs Over Broadway*.

As much as this book is about big dreams and big stages, it's also a love letter to Nebraska—that beautiful land and people who gifted Mazie fertile ground to stand on and the gumption to test her wings.

With deep thanks to my editor for allowing this book the time it needed to flourish, I was able to consult writing colleagues, proud Nebraskans, dancers, and theatre experts to soak in their wise feedback. Immense thanks to Nanci Turner Steveson, Shana Targosz, Meg Wiviott, Greta Birch, Anna E. Jordan, Jennifer Bertman, Allison Pearce, Lisa Walter, Kristin Derwich, Tiffany Crowder, Tara Dairman, and Emily France. Thanks also to librarians at Jefferson County Public Library, Fairbury Public Library, the NYPL Billy Rose Theatre Division, and the Special Collections and Archives at the CU Norlin Library, who assisted with my research. And special thanks to Lynne Collins, Christine Moore, and the Arvada Center repertory group for allowing me a glimpse into the intricate world of professional theatre.

Every book is its own unique journey, and this one was pure joy. I'm so grateful to have been given the opportunity to dream alongside Mazie. Thanks to my agent, Ammi-Joan Paquette, who wholeheartedly supported this book from the beginning. And thanks to my extraordinary editor, Liza Kaplan, whose keen insight and expert guidance transformed the story. I'm grateful to the phenomenal team at Philomel—none of this would be possible without you: Kenneth Wright, Jill Santopolo, Cheryl Eissing, Kate Frentzel, Krista Ahlberg, Elise Poston, Tim Fox, Maria Fazio, and Lindsey Andrews.

Finally, I'm sending love and gratitude to my friends and family, and back through the years to my great-grandmother Mazie Gossler Goodpasture.

A standing ovation for you all.